FINAL DRIVE

FINAL DRIVE

D.K. MORSS

Book cover and interior design by Jean Boles
http://jeanboles.elance.com

This book is dedicated to survivors of domestic violence and those who still suffer from physical and or psychological abuse.

About the Author

––––––––––––– ⟡ –––––––––––––

D.K. Morss was born and raised in the state of Wyoming. She has been legally blind since infancy due to a pituitary brain tumor. Her mother refused to send her out of state to a residential school for the blind because of her pan-hypopituitary condition. Therefore, she was one of the first legally blind children mainstreamed in the public school system in Wyoming.

D.K. Morss earned a BA degree in psychology and a MA in Agency Counseling with an emphasis in women's issues at the University of Northern Colorado in Greeley. She was employed as a rape crisis and domestic violence counselor. She also volunteered for suicide prevention and domestic violence hotlines.

When D.K. Morss moved to California to get married, she changed careers and was employed by the U.S. Government. At the time of her retirement she worked on the national level as part of a team of six management analysts in California. Upon her retirement she received the Albert Gallatin Award, the Department of the Treasury's highest honorary career service award. She resides in California with her husband and their two Maltese dogs, Destiny and Freddie.

Chapter One

Clouds pregnant with rain hang over the Seattle skyline, and black sugar maple, empire white ash, and Italian oak trees line both sides of Cherry Street. The leaves have turned yellow, red, and orange, clinging to their final stage of life before joining the tapestry of leaves carpeting the ground. The gentle breeze blows more leaves from the trees and some are scattered on the street. A frosty moon-shaped cluster lamppost stands adjacent to the entrance of an apartment building, converted from an early twentieth century, brick fish cannery. A black 1959 Chevy Impala sits perfectly parallel parked at the curb. An ambulance and a police cruiser drive up and pull into the curb in front of the Chevy.

Rachel's hair, a warm chestnut brown, is worn in a bun, and her blue eyes are shielded with wide-rim, brown bifocal glasses. Her makeup-free face gives her a schoolmarm appearance. She is dressed in Calvin Klein jeans, baby blue wool turtleneck sweater and sneakers. She walks slowly down the stairs where her ride to San Francisco waits. A ride from total strangers that seems risky and unsafe.

The primal urge to see her mother took precedence over safety, and it even took priority over seeing Aaron, her boss. He'd called her and said they needed to talk when he returned from Denver on Tuesday. Yes, she clung to going home to Mom. It was like being five again and attending the first day of kindergarten; she remembers being alone with strangers and crying when her mother walked out of the classroom.

She'd packed her suitcase and moved about her apartment in a daze. A lump forms in the pit of her stomach as she tries to remember how she'd gotten this ride.

Two police officers, followed by two paramedics, race up the stairs and pass her like she isn't even there. Why are they here? One of the policemen reminded her of Kenneth Hamilton, her ex-husband.

Seeing the policemen jogs her memory of lately beginning to feel uneasy, as if she's being watched by someone. Her seven-year marriage to Kenneth had always kept her on edge—anticipating and managing his moods to minimize his explosive anger towards her.

A young woman in her late twenties, stepping out of the front passenger side door of the Chevy Impala, smiles at Rachel. Her large, brown eyes meet Rachel's. The lady has perfect movie star white teeth, and her shiny, ebony-black hair is styled in a chin length bob with bangs.

"You must be Rachel?"

"Yes, I am. And you're Marie?"

"Nope, Marie is my mom. My name is Sherry."

"It's nice to meet you, Sherry. I really appreciate the ride. Wow, that's a really classic car you have there."

"My dad collected vintage cars, and this 1959 Impala was his favorite. Mom likes driving it because it's big, and she feels safer in it than in some of these newer cars. Let's put your suitcase in the trunk."

"Great!" Rachel walks to the back of the car and could not help but admire the car's bat wing fenders and cat's eye tail lamps. Sherry adjusts the luggage in the trunk, making a space for Rachel's black leather suitcase. Slamming the trunk shut, she said, "Let's go, shall we?"

"I'm ready."

Sliding into the back seat of the car, Rachel introduces herself to Sherry's mom. "Hi Marie, I'm Rachel. I really want to thank you for giving me a ride to San Francisco."

Marie, a matronly woman in her late fifties, wore her silver blue hair in a short perm. "Not a problem, we're going there anyway. Hope we can get out of Seattle before it starts to rain. It seems we've had nothing but rain every time we want to go somewhere." Marie turns the key in the ignition and the car sputters and stops. She pushes the gas pedal and again turns the key in the ignition. The big engine caught, and shifting the car into drive she turns the wheel, edging the car out of the parking place. "I need to get my son to check the carburetor. Maybe this drive will clean it out some."

"September is usually still warm, but we seem to be getting more rain than usual. I heard city driving can be hard on big cars."

"Rachel, that's exactly what my husband always said; town driving is hard on these v-eight engines."

Suddenly, like rapid clicks of camera flashes from a crowd of frenzied paparazzi stalking a celebrity, Rachel's eyes fed images of the car's interior to her brain. Rosary beads and a pyramid-shaped crystal hung from the rear view mirror; picture albums and loose pictures were strewn on the backseat floor behind the driver; the car seats were covered with a grey felt material, and a half box of tissues sat in the seat next to her. A heavy scent of roses filled the car. Gram's funeral smelled exactly like this! Part of her service included attendees placing a single rose on the pillow in her casket. The intense sweet smell of incense and roses in the hot un-ventilated mortuary chapel had been suffocating. She shivered, wrapping her hands in the bottom of her sweater. How did she get this ride?

Wondering how long it would take them to get out of Seattle, Rachel looks at her watch. It was nine o'clock, but the second hand was not moving. The watch was dead. Her lips soundlessly lip-synched the word, dead. "Do you know what time it is?" She asked aloud.

"Rachel, my watch says it's ten minutes to nine," Sherry said. "But that doesn't seem right. I think the battery must be dead."

Marie glances down at her wrist. "Oh, I forgot to put my watch on this morning."

"Aren't watches so undependable? The batteries die at the most unexpected or inconvenient times," Rachel said as she leaned back in her seat and sighed, thinking of the policemen who had passed her on the steps of her apartment building and reflecting on how Seattle had been so wonderful for her. Seven years ago, Aaron Townsend hired her as his executive secretary, giving her a fresh start in life. All of the employees at the Coffee Genie liked and admired him. He gives his employees gift cards on their birthday along with a half day off with pay.

He enjoyed working out, had a muscular build, and stood five feet eleven inches, with dark brown hair and graying sideburns. His soft brown eyes sparkle and his voice is deep and masculine. Lots of women flirted with him, especially Sandy Delray, the office manager.

Yes, life had been so much more satisfying since the divorce. It took a couple of years just to relax and feel safe. She was probably in her junior year at Washington State when she stopped looking over her shoulder.

Her parents had warned her about Kenneth's hot-blooded temper, but she was blinded by love and never could've imagined how unhappy she would become during her marriage to him. They met when she was a sophomore and he was a senior at Hayward High. He played football and was so good looking, with black wavy hair, hazel eyes, and a smile that could melt a glacier. He was six foot tall and slender. A month after high school graduation, he joined the Army. They stayed connected through email, letters, and phone calls. Two years later, when he was halfway through his enlistment period, they were married.

They were in El Paso, Texas when he began calling her names and slapping her. Each time begging her to forgive him and promising never to hit her again. He would be so sweet, and the makeup sex was filled with emotion and intense passion. This cycle had repeated itself throughout their marriage.

She'd hoped when he became a police officer in Lincoln things would get better. However, the abuse only escalated. Calling the police a few times turned out to be useless, and as time went on she felt herself becoming more submissive and feeling like a nonperson. The times she called the police the messages were all the same. *Wouldn't you say this is partly your fault? Couldn't you just try a little harder to get along with him? Doesn't Kenneth have so many fine qualities? All his coworkers really like him. Don't you understand how dangerous and stressful his job is? If they took him to jail he would lose his job. You don't want that, do you?*

Talking with some of the other wives of policemen in his department, she learned that one out of every two women who are married to, or have boyfriends who work for the police department, are physically or emotionally abused. The general United States statistics is one out of every four women will experience some kind of abuse in their lifetime. The other police wives cautioned her saying, "Don't call one of those shelters. The police know where they're located, and shelters are not a safe place because your husband works for the department."

Feeling worthless and powerless to change her life, she accepted the abuse. Besides, he told her he would kill her parents if she left. Feeling the tension building between them she would purposely say things to him just to bring things to a head. It surprised her when he hit her when she was pregnant, because he always seemed to love children. One night he shoved her out of bed and kicked her in the back when she was in the fourth month of carrying their daughter.

Most definitely, he and Aaron were like the difference between daylight and darkness. One day when Aaron walked into the office while she was cleaning her bifocals, he told her, "You have beautiful blue eyes, Rachel. You should check out getting contacts or laser surgery and not hide your beauty."

He had apologized when he saw her face flush sunburned red. She told him an apology was unnecessary and graciously accepted his eye specialist's business card. The last thing she wanted was for some man to notice her. No, hadn't she been through enough hell?

Marie enters the I-5 South Freeway and steers the car into the center lane. A few minutes later she said, "Wow, look at all this traffic. I sure hope we can get out of Seattle pretty soon."

"Mom, why don't you switch to the right lane; there's very little traffic there."

"I thought about moving over, but it seems whenever you change lanes it slows down and becomes just as slow as the others. But it's worth a try." Signaling and stepping on the gas, she turns the wheel to the right, edging the car over.

After driving for about twenty minutes, an underpass appears approximately a quarter of a mile away. "Girls, the traffic's too heavy. I can't change lanes, and I don't remember seeing an underpass in this area before."

"Mom, did we take the wrong freeway?"

"Honey, I don't think so." The car moved smoothly down the hill into the underpass. When they emerged they found themselves on an old highway, filled with potholes. The rear tire made a thumping sound as it went flat. Driving the car to the side of the road, Marie said, "Well, girls, we need to get out and change the tire."

The old highway stretched out before them; both sides of the road is littered with rusty cans and bottles; a bent up tire rim, half covered by dead weeds, lay on the roadside in front of their car, and junk cars are scattered across the landscape as far as the eye could see. A grey field mouse scurries across the highway.

"Look at this place!" Sherry said. "Where are we?"

"Sherry, I don't have a clue where we are. It feels like a hot day in August, and just look at all this trash and dead brush," Rachel commented as she surveyed the area around them, wondering about other travelers who had found themselves on this old highway. Wondering, did the people find themselves stranded in dire circumstances? Are we stranded and in dire circumstances?

"This place gives me the creeps," Sherry said.

Suddenly, an old man, with a thick grey beard, appears and knocks on Marie's car window. The only sound is the mechanical whine as the window is partially opened. A blast of dusty, hot air and a large, black blowfly invades the car.

"Howdy, Marie, I see you've got a flat tire."

"Unfortunately, we do." Marie swats at the fly with her left hand, shooing it back out through the car window. "We're not familiar with this area. One minute we were on the freeway, with busy traffic going in both directions, and now we're on this old highway. Where are we?"

"You're on Final Drive. Those people on the freeway should've taken this exit, but they didn't. They're all people driving nowhere. They've not yet arrived at that state of knowing."

"Final Drive? We've never heard of that road. Anyway, we want to get back to the freeway once we change the tire."

"Marie, I'll change it for you."

"Thank you," Marie said, and she reaches for the car door handle.

Grabbing her mother's arm and whispering, Sherry said, "No! Wait, Mom! How does he know your name? He talks strangely. Didn't he say people are on the freeway going nowhere? That doesn't make sense. I'm not sure we can trust him! Let's call the operator from my cell phone and get someone to come help us."

"Well, dear, you might be right. He does talk a little odd."

Pulling her cell phone from her purse and flipping it open, Sherry quickly dials the operator, but the resulting sound is a static hum. "Oh, no! We're out of the service area!"

"Girls, we don't have any choice. We need to get out and let this gentleman help us change the tire." Outside, unlocking the trunk, Marie steps back, and the old man pulls out the spare tire.

"Hmm, this tire ain't going to take you very far. It's flatter than what's on your car."

"Oh, darn! I told my son to put the new tire in the trunk and he forgot to do it! Is there a gas station around here?"

"Nah, there ain't no gas station in these parts. I'll get your tire fixed, but not today. It's getting late. You need to take that path on the left, and you'll be given help and lodging for the night."

"Look, we're in a hurry," Sherry said. "We don't want to stay the night."

"I'm sorry to hear that, Sherry. Trust me; you don't want to be in these parts alone in the dark."

"How do you know my name?"

"That's a complicated story, but the important thing is I'm here to help you on your journey."

Rachel chewed her fingernails as the old man convinced Marie and Sherry that they needed to spend the night. How could morning be turning so quickly into early evening and September turn to a hot day in late summer? Who were Marie and Sherry anyway? Did they take this road on purpose? Were they going to harm her? She could feel her breath quickening, her heart rate increasing, and she had to root herself into the ground to keep from fleeing. Stop, you're being silly, she scolded herself.

Rachel, Marie, and Sherry stood holding their suitcases as the old man pointed with his yellowed, withered index finger to the embankment on the right side of the road.

"Climb up there and you'll see two pathways. Take the path on the left."

Chapter Two

Walking on the hilly, uneven ground, twigs and dead grass crunched under their feet. At the top of the small embankment they begin following the path on the left. The terrain soon changes and they stop abruptly and soundlessly gaze upon a small, wooden bridge directly in front of them. A dirt road descended into a valley that was filled with wild green grasses, pink and purple New England asters, purple prairie clover, lavender, wild bergamot, yellow with red centers Mexican hat, and other wildflowers. The sky was azure blue, and it seemed to bend and touch the ground like an artist's canvas contrasting the brilliant colors of a panoramic nature scene.

Rachel caught her breath as a dark brown cocker spaniel with a white chest stood just on the other side of the bridge. She touched her breast, and her eyes welled up with tears. "Cookie," she muttered.

Marie turns to look at Rachel. "Did you say something dear?"

"The cocker spaniel on the other side of the footbridge, she reminds me of Cookie, a pet I had as a child."

Marie looks at the bridge. "Dear, I don't see her."

"Rachel, I didn't see a dog either."

"She's right there! Don't you see her?"

"Sometimes our eyes can play tricks on us. Sounds like your childhood pet really meant a lot to you."

"Marie, I didn't imagine it, Cookie was right there! I saw her!" She looks on both sides of the footbridge but the dog had vanished. "Well, of course it wasn't Cookie, but the dog did look exactly like her."

Rachel continued, "I was ten when my parents took me to Tel Aviv to see my great grandmother. I came down with strep throat that later turned into rheumatic fever. I was in and out of the hospital. When I was home, Cookie shared my pillow. In fact, Mother had to move Cookie's food and water dishes to my room because she refused to leave my side."

Touching Rachel's elbow, Sherry said, "We can see why you might think you saw Cookie."

Pulling her arm away from Sherry, Rachel sets her suitcase down. Her face turns red, and trying to regain her composure, she inspects her sweater, brushing off imaginary lint and straightening it. She didn't care what they thought. She wasn't going to start crying in front of total strangers. She remembered Cookie's soft, silky ears, her warm tongue on her skin and the love in her eyes.

Cookie died when Rachel was seventeen, and the grief cloaked her soul in a heavy black and grey dampness. Several weeks after Cookie's death, her dog had visited her. It happened in the early morning hours, just before dawn, while in that state between sleep and wakefulness. The dog jumped onto her bed and licked her on the nose. The nerves in her arms detected a gentle ebb and flow on her skin, and images of the ocean played in her mind like a movie. The scent of ocean air filled her bedroom while the song of seagulls played a symphony in her ear. Love and warmth emanated from every core of her being. It seemed like only an instant, and Cookie and the experience evaporated like the dew on grass on a hot day. What remained was a sense of boundless love and knowledge of how life is a complete circle, ebbing and flowing like the unending tides of the oceans.

She always felt her dog's presence when traumatic events happened in her life. Is something bad going to happen to me? The word DID floats into her mind and sinks like a rock. Shivering, she thinks again about how the weather has changed from fall to late summer and how time seems to melt away.

"Mom, do you see Nana and Dad?"

"Sherry, I believe they're standing on the other side of the little bridge."

"Nana!" Sherry shouted, but there's no response.

"I don't see anyone," Rachel said.

"Something bizarre is happening here," Sherry said as they walked across the footbridge.

"Girls, let's try to get to the place where we're supposed to stay, as it seems like we're all hallucinating."

Shortly after crossing the bridge a sign appears which reads, Souls Inn, with an arrow pointing towards a dirt road. Following the path for about a half mile they find themselves in a courtyard.

A rainbow hangs over the cherub fountain where water was cascading over the three ceramic levels. The fountain stood in front of a tall building resembling a spool of thread, with indigo walls and a white flat roof. A cobblestone pathway followed the perimeter of the building. A lavender sign with gold and black gothic print hung prominently on the door: ENTER ALL GOOD SOULS. For a few minutes they stare at the sign and their surroundings.

"Does the sign mean like spirit?" Sherry asked.

"Sherry, I was thinking the same thing," Rachel said. She thought, if only Aaron was here, he'd know what to do. In fact, he always seemed to have the answers—except for the morning after they'd made love in Denver. He withdrew from her and abruptly sent her back to Seattle. She felt used and brushed off, and wondered if she's now a tramp in his eyes?

Making love with Aaron in Denver complicated their relationship. She left because he wanted her to go back to Seattle. But she was torn between wanting to go and wanting to stay. Leaving him and Denver just seemed easier. Besides, how could she tell him about Kenneth, who beat her, and about the death of her precious little baby, Sara? Maybe it really didn't matter anyway because he couldn't possibly have been interested in her. It was no secret that Sandy was attracted to Aaron and wanted a relationship with him.

Sandy fawned and bent over backwards for Aaron when he was in the Seattle office. She told her on numerous occasions that their boss could park his slippers under her bed anytime. She was always asking Rachel if she knew if he's involved with anyone. Rachel reminded her that he didn't approve of office relationships and she had no idea who he was seeing or not seeing. No matter how she tried to discourage Sandy's chatter about Aaron, there was just no stopping her. Maybe he was interested in Sandy after all, because it was apparent to her that Denver was simply just a one-night stand.

"Well, girls, I guess we should go in," Marie said, gripping the sun-warmed colonial iron door handle, pushing down with her thumb on the latch and opening the squeaking oak door. A rainbow vapor eddied into the open air, accompanied by a melodious sound.

Marie and Sherry hesitatingly step inside a large, dimly lit, circular room. Sherry asked, "Rachel, are you coming?"

"Yes, sorry. I wasn't paying attention," Rachel replied, stepping into the circular room and noticing the unpolished, antique pine floor. Several feet in front of her are ceiling to floor, thick, black velvet drapes. To the right of the drapes is a square oak table with an open book. Left of the drapes is a tall, three-headed grandfather clock with a single pendulum and a wave-shaped base. The base incorporated decorative aspects of all three clocks. The left side of the base is a dark cherry. A light-colored oak formed the bottom, and wenge—a dark brown hardwood with black grain—completed the base on the right side. The dark cherry clock on the left has an antique white face with baroque style carving, gold gilding, and Roman numerals that slant backwards. The center clock made from oak is a square box with numbers that are perfectly aligned. The final clock on the right is a simple, round shape, made from wenge and contains a polished chrome finished bezel, surrounding a glossy white dial. The black hour markers on this clock slant forward.

Mounted on the wall next to the clock is a giant wheel with golden spokes emanating from a pure white center. On the wheel, hundreds of pinhead lights twinkle off and on.

Walking over to the table and peering down at the book, Rachel examines the luminescent page. At the top is gold embossed lettering which reads September 26. Included in the list of names was Rachel Millicent Goodrich, along with two undecipherable words next to her name.

Startled by a movement beside her, Rachel looks up as a young woman comes through the drapes. She wears a green robe, and emanating from her head and shoulders are colors of soft pinks, gold, blues, magenta, along with a strand of indigo.

"Welcome to Souls Inn. My name is Anna."

"I'm Marie; this is my daughter Sherry, and our new friend, Rachel."

"I know."

"Anna, this is a very strange clock," Sherry said.

"Sherry, it symbolizes soul progression and the past, present, and future tenses."

"How so?" Marie asked.

"Marie, the clock on the left symbolizing past life experiences and its numbers slant backwards. The center clock represents the here and now in which we atone for past mistakes. Working through negative and positive karma. The numbers are vertically aligned. The clock on the right represents hope for the future and the black marker numbers slant forward. Finally, the pendulum represents our goal of achieving soul balance and that our past, present, and future are all entwined."

"Interesting, very interesting, and what about that wheel over there, what does that mean?"

"Marie, as souls enter and exit the physical plane, the lights twinkle on and off. The white light in the center of the wheel means all souls are connected in eternal love to the God consciousness."

"Are we dead?"

"Sherry, do you think you're dead?"

Tears glisten in Sherry's eyes. "I don't know. I just know I'm afraid."

"Fear not. Death only happens on the physical plane. When the soul departs the physical body it returns to the earth, as you no longer have need for it. It is a mere prop used in the journey of soul growth. A joyous reunion with the Creator awaits you. Please follow me, for a place has been prepared for you and your mother."

"Please! No!" Rachel cried. "I want to be with Marie and Sherry!"

"Rachel, you must wait, as it's not yet your time."

"Please, we came together and we want to stay together!" Sherry said.

"Sherry's right," Marie added. "There's no sense in Rachel being alone."

"No, she must remain."

"I've got one more question, what's on the other side of those drapes?" Sherry asked.

"Sherry, the drapes open to a tunnel souls go through to reach the spiritual plane. It is the true home of all souls and is a place of love and light. This space is referred to by many different names such as heaven, Swarga Loca, and paradise. It's a place of limitless instant knowing through vibrations like the feeling of colors. Come with me; it is time. Our Father has prepared a place for you."

Chapter Three

*T*ears stream down Rachel's face as she watches her new friends being enfolded in the black velvet drapes and disappear like flies being ravenously consumed by a Venus fly-trap. Suddenly, Cookie appears, brushing her body against her leg. Rachel sits down on the floor cross-legged, and the dog steps into her lap. She caresses her silky ears and feels her wet nose. "Cookie, I love you!"

The dog turns towards the drapes and barks at a young man coming through the drapes. He has long, golden blonde hair and appears to be in his late twenties. He, too, has colors similar to Anna emanating from his head and shoulders.

"Rachel, welcome to Souls Inn. I'm Michael, your personal guide. Please come with me and bring Cookie."

"Michael, I don't understand what's happening to me or where I am. I will go with you because my dog is wagging her tail like she knows you. But please, couldn't you just explain all of this to me, like why I'm here?"

"Rachel, your questions will be answered when the time is right; all will become crystal clear."

Rising, and walking with Cookie, an invisible magnet grips her firmly, pulling and guiding her through the drapes. The thick, soft velvet caresses her body and a blend of sandalwood and patchouli fills her lungs as she begins to tumble forward into the blackness, passing wispy ghost figures who reach towards her with unrecognizable pleadings and moans. They enter a hallway lined on both sides by many doors which are framed with soft white lights. At the opposite end of this space is a brilliant, white light.

Michael touches a button and a door on the left slides open. "This is your room. If you need help, all you have to do is visualize the word *come*, and I'll be at your side instantly."

"Thank you, Michael."

Rachel steps over the threshold with the dog, and the door closes behind them. The room resembles her childhood bedroom. There is an Edwardian single bed, covered with a lavender and silver damask bedspread, along with a matching mahogany night table. An angel statue lamp sits in the center of the table. Across from the bed is a small closet. She opens it, and hanging on the rack is a white, silk and lace gown along with a white velvet robe trimmed in gold. The round collar has her initials RMG in gold silk lettering. Taking the robe and gown she enters the bathroom, which is located to the left of the closet. Undressing and climbing into the shower, she turns the spigots to adjust the temperature. Instead of water a pure white light pours from the shower-head, spilling over her. Out of the shower and dressing in the gown and robe she becomes aware of feeling light and airy—like vapor.

Entering the bedroom she sees for the first time a desk in the corner of the room. On the desk is a lavender-colored book which contains her name, centered in silver lettering.

Sitting down and opening the book, she sees the first page lit up like a movie screen. It shows the moment her soul enters her mother's womb, and a metallic clank sounded as she flips the page to her birth.

A quarter of the way through the book is her wedding day. She is wearing an ivory full-length gown which had been her mother's. She watches her father walk her down the aisle at the Lutheran Church she attended part of the time with her grandparents, Emily and Henry Bender. Her father is Jewish and her mother is a Lutheran. Her dad's parents had wanted him to marry within their religion and had been opposed to the marriage. Because of that, Stanley and Susan had encouraged Rachel to experience other religions and to select a religion of her own choice. The church is packed with family and friends.

Several pages later she watches the birth of her daughter, Sara. Kenneth cries as he holds Sara for the first time, cuddling her as he counts her fingers and toes. Turning the pages, she sees her daughter's death. It is in the middle of the afternoon when she finds her blue and unresponsive in her crib. The paramedics try to resuscitate her, but when they couldn't, they rush her into the ambulance. Tires screeching and sirens blaring, she's transported to the emergency room where the doctor declares her deceased. Rachel sniffles, thinking of Sara's soft, wispy hair and the big smile she'd get on her face when she was changing her diaper; her little fist shoved in her mouth when she was hungry, and the way the baby nuzzled her neck when she'd held her.

After Sara's death, living with Kenneth was like being in hell. Sometimes he didn't come home and when he did, often he was drunk. Many dinners went uneaten. One night after weeks of eating by herself and refrigerating the rest, she didn't cook dinner. He came home in a bad mood and she'd tried to prepare spaghetti in a hurry. He'd thrown the spaghetti sauce on her and burned her skin. The sauce was all over her and the floor in front of the stove. He grabbed her by the hair, throwing her on the floor. He made her clean it up on her hands and knees. The whole time he screamed at her like a drill sergeant in the army. He blacked both of her eyes. He told her that she repulsed him and it was all her fault Sara died.

When she found lipstick on the collar of his uniform she knew he was seeing someone else. Later, she learned it was the police cadet he was training. She begged him not to leave her as she loved him and she was nothing without him. The threats he made to hurt her parents finally brought her into submission and she signed the divorce papers.

The book made a series of beeps as she quickly flipped to the last few pages and there it was! It all came back like the flip of a light switch in a pitch-black room.

Rachel and Sandy had worked late at the Coffee Genie, and they stopped for dinner at Harry's Seafood grill across the street from the office. Rachel declined Sandy's offer to drive her home, as it was out of her way and she only needed to take one bus to her apartment. She feels the cold damp air as she exits the city bus two blocks from home. Walking about a half a block, she hears footsteps behind her. The street looks shadowy in the partial darkness and an uneasiness sweeps over her. Picking up her pace she tells herself, stop being so silly. Seeing her building, she quickly walks up the steps and enters the hallway to her apartment. Someone comes into the hall shortly after her but she doesn't look up. Hurriedly locating her keys, she inserts the key into the lock. A touch on her shoulder startles her and she turns her head and sees Kenneth.

"Rach baby, didn't mean to startle you. I brought you some posies."

"What are you doing here and how did you get my address?"

"Baby, maybe you've forgotten. I'm a cop and we can get anything. I miss you and I want to talk about us."

"Kenneth, we finished *us* with the divorce and honestly, I'm tired. This isn't a good time."

"Then when is a good time?"

"Never!"

"Come on, Rachie. I won't stay long. For old time's sake, please just let me come in for a few minutes."

"Okay, but just for a few minutes." She turns the key in the lock, opening the door, and he follows close behind her. She feels for the light switch and flips it on just as he closes the door behind them. "So Kenneth, why are you here?" she asks as she lays her coat and purse on the sofa.

"Aren't you going to offer me a drink or a cup of coffee?"

"No! You want to talk, so get to what you came here for."

"Baby, I've missed you so, and I was such a fool about us. I need you back in my life. I'm no good without you."

"Remember, you left me for Debbie. And to be honest, I've moved on. I don't love you anymore."

Grabbing her wrists, he says, "Rachel I'll kill myself if you don't take me back. We had great sex, don't you remember?" Putting his arms around her, he kisses her.

Pushing him away, she says, "You've been drinking! I want you to leave!"

"I'll leave when I'm ready! Besides, where the hell have you been? In bed with him?"

"I don't know what you're talking about. I just came home from having dinner with Sandy. Now get out!"

"I ain't goin' nowhere, baby! I came to take your sorry ass back to Lincoln."

"You must be insane to think I'd ever go anywhere with you!"

"You've gotten a little spunky in your old age. Guess you forgot what happens when you talk back to me, bitch! Besides, you're probably sleeping with him!"

"What are you talking about?"

"You know who I'm talking about! Your boss! The guy you were all lovie dovie with in Denver. I saw you that night at Mazuna's restaurant, sashaying in with him and some other guy. You were oozing with sexiness in that short skirt and silky blouse. I would've never allowed you to dress like that in public. Believe me, I saw the way he looked at you!"

"That's one thing I don't miss about you is your insane jealousy. My personal life is none of your business. Now leave!"

"I'll leave when you give me what you gave your boss." Grabbing and holding her tightly against him, he kisses her again.

She bit him on his upper lip, trying to free herself from his grip and from the stench of alcohol on his breath.

Releasing her, he quickly wipes the blood trickling down his chin with the back of his sleeve. Slapping her hard across the face, he nearly knocks her to the floor. "You dirty bitch! You whore!"

He grabs her by the hair as she tries to break free and run for the door. She wrestles against him, but she is no match for his six-foot frame. He slams her hard against the wall and her body bumps the lamp on the table, causing it to crash to the floor, shattering. "Now I was hoping for more of a welcome from my ex-wife."

"We were finished twelve years ago, and you're the last person I want to be with!"

"Got news for you, sugar cakes, it ain't over until I say so. We're getting married again."

"No we aren't! I've worked hard to change my life, and I don't love you anymore. What we had died a long time ago!"

Encircling her neck with his hands, he said, "I could slit your throat right now, you whore, and throw your body into Puget Sound. No one would ever know what happened to you! And you know I could do it, too, baby. I'm a cop, and I know how to do these things and not get caught."

"Go ahead! I'd rather be dead than be with you!"

He is choking her and she is turning blue. He releases his grip, and she bends over gasping for air as his fist hits the side of her ear.

"This is all your fault! You always make me do these things to you. I hoped it would be different this time. But you're the same dirty bitch I divorced twelve years ago. Now I want some sex, and you better make me happy!"

"No, I'm not having sex with you!"

Pushing her towards the bedroom, he yelled, "I've had enough of your shit! Undress or I'll kill you!"

Entering into the old familiar survival state she'd known throughout their marriage, she begins undressing. With trembling fingers she is unbuttoning her blouse, slipping out of her bra, unzipping and stepping out of her slacks and removing her pink, silk panties. She is standing naked before him in a zombie state as pain from her injuries engulfs her.

"Rachie, you still have a really hot body. It's been a long time. Come to big daddy, bitch. I'll help you remember what a little racket in the sack is like with me." Shoving her on her bed, he climbs on top of her, kissing her neck and fondling her breasts. Kissing her on her lips, he forces his tongue inside her mouth. Next, he moves his mouth back down to her breasts as his penis pushes against her lower abdomen. Groping her vaginal area and moving his hands to her inner thighs forcing her legs apart, he raises up, pushing himself roughly inside her and begins pushing deeper and deeper within her as he grasps her buttocks with his hands.

For a brief time the fog clears and she begins to scream, hoping to save herself. He quickly places his hand over her mouth and she bites him. He hits her in the nose with his fist, blood spurts and trickles down her cheek, and she feels herself sinking lower and lower until she leaves the body, becoming a pinpoint of light in the corner of the bedroom. Emotionless, she watches the rape and sees Kenneth falling into a fitful sleep, moaning on top of the body. He looks like a crazed dog dozing, ready to spring to action, ripping out her throat if she dared to try to escape.

Minutes become hours, and the agony of the night gives way to the dawn of a new day. The early morning light sparkles on the vanity mirror. Simultaneously, they both notice when the body's shallow breathing stops and it lays lifeless, battered, and bleeding.

Oh shit! She's isn't breathing! He begins chest compressions and counting until her breathing resumes. "We need a paramedic; there's been an accident," Kenneth says as he provides the 911 operator with the address. "It doesn't matter who I am, just get someone over here!" He slams down the phone.

"I didn't mean to hurt you," he mutters. "You made me do it. I love you. Christ, I should've used a condom. I've got to get the hell out of here."

Closing the book of her life, she begins to weep. Picking up Cookie, she holds her in her arms, the dog snuggling to her and licking her in the face. She'd married Kenneth when she was nineteen. He could be so kind to the homeless, kids, and the elderly. Yet, with her he was often condescending and absolutely brutal.

Aaron was so different from Kenneth, and with him she had learned to trust. It was uncanny how sometimes she and Aaron would be thinking of the same thing at the same time. Other than the men in her family, Aaron was the only other man she felt totally safe with.

Suddenly, she realizes they weren't alone. Standing on each side of her are her maternal grandparents, Henry and Emily Bender.

"Sweetpea," her grandfather said, as he stroked her shoulder. "You've been through a horrible time but you're not alone. We've come to help you make the crossing."

"Yes, that's right honey; we're with Cookie to take you across," her grandmother said. "That is if you're ready. We've got a big family reunion planned before you're placed in the reflectory for meditation and a full review of your life."

"Gram, am I really dead?"

"Well, yes and no. Your silver cord has not yet separated from your body, but that is a small technicality. Your cord will separate when your physical body can no longer support life and part of that is when you let go."

"I don't understand what a silver cord is."

"The silver cord is the connection between your physical and your astral body, and it's usually connected in the area of your belly button."

"What happens when I die?"

"Did you see the bright lights at the end of the corridor?"

"Yes."

"We'll travel with you through the tunnel, and you'll cross over into the light. A short distance into the light, your physical body will separate from your soul and it'll die."

"What if I don't want to die?"

"Honey, this is not the Wizard of Oz. You're not Dorothy and there aren't any ruby slippers."

"Gram, when I came here there was something in the book by my name, but I couldn't make it out. Do you know what it said?"

"Yes, it said, and unborn son."

"Am I pregnant?"

"Yes, didn't you get sick at your stomach on Friday morning?"

"I thought it was food poisoning."

"Now honey! That was some steamy night in Denver. You gave the people up here who love you something to talk about." Rolling her eyes. "Your Aunt Margie said you two looked like Scarlet O'Hara and Rhett Butler. The way he picked you up like a cream puff and carried you into your bedroom. We were placing a little side bet on whether you would get pregnant."

"Gram!"

"Well, sometimes the God Council can be so stuffy. Anyway, they said we were supposed to be dignified souls and not behaving like physical beings. All I can say is it's a good thing your mom hasn't crossed over yet. She wouldn't be happy. I always was more liberal than your mom."

"Birds do it, Bees do it, and we did it, too," Henry said.

Her grandmother smiled, patting him on the shoulder. "Now Henry, stop being a dirty old man."

Blushing, Rachel couldn't believe her grandmother still talked like this in spirit form. "I don't want to die. I want another chance to be a better mom."

"Sara was meant to have a short incarnation, and her death was not your fault. Crib death is not uncommon."

"Gram, Kenneth blamed me and said I was a horrible mother."

"He's not a nice man, and he's got a lot to atone for, you know."

"Do you know about Marie and Sherry?"

"Yes, they've crossed over and their physical bodies have died," her grandmother said.

"What happened to them and why was I with them?"

Her grandfather explains, "Sherry was driving her mother to the mall in her Toyota and she ran a red light and they were in a head-on collision. Running a red light is never a good idea. You ended up on the same soul path with them. We don't always know why souls cross paths on transition. Perhaps it was because you all experienced traumatic events. Only God knows."

Chapter Four

*A*aron exits the elevator on the third floor housing the intensive care unit of County General.

"Excuse me, may I help you?"

Aaron stops abruptly to avoid a head-on collision with a nurse. "Yes, I'm looking for Rachel Goodrich."

"Are you a relative?"

"No, I'm her employer."

"I'm sorry, but right now there are restrictions on visitors for Rachel."

"Can you tell me how she is?"

"Sir, I'm sorry, but we can only provide that information to the family."

"I do have a medical power of attorney."

"I'll need to see it and make a copy."

The grey-haired nurse looks through the lower part of her glasses at him. He thinks she's analyzing him like a bacteria sample under a microscope. "I'm sorry. I came straight from the airport, and I don't have it with me."

"Okay. Wait here."

Minutes later a plain clothed detective appears, flashing his credentials and introducing himself as Sergeant Gerald Hershel. He's a bald man in his middle fifties with a stocky build. He escorts Aaron into an empty waiting room. "Have a seat. Could I get you something to drink?"

"No thanks. I'm anxious to check on Rachel."

"Sure, I understand. We're investigating a crime and need to gather a little information. I'm sorry for the inconvenience. Sandy, your secretary, told us you were in Denver."

"That's right, I was, but I caught the first available flight when Sandy called me."

"How well do you know Rachel?"

"She's worked for me for seven years and we often travel together, so I know her pretty well."

"Do you know if she's currently seeing anyone?"

"Not that I'm aware of."

"Do you know if she had any enemies or problems with someone that might cause her harm?"

"I can't think of anyone who would do such a thing!"

"I may have further questions later, but for now let me see if I can find her parents. By the way, the Coffee Genie makes a good cup of mud."

"Thank you."

Leaning back in his chair he thinks about the day. He was in the middle of the big, grand opening of the Denver Coffee Genie when Sandy called him on his cell. She was in her car on the way to the office to find Rachel's personnel folder.

"Something has happened to Rachel, and the police and the emergency room at County General called our office! The answering service called me at home. It may've been a home invasion, but no one can say exactly. I've got to find her parent's contact information!"

"Sandy, try to calm down. Her personnel file is in my office in the brown filing cabinet by the window. Her parents live in Hayward, a suburb of San Francisco. Call her parents, and I'll get the next available flight home. If you hear anything, call me."

It seemed like forever before he heard footsteps in the hall and the detective returned with Stanley Goodrich. Aaron stood up, extending his hand. "Hello sir, I'm Aaron Townsend, Rachel's employer."

"Nice to meet you. Rachel's told us a lot about her job and how much she likes working for you."

"If you gentlemen will excuse me," the detective said, "I need to leave and continue my investigation on this case."

"Thank you, Sergeant Hershel. Her mother and I appreciate anything you can do to bring the perpetrator of this horrible crime to justice."

Looking at Stanley, Aaron asked, "Is there anything I can do to help?"

"Mr. Townsend, there's not much any of us can do but pray. Her mom and I've been doing that since we heard about her condition this morning. Your office called us when she was in the emergency room, and we caught the next flight out of San Francisco. She was moved to the intensive care unit about a half hour or so before we arrived. It's a terrible shock for her mother and me to see her in such a lifeless condition."

"Please call me, Aaron. I'm so sorry."

"She's still unconscious, but you could see her if you want. She's been beaten up pretty badly, raped, and she's got a concussion and other injuries. Rachel's in critical condition, and the hospital is doing all it can to pull her through this.

Gerald Hershel asked if Rachel was seeing anyone or if we knew of anyone who might want to harm her. Of course we don't."

"He asked me the same questions and I'm dumbfounded and shocked about how this could've happened to her."

"Well, it's been about twelve years since her divorce to that creep, Kenneth Hamilton. Back then I would've said he was guilty. But as far as I know she hasn't seen or heard from him after she left Lincoln, Nebraska. He remarried, so I told the detective I was pretty sure her ex wouldn't have anything to do with this."

"I knew Rachel was divorced, but she never talked about him, so I, too, think it unlikely he would be involved."

"They completed a rape kit when she came in, and they said they'll compare any DNA they find with their known sex offender data base. I'll tell the charge nurse that you can see our daughter."

"Thank you."

Kenneth timed his debut at the hospital to arrive after things had a chance to settle down a bit, along with reducing the probability the police would still be there. Inquiring of Rachel's condition, he was directed to the ICU nurses' station. The nurse pointed to a waiting room where her father could be located.

"Stanley, it's been a long time! One of the nurses said I could find you in this waiting room," Kenneth said, offering his hand.

"Oh Lord, what are you doing here?"

"I went by Rachel's apartment to see her, and her neighbors told me she'd been hurt, that I could find her here. What happened?"

"She's near death; someone almost killed her. That wouldn't happen to be you, would it?"

"How could you possibly think or say that?"

"With your history it's not a far leap to make."

"I'm hurt and offended you would think that I'd harm Rachel. I've loved her since we were kids."

"Look, Kenneth, I've no energy to rehash the past. My daughter might not make it through the day, so if you don't mind, please leave me the hell alone!"

"Fine! I want to see Rachel, too. I also care about her. If you remember Stanley, she was the mother of my child. And who are you?" he asked, turning to Aaron.

"I'm Aaron Townsend, Rachel's employer."

"Nice to meet you, Mr. Townsend. I hope her dad treats you better than he treated me."

Stanley speaks to the charge nurse and Aaron is directed to Rachel's bed in ICU.

Aaron's hands grip the cold, hard, metal rail of the hospital bed. A blood pressure cuff is attached to Rachel's left arm and a computer screen is deciphering all the data from the tubes and wires connected to her. The sound of her ventilator rhythmically pumping oxygen seems loud in the quiet room. Her body is swathed in bandages and the small amount of skin showing is a pasty grey. The smell of alcohol and cleansers drifts through the large ICU that provides care to several patients. Aaron shook his head, wondering what could drive someone to such brutality. Did Rachel know her attacker? Was he a lover, current or past? Could it have been her ex-husband? He never had any indication Rachel was seeing her ex, but it's quite apparent her father has a very low opinion of him. Aaron used to think of her as a timid mouse.

He'd never been aware of her dating anyone. In fact, he thought she was leery of men.

He remembered when he first met Rachel. He agreed to give her a job interview because of Cash Wilson, an old UCLA buddy. Cash was her advisor at Washington State and thought she'd be a gem for Aaron's business. She seemed timid and was not pretty to look at. Her hair was severely pulled back in a bun, no makeup, and she wore these god-awful brown-framed bifocal glasses. She was about five feet six inches tall and was dressed in a pantsuit and black flats. But he was not looking for a date and she seemed pretty sharp. It had been a good fit because she was a whiz when it came to computers, accounting, and communicating with the other staff.

Three years ago he began expanding the Coffee Genie on the west coast. He hired Sandy to manage the office while he and Rachel were out of town. Spending more time together, they became the best of friends. He liked watching her blossom.

In Los Angeles, they were window-shopping to kill some time before a meeting. There was this beautiful sky blue dress with French sleeves and straight skirt. Rachel tried it on, and he told her she looked stunning in the dress. The next day he coaxed her into having her hair done and having a spa treatment. The makeup, light and perfect, accentuated her high cheekbones. The dress hugged her curves and fell just above the knee, exposing her shapely legs. Later, they'd gone out to dinner, and he told her over a glass of Chablis that she was beautiful. When they returned to Seattle she changed to contact lenses. Sometimes he felt like her father even though there was only a seven-year difference between their ages.

Watching and participating in her transformation made him happy.

Six weeks ago he and Rachel were in the final preparation of expanding the Coffee Genie into the Denver area. They were sitting in the living room of their two-bedroom suite, reviewing his accountant's cost analysis. She was leaning over his chair pointing out one of the expenses.

It was late in the evening, and maybe it was the wine on an empty stomach, her chocolate-scented perfume, or the soft rock instrumental music that played in the background. Who could say? Pulling her close and kissing her, he had momentarily felt her hesitancy and then her response. Wrapping his arm around her small waist, he gently guided her onto his lap as he kissed her. Kissing her ear, his lips then slid down to her creamy, slender neck. Pulling the combs from her hair, he placed his hand into the soft, silky, chestnut brown hair tumbling down her back. Placing his hands under her knees and standing up, he carried her to her bedroom. "Darling, I need you. You're so beautiful. Please let me make love to you tonight."

She had murmured, "Oh, Aaron."

He looked at the sleeping Rachel in the early morning light, realizing he'd made a big mistake. She was special and not like the other women he'd casually dated. Since the accident, he found it difficult to form a lasting relationship. Abruptly, he had sent her back to Seattle to take care of the office while he remained in Denver to oversee the opening of the new coffee shop.

Meredith and Aaron Michael Junior had been killed in an automobile crash in Los Angeles. They were side swiped by a drunk driver on their way home to Irvine from a regional soccer game. He played the scene over and over in his mind, wondering if he could have saved them if he'd been driving the car. Damn, he should've been there.

He was the junior partner in the law firm of McCormick, Ellis, Miller, Schumer, and Townsend. He and Chuck Schumer had been preparing for weeks for the upcoming multimillion-dollar lawsuit on behalf of the developer in a real estate partnership that had gone amuck. They both canceled family times to work late evenings and Saturdays.

Meredith had expressed her fear of driving in Los Angeles and pleaded for him to take them to the soccer game. He had been trying to explain why he had to work on Saturday. One thing led to another, and they quarreled in their bedroom while he was getting ready to leave for the office. Meredith was accusing him of always putting his job first. Didn't she see how he was trying to provide for their financial future? She retorted, "Well, money isn't everything!" Snapping back, he said, "Well, tell that to your food cooperatives, your charities, and your political action groups." My God, if only he had gone with them.

The house felt so empty after their death. Walking through the rooms, reliving memories of his son's first birthday, cuddling him when he had that bad ear infection, his first Christmas. He could still remember the sound of Mikie's squeals when he walked in the front door, "Daddy! Daddy! Daddy!" He had picked him up, bouncing him in the air. He would carry the toddler into the kitchen to kiss his wife, who was making dinner. Then there was the first bike with training wheels. The soapbox car kit he helped Mike build when he was nine. Gone all gone, and all that remained were haunting memories of a time never coming back.

Time seemed to drag by. It felt like a decade since their death when it actually was only about a year. Work was the only thing giving him structure and a certain normalcy, but at the end of the day, people returned home to their families, and he to his empty house, filled with nothing but memories. Sometimes he thought he could hear Mike calling him, "Dad, where are you?" or Meredith's laugh.

Drinking wine to a state of stupor, falling into bed and snuggling his pillow night after night, shedding rivers of tears—nothing could bring them home to him. Eventually, realizing he needed a change, he began cleaning out drawers and cabinets to keep his mind busy. He found some of Meredith's old psychology tapes of Leo Buscaglia, a professor at the University of Southern California and an author who lectured on love. Buscaglia spoke of growing up with Italian immigrant parents and talked about the human condition and making a difference in the lives of those around you. He provided a poignant story of a young woman in her early twenties who committed suicide. She must have felt so alone, and no one even noticed. Aaron listened to those tapes over and over. He realized that he'd over emphasized the material side of life. He had worked three years for the public defender's office and five years as a private practice attorney. He now believed that he had failed in fully living in the moment with his family.

He wanted more out of life and though he could never bring them back, by God, he was going to go out and find a way to make the world a better place! But what? Coffee? Yes, a simple, cheery cup of coffee. He wanted to leave Southern California far behind, and if he was going to sell coffee he couldn't think of a better place than Seattle. Doesn't all good coffee start in Seattle? Yes, just about anything great starts in Seattle.

He decided his coffee shop would be a memorial to Meredith and the principles by which she had lived. He wouldn't sell anything that was not organic! Baked goods of the highest quality made with real butter from cows grazing on grass, unbleached flours, quality oils like cold pressed coconut, and free from preservatives. He would make sure his products were soy free and free of genetic engineering. Meredith would be proud if she was up there looking down!

His first coffee shop was a huge success. In those days he only carried a few things like bagels, cheesecake, brownies, and cookies. By word of mouth, he found a French pastry chef, Bernard Beaumont, who shared Meredith's views on food. Bernie had worked with him all these years, creating the finest pastry money could buy. Of course, the prices are a little higher than regular coffee shops, but his customers never seem to mind. Most people frequenting his coffee shops were of a similar mindset, never buying into the cholesterol hoax perpetrated on the American public. All one has to do is look at the diet of the French to realize Ancel Key's lipid hypothesis doesn't hold water, or so Meredith always said.

He was now choking down sobs as the realization hit that he might not ever have the chance to tell Rachel why he sent her back to Seattle. Never tell her he was in love with her. He touches the bulge in his suit pants pocket, a small velvet box. If he could find the son of a bitch that did this to her, he'd kill him! Oh God, why was this happening?

Chapter Five

Late Saturday afternoon, Stanley and Susan Goodrich, Rachel's Aunt Amelia, Kenneth Hamilton and Aaron Townsend are ushered into a medical office on the ICU floor of County General. The hours had ticked by while waiting for news of her condition—any news.

"Mr. Townsend, you could go ahead and leave. This is a family matter and we'll take care of Rachel and her needs," Kenneth said.

Susan dabs at her eyes. "Kenneth, I'd prefer Mr. Townsend stay. After all, he's been so helpful to her father and me. He arranged with the hospital to give us a place to stay so we could be close to Rachel."

"Sure, Mom, if you'd rather. I just thought we could take care of things and keep it simple. You know, just the family."

"I'm not going to sit here and pretend that we're family, or that I even like you Kenneth," Stanley said.

"Stanley, I do understand how you feel."

"Kenneth, you couldn't possibly!"

"Stanley, please!" Susan said.

"Honey, I'm sorry. Please don't cry." Stanley places his arms around her shoulder.

Amelia touches Susan's arm. "Honey, Rachel's a strong girl. She'll be okay."

"I don't know, Amelia. She looks so pitiful and she does have a weak heart."

Rapping on the door and walking in, the young doctor spoke. "Hi, I'm Doctor Johnson, Rachel's primary care doctor. I know you're all anxious for news of her condition, so let's—"

There's a knock on the door.

"Yes, come in," Dr. Johnson said.

"I'm Sandy Delray, and I've got some papers for Aaron Townsend."

"Please excuse me a moment," Aaron said as he left the room.

Aaron, flipping through Rachel's folder, removes the durable medical power of attorney.

"Thanks, Sandy. If you don't mind, could you please wait here until this meeting is finished? I'd appreciate it if you could take her file back to the office."

"Sure, is there anything else I can do?"

"I can't think of anything right now."

Returning to the meeting, Aaron said, "I apologize for the disruption."

Dr. Johnson clears his throat. "We've gotten back most of the medical tests. Rachel has a broken nose, bruises, contusions, and cracked ribs. These by themselves are not really life threatening. However, due to blows she received to the head, she has cerebral edema. This is an accumulation of excess fluid in the extracellular spaces of the brain. We've started her on an intravenous osmotic therapy to dehydrate and reduce the cranial pressure. In addition, she has an arrhythmia and her heart has stopped a few times since she was admitted to County General."

"Rachel had rheumatic fever when she was ten and it weakened her heart," Susan explained.

"Susan, you're right; this is a complication. One area we're concerned about is her pregnancy. Even though the pregnancy is in the embryonic stage, we do want to take precautions and consider this aspect of her condition as we try to help Rachel recover. Of course, since this is an embryo, we're not going to avoid doing everything we can to save her."

"Pregnant! Oh my God! She isn't even married and she never mentioned any boyfriends to her dad and me," Susan said.

Amelia interjected, "Rachel's a good girl. Times have changed, Susan, since we were kids. No one pays much attention to unwed mothers these days."

"Amelia, how can you talk like that?"

"Mom," Kenneth said. "Rachel probably didn't want to tell you right away, but we're trying to reconcile our differences. I was out here for a weekend in July. The baby is certainly mine. I flew in yesterday so we could go to the courthouse and get remarried. I'm just devastated this happened to her—to me!"

"Kenneth, are you sure? What you're saying seems unbelievable to me."

"Sue—unbelievable? Let's face it; he's a God damn liar!" Stanley shouted.

Susan, embarrassed by Stanley's outburst, said, "Stanley, please calm down, and don't talk to Ken like that."

"Susan, I'm sorry, but he grates on me."

Dr. Johnson spoke again in a calm voice. "Our tests indicate she is in her first trimester and approximately five to six weeks pregnant."

"Dr. Johnson, do you think she'll come out of the coma?" Kenneth asked.

"I'm hopeful, but right now there's no way of knowing."

"Rachel would never want to be kept alive on life supports," Kenneth said. "Mom, don't you think the humane thing would be to take her off of the life supports and let her pass away naturally if she's meant to?"

"God, I just can't," Susan sobbed.

Touching Susan on the knee, Amelia turns to face Kenneth. "Really, Kenneth, shutting off her life supports seems a bit premature. Sue, please don't cry. You need to be strong for Rachel. She needs you."

"I know Amelia; it's all just so upsetting."

"Susan, can we get you some water or something," Dr. Johnson asked.

Aaron offers her his handkerchief. "This is so hard. Why don't you and Amelia go with my office manager and have something to drink?"

"No, I need to stay."

"No, Sue," Stanley spoke firmly. "Aaron is right. I'll take care of everything."

Aaron walks out into the hall. "Sandy, Mrs. Goodrich is very distraught. Could you please take her and her sister to the cafeteria and get them something to drink?"

"Sure, I'd be happy to."

Returning to the room, Aaron introduces Sandy as he helps Mrs. Goodrich to her feet.

When the door closes behind them, the doctor asks, "Kenneth, why did you suggest that Rachel be taken off life supports?"

"Dr. Johnson. I'm just thinking of her parents, really."

"Now that's bull and you know it!" Stanley yelled. "In other words, you're full of shit! You never cared about my daughter, her mother, or me."

Kenneth's jaw quivered and Aaron notices the cut on his lip. "Excuse me, I think what we need to focus on is Rachel and what's best for her."

"I totally agree. I didn't come here to fight with her father, or be insulted," Kenneth said.

"I know Rachel wouldn't want to be kept on life supports if there was nothing more that could be done," Aaron said. "However, she hasn't even been here twenty-four hours. I think we need to allow more time before we consider taking her off life supports."

"Mr. Townsend, that seems really presumptuous," Kenneth said. "How is Rachel's condition any of your business?"

"I'm sorry you think I'm presumptuous. However, I have her durable medical power of attorney. It is recorded at the King's County Courthouse here in downtown Seattle. This document is in compliance with Chapter Eleven of the Code of Washington State. I, along with her parents and doctors, will be making the final decisions on Rachel's care. By the way, you have a nasty cut on your lip; you might want to get someone to look at it." Aaron was trying not to lose his cool and was thinking: you're a jerk. He was willing to place bets that the baby Rachel was carrying was a Townsend and not Hamilton's. If he found out he was the one that hurt her he would smash his face in.

"I did it shaving. Why do you have a power of attorney for Rachel?" Kenneth asked.

"Did you get the cut on your hand from shaving, too?"

"Yah, it seems when I cut myself with my shaver I always end up doing it a couple of times before I'm finished. I guess guys would call that a bad hair day. Like I asked, why do you have a medical power of attorney for Rachel?"

"She and I travel outside of the country on business, and we have had power of attorneys for each other for a few years."

Drumming his fingers on the medical file before him, Dr. Johnson said, "There is one final treatment I wanted to discuss with you which could possibly improve Rachel's prognosis. I'm not sure if you ever heard about hyperbaric oxygen therapy—HBOT?"

"I think I've heard something about it. Don't some athletes use HBOT to heal sports injuries?" Aaron asked.

"Aaron, the very same. Rachel would be put into a hyperbaric oxygen chamber and administered oxygen under pressure. It's been clearly demonstrated to reduce edema and increase healing in traumatic brain injuries. This treatment is contraindicated during pregnancy. However, it's been used a number of times with pregnant women in the case of carbon monoxide poisoning with no damage to the fetus. But this is the rub; this therapy could be of a huge benefit to Rachel but she could lose the baby. In addition, insurance may cover some of the cost, but HBOT is quite expensive—around twelve hundred dollars a treatment. If we wanted to do this, the sooner we start, the better the prognosis."

"Doctor, I want my daughter to have the best chance of survival and I know it's what her mother would want. I think we've got to take the risk."

"I have to concur with her father," Aaron said.

"It does make sense what you're saying Doctor, but Mr. Townsend and her father don't understand how important this baby is to Rachel and me. We lost our daughter to crib death, and we were excited about this baby. I'm not sure Rachel would want to risk it. But of course, I love her and want only the best outcome. So I think I'm outnumbered. So, yes, go ahead. But I'm embarrassed to say that unfortunately, this has caught me at a bad time. I'm a little strapped for cash."

"That's fine," Aaron said. "Let's just get Rachel the best chance of recovery. Her dad and I'll deal with the finances."

"Wow, that is generous of you. I want you to know how much Rach and I appreciate your financial assistance, Mr. Townsend."

"You act like you're back with Rachel, and to be honest, I seriously doubt it!" Stanley said.

"Stanley, I'm not here to argue with you, man; I'm here for Rachel and our baby."

"Well, okay. It's settled," Dr. Johnson said. "I'll try to get her scheduled for this hyperbaric oxygen treatment. If there are no further questions, I'll be in touch when we have new information."

"As it's been a long day and there's nothing further I can do, I'm going to go get some rest and I'll return tomorrow to check on our girl," Kenneth said.

"Great, you do that," Stanley said.

Chapter Six

After the meeting, they had taken turns standing vigil at Rachel's bedside until her nurse suggested the family might want to go and have some dinner while she bathed Rachel and took her vitals. The nurse recommended Rosa's kitchen across the street from the hospital, which served Mexican and American cuisine.

The smell of chili spice and onions oozed from the little café, and when they opened the door the smell intensified. A plump Hispanic lady seated them at a round table near the entrance to the kitchen. Wonderful aromas of enchilada's, beans, and chili drifted by, making their mouths water in anticipation. A large dish of corn tortilla chips, salsa, and guacamole was placed on the table before them.

Looking at the menu, Susan said, "I don't feel hungry. Maybe I'll just have a glass of water."

"Susan," Amelia said. "You really need to have something. How are you going to be of help to Rachel if you become ill from malnutrition?"

"Really Amelia, missing one meal is hardly malnutrition. Besides, I don't feel like eating when I think of this horrible thing that has happened to her. She isn't even married and being pregnant. We never raised her like that!"

"Yes, I find it hard to believe she's back with Kenneth, who's such a low life scum. There has to be some other explanation! Aaron, did she ever tell you she's divorced?"

"Yes, she did Stan, but she never really talked about it."

"Well, let me tell you, he was a low life from the very beginning. Her mother and I grounded her and we did everything to keep her away from him. We knew it wasn't going to be good. Rumor in Hayward was his parents use to fight like cats and dogs. Anyway, his mother ran off with a used car salesman. He used to slap my daughter around on a regular basis. To add insult to injury, after their daughter died of crib death he started running around with some blonde bimbo. He left Rachel for this other woman. Her mom and I were more than happy to go to Lincoln and get her. I fail to see why we've got to let Kenneth see her."

"Stan, please," Susan said. "Maybe Rachel wouldn't want you to divulge all this information. It's embarrassing, you know. Plus, we already talked about this; we don't know if they've made up."

"Sue, it all happened such a long time ago. There's nothing she should be embarrassed about," Amelia said.

"Well, maybe not, Amelia, but we don't need to be rehashing dirty laundry in public. And you're so liberal—like Mom."

"I suppose I am, but I like to take life easy, and I'm not stuffy like you. By the way, do you remember your purple hair experience?"

A smile spread across Susan's face. "Oh, that again! You know full well I do because everyone teased me so much!"

"Aaron, you should've been there!" Amelia said, as she began to laugh, thinking this little story may reduce the tension now surrounding them. "Let me tell you. My sister was getting ready for the junior prom. She had her dress, and her date, Doug, was the most popular boy in high school. She had to top it off with blonde hair. Mom recommended she not do that and Dad said, 'Let her do it. Why not?' Anyway, she went to the beauty school near where we lived, and because of the red highlights in her hair, the bleach job went totally wrong and she had purple hair. It took six hours and they finally toned it down to just purple highlights. When she came home she was like a poodle that runs and hides under the bed after its first shearing. Mom saw it and burst out laughing. Dad told her not to cry, that it looked nice on her. He tried to reassure her and told her it would go with her dress. Anyway, Doug came to take her to the dance and his eyes got as big as saucers. 'Can you see the purple in my hair?' Susan asked. Now that is like a woman asking her husband if he thinks she looks fat. He better not say yes. In a consoling voice he said, 'Your hair is beautiful and I barely see any purple.' At the time it was so hard to keep from bursting out laughing, just watching the dynamics between those two.

"Anyway, they went to the dance, and when uppity Margie Benson was dancing the twist with Doug, she asked about your hair. 'Well,' he told her, 'she did it on purpose; after all this is California and we are more modern thinkers.' Many of the girls in your class were trying to replicate your hairdo. On the way home you fretted over it, as you do with many things, and do you remember what he told you?"

"He said, 'There are two basic types of people, those who are trend setters, living boldly, and the ones who are like plain vanilla wrappers, blending into obscurity in the world. The rest of our society falls somewhere in between these extremes.'"

"Exactly right, Susan. He was wise beyond his years. Too bad he was killed in Viet Nam. Different theme with the same results. Sue, you take life way too seriously dear; stop being so stuffy! Think if Rachel lives how wonderful this grandbaby will be. So let's be cheery and have something good to eat. I'm having a chicken chimichanga."

Aaron really likes Rachel's Aunt Amelia and thinks she's a real card. He refrains from laughing but finds her amusing even at this somber time. She's like a ray of sunshine. Susan, on the other hand, could be best described as Victorian. Everything with her has a place and time. One might say she's a proper lady. He also likes a guy like Stan who speaks his mind.

Returning from dinner, the nurse tells them there are some improvements in Rachel's condition. Although she is breathing on her own, she's still in a coma, and the brain swelling has marginally improved.

At nine thirty p.m. the speaker on the public address system announces, "Visiting hours are closing for the day, please make your way to the elevators." Even though ICU had no real visiting hours per se, at nine thirty p.m. they discouraged family from remaining, partly for the comfort of all of their patients as well as the knowledge that family members, too, needed their rest.

Rachel's family was given a room near the ICU, so after hugs and bidding them goodnight, Aaron leaves the hospital to go home.

Unlocking his front door and walking into his bedroom he sits his suitcase by the bed. Tired and unable to sleep he goes into the kitchen and opens a bottle of water. He carries it to his favorite brown leather recliner in the living room and sits down. It's been a long day, starting out in Denver at the grand opening, flying home, and spending hours in the waiting room at the hospital. He begins hashing through the day's events and allowing his mind to wander.

It's kind of strange that Rachel never mentioned she'd had a baby or what she'd gone through in her seven-year marriage. How well did he really know her? Thinking they were really close and she might've at least mentioned something. But then, did he tell her about his family? No, it just never felt like a right time to tell her. Maybe it was the same for her. She must've gone through hell with Kenneth. No wonder she never wanted to look like she was shopping or available for a man. He can see now the wariness she'd had in her eyes when she first started working for him. What could drive someone to hurt her like that? Violence just never made sense to him. Meredith used to say mentally disturbed people and those who hurt others were nutritionally unsound. She believed it was a sign of the degeneration of our society. Yes, my girl Meredith almost always talked this way.

He was all prepared to pop the question on Tuesday and now he didn't know if she'd live. If she lived, is she going back to him? It didn't seem to ring true and her family didn't believe it. Yet what if she did want her ex-husband back? Where would it leave him? Us? He mused to himself, when did he begin thinking of Rachel and himself as *us*? It was way before the night in Denver. Could this be his baby? Or had she been having conjugal visits with Kenneth? So many unanswered questions.

He guesses it doesn't matter because he loves her, totally loves her! No matter the outcome, he'll be there for her in a way he wasn't for Meredith and Mike.

Meredith and Rachel were very different from each other. Meredith had often worn her long, blonde hair pulled back in a clip. She loved dogs and kids. She was thrilled with the chaos of having all of Mike's friends at the house and whipping up a batch of organic cookies. Rachel, on the other hand, always kept her hair in a French twist or a bun—there wasn't a hair out of place. She didn't enjoy cooking. He smiled, thinking of those cookies she made for their last company Christmas party. They could've been lethal weapons if thrown. Someone had to go to the dentist for a chipped tooth over one of those cookies. He couldn't help but laugh. Yes, he was sure she was pretty inept in the kitchen, but not everyone can be a Julia Child.

Rachel is such a sweet and thoughtful person. A couple of years ago she found out the lady who cleaned their office was not going to be able to buy Christmas presents for her four children. Her husband had recently been laid off from his job. She went on a shopping spree, buying food, clothes, and toys for the lady. Rachel never mentioned it to anyone, but the cleaning lady had told him of her kindness.

Meredith was so much like her father. Dwayne Turner was an MD who had gotten into trouble with the medical board over his naturopathic ideas. He was into anti-aging medicine in its infancy. He believed nutrition was the key to healing, not pharmaceutical drugs. When his mother died of colon cancer it changed him. He often raged about chemotherapy killing the immune system.

He remembered that when Meredith was pregnant with Mike she was meticulous about her diet. She drank raw milk, ate real butter from grass-fed cows, and supplemented her natural diet with cod liver oil. It seemed like she was always making bone broth or lacto fermenting vegetables. She had also chosen natural instead of drug-assisted childbirth.

She watched over their diets and they were rarely sick. She didn't believe in vaccinations, as she said it damages the immune system and doesn't allow the body to develop natural immunity. She was adamant that Mike would never have childhood vaccines. She'd often rave about the flu vaccine, of how it was full of toxins like aluminum, something about chicken blood and baby placenta. Quite honestly, when she described it, Aaron knew he would never have the flu shot.

One time he came home and Mike was in his crib, wailing at the top of his lungs, and she was in the kitchen. It looked like a war zone. She'd left the lid on too tightly on of one of her fermenting jars, and the gas from the fermenting sugar built up, exploding. It left shrapnel in the kitchen ceiling and glass had gone everywhere. He remembered how relieved he was when he determined neither of them was hurt. When it exploded she'd been in the laundry room putting a load of clothes in the dryer. He told her to go take care of the baby and he would clean up the glass and the mess.

The vegetables and the fermented liquid were dripping down the sides of the wall and the kitchen cabinetry. At the time they'd been living in married student housing. They couldn't get the glass out of the ceiling. When they moved out the school staff never noticed the kitchen ceiling during their closeout inventory. He cleaned up the mess and Meredith changed and fed the baby. The full realization hit him how serious this could've been. He angrily told her, "You've been so careless! What if the baby would have been killed or hurt, or you?" She cried and he felt like a jerk. He went out and bought some flowers. He also went to a beer-making place and bought some lids with valves to release the pressure so this would never happen again. She forgave him and they made love like newlyweds even though he needed to study for the state bar exam. He often loved to tell their friends the story of how she almost blew up their kitchen. It was always good for a laugh. Gosh, how he still missed her.

He remembered when they first met; it was at the student bookstore at UCLA. He was prelaw and her double major was early childhood education and psychology. Meredith was a year older than he was but they were both freshmen, as he graduated high school when he was seventeen.

Hyperbaric oxygen sounded like a great approach for Rachel. Because of Meredith, he was kind of skeptical of anyone with an MD after their name. Oh sure, they were wonderful if you broke your neck or an arm. When it came to chronic diseases they were almost complete failures. Meredith and her father always said they suppress symptoms but they don't help people regain their health. He'd heard how big pharma wined and dined them, sending them to places like the Bahamas on medical conferences. Dwayne, and his clone, Meredith, had said what they know about nutrition you could put in a thimble. If he heard her say it once, he'd heard it a million times: "They don't know an amino acid from an antioxidant." Sometimes he would tease her for being so radical. She'd retort, "No, I'm a realist. Prescription drugs have side effects. The only true way to real health is through clean food and taking responsibility for your lifestyle."

It didn't bother him if she thought there was a new world order that was out to kill baby boomers with statin drugs, painkillers, and antidepressants. He loved women to be free thinkers and have their own opinions.

He did have to agree with Meredith about raw milk; it tasted so much better than the pasteurized stuff. He couldn't ever see why the Department of Agriculture harassed small farmers and people in food cooperatives. For God's sake, it is only raw milk, not bootleg gin from the nineteen twenties.

The other thing Meredith would get on her bully pulpit over was dentists and root canals. According to her, there was this dentist in the early part of the twentieth century who planted infected teeth in the stomachs of rabbits. A short time later the rabbits all died from similar afflictions plaguing the people from whom the teeth were extracted. He couldn't remember the name of the dentist; he thought it might be something like Price or Rice. Anyway, this dentist was considered the father of nutrition. Her other pet peeve were silver fillings.

It was too bad, but after he lost Meredith and Mike his in-laws severed all ties with him, blaming him for not being with them in Los Angeles. They were their only daughter and grandchild. He could see how hurt they were. It'd been fourteen years and sometimes it still felt like yesterday.

It will be different this time. Rachel and her family can count on him being there even if she is going to marry Kenneth. Which he hopes is not the case.

"Rachel, please don't die. I love you sweetheart." He threw his tie on the dresser, unbuttoning his shirt. "God, if you are up there, please let her live, even if the baby is not mine or she chooses Kenneth."

Parking in the lot of his studio apartment in the Belltown area of Seattle, Kenneth slides out of the car. Locking the car door then tucking his thirty-eight-special handgun into his left front pocket. It had stopped raining but the wet pavement glistened like lip gloss against the orange-yellow city lights. Trees and other objects look shadowy in the dim light. He's prepared for anything which may come his way; after all, this is downtown Seattle.

Walking down the street he looks at all the flashing neon signs of hotels, cafes, and bars. He wasn't sure when he had felt so alone.

Opening the door to the Twilight Bar, he feels a warm blast of air on his face. The bartender, a short, half-bald, pudgy man wearing a topaz ring, was wiping the shiny, dark oak counter with a peppermint stick colored rag. A Hank Williams tune played on the jukebox and the place was nearly empty. The people in a dump like this on a Saturday night were probably just a few losers—just like himself.

"Hey, man, what can I get ya?"

"Give me a double scotch on the rocks with a twist of lime." He needed a drink, and he couldn't wait to feel the warm, numbing fluid go down his throat.

"Here you go, it'll be four dollars. Do you want to run a tab?"

"No." Paying and taking the drink, he walks across the dark wood floor to a corner booth.

Sighing, he thinks, what is that cliché? Something about the fruit never falls far from the tree. He's just like his ole man. A chip off the ole block. He snickers and raises the glass to his lips, feeling the liquid warm his throat. God, no! He would've never predicted he'd live like his parents.

Glen and Stella would leave him and Rodger home alone on a Saturday night while they went bar hopping. Mom would wear a short, tight, black dress a size too small, with four-inch heels. She reeked of cheap, dime store cologne, and her makeup was heavily applied. She always wore these long dangly faux diamond earrings she purchased at Woolworth, a dime store a few blocks from their home.

There were usually snacks and candy for them along with strict instructions to not open the door to anyone and don't play with matches. The feeling in the pit of the stomach when they would hear the car make the turn into the parking lot in front of their building around two o'clock a.m., shortly after the bars closed.

Having a ground floor apartment, the headlights lit up the side of their bedroom wall. The moment dreaded all evening finally arrived. As soon as they walked in the door, the arguing started, along with the angst and feeling of helplessness. The sounds of thuds as flesh contacts flesh, along with their mother's cries. Sometimes they'd plead for him to stop. He also remembered the nauseating smell of alcohol on their clothes and breaths. The neighbors in the other apartments would bang on the walls, telling them to shut up or they'd call the police, and sometimes they did. The cops would come and cool them down and sometimes Dad would end up in the county clink. Then Mom would have to go bail him out. He'd sworn he'd never behave like them, and especially not around little children.

One day returning home from junior high school, he discovered Mom had packed her bags and left town with a used car salesman. After she left, the three of them moved to a small mobile home park near the garage where Dad worked as a mechanic.

He remembered when he met Rachel. It was the beginning of his senior year at Hayward High, and she had the locker next to his. She was definitely a sweet and beautiful girl. He flirted with her and invited her to the game. They were both popular in those days, but it seemed like destiny for them to be together. He pushed her at school once and the principal called their parents. Her parents never liked him after that and did everything to keep them separated. Her dad probably thought she was too good for the guy on the wrong side of town.

After graduation he couldn't wait to leave home and did what many poor boys do—joined the Army. Rodger was different; he got a scholarship and went to college, where he met Cathy. They finished their education and had four kids. Rodger's childhood memories are relics of the past. He told him, "You know, Kenneth, life is what you make it. Why dwell on what happened when we were kids?" It's hard to believe they grew up in the same house, as he never heard him raise his voice to Cathy or their kids.

He went on the job interview in Denver as a diesel mechanic at the suggestion of his therapist and his parole officer. They said he needed a fresh start and to get out of Sioux Falls. He stayed at Rodger and Cathy's house in Arvada. Seeing their happiness emphasized the fact that all he had to his name was a steamer trunk they'd kept while he was in prison. He went through it—the remnants of a broken life—in the basement of their home. A wrinkled army hat; his discharge papers; certificate of completing the police academy in Nebraska; two sets of divorce papers—one from Rachel and one from Debbie—some fake identification cards issued to him when he worked undercover for vice; a thirty-eight-caliber gun he'd purchased on the black market; and some sweaters that were too small.

At the completion of the undercover assignment, the police department required him to turn in the fake IDs, but they were lost. He and Debbie had torn the house apart looking for them, but they came up empty handed. The captain had chewed him up one side and down the other for his carelessness and wrote a negative job appraisal on him. Months later they were cleaning out some boxes in the garage and he found the IDs shoved into a book he'd been reading at the time. Debbie told him he should turn them in to the department. He told her, "Fuck it! I'm not turning them in to my boss; he was a prick about me losing them. Besides, you never know when they might come in handy. I might decide to rob a bank or something."

He was only kidding, but who knows what can happen in life. One minute you're an upstanding citizen; the next thing you know things turn sour and you're on the other side of the law. How many prostitutes had he busted who were tricking because some event in their life forced them on to the streets. Yah, you just never know.

Being out of prison, he thought these could come in handy and shoved the gun and the ID's into a duffle bag. The sweaters, the certificate, and all the remaining stuff Cathy could just put it in the trash. His life as a cop was over and there was no turning back. No sense crying over spilt milk, like his mother used to say.

It's all in the past, he thought, as he raised his glass, allowing more of the scotch to go down.

I never meant to hurt her. Things went so wrong, and if she'd have just been more welcoming. What a bitch she could be. Yet, she was a lot more submissive than Debbie. She learned early on that it was a waste of time to call the cops on another cop. All they would do is suggest how both parties were responsible and ask would she want him to lose his job.

Now that bitch Debbie fought like a man. Almost choking on a piece of ice, remembering the time they were fighting and she kicked him in the balls. His genitals were bruised for weeks. Well, Rach never dared to do such a thing to him. Rachel was more fragile, and he'd have beaten her senseless if she even tried it.

He truly hated Debbie. It was her fault he lost his job, her fault he ended up behind bars for two years with three years of probation. Come to think of it, he was sure it was mostly her fault he split up with Rachel. Yah, sure when the baby died they were going through some rocky times in their marriage. Things would've probably settled down if she'd not been assigned to him for her ninety-day training period. She was flirtatious and came on to him first. He was certain that was exactly how it went down. If he hadn't got involved with her none of this would have happened. Rach would have probably gotten pregnant again and he'd still have his job in Lincoln.

Debbie's dad was a politician in Nebraska and so when they got into fights the captain was forced to take disciplinary actions. He was put on probation at work and required to take anger management classes. Yah, wasn't Sioux Falls supposed to be a fresh start for them? His partner had moved there and helped them get on with the Sioux Falls Police Department five years ago. Well, so much for marital bliss.

Thinking back to when he saw Rachel in Denver at Mazuna's restaurant. He had nearly finished his dinner when he saw her walking in with Aaron Townsend. The waiter had told him the man was Aaron Townsend, a coffee tycoon from Seattle.

Rachel was obviously doing all right for herself, and she looked really hot in her short skirt, oozing with sexiness. Just looking at her made him want her. He undressed her with his eyes. Yet, she never even saw him; she was so caught up in conversation. He had to have her back. They'd had a lot of bad blood between them, but he figured it would be a piece of cake; she was easy to manipulate and control.

Oh shit, what has he done? If only he could just dial back the time and not taken the shot at Debbie in her car. He was on his way back to his apartment, tired and in his greasy clothes from welding all day when he saw her near West 60th and I-29. He was certain she gave him the finger. Rage rolled over him like a can of gasoline touched by a match. Stepping on the gas, catching nearly up with her, swerving as he reached for the thirty-eight-caliber tucked under the driver's seat. Turning a little to the right, he stuck the gun out the side window, pulling the trigger. The bullet went through her back window, narrowly missing her. The sound of squealing tires as she swerved and then floor boarded her Lexus. His Honda was no match for her newer car.

The trip to Seattle was going to be a week sooner than he and Sandy, the chick who worked for Aaron Townsend, had planned, but he knew the cops would be after him, and he had to go and pack a suitcase and get out of there before they had him back in the slammer. Remembering how he ran through stop signs and stop lights screeching around corners. Racing through his apartment throwing stuff together, clothes, laptop, checkbook, and brief case. There was no time to clean up, so he threw everything in the trunk. He had to get the hell out of South Dakota. There was no way he was going to show up for the meeting with his parole officer on Tuesday. What would be waiting there would be a pair of handcuffs. Too bad he didn't hit the bitch; guess he was out of practice.

Wasn't those anger management classes a fucking waste of time. Stay calm and figure out what to do. If Rach dies and they find out he did it, he would be back in the pen. If she lives, she'll probably tell what happened. There has to be a way out.

"Mister, could I get you another drink?"

"Yah, sure."

Thinking he needed some cold, hard cash in case things went bad. A goal for Monday would be to put a little squeeze on Sandy. Yah, she paid the rent on this studio apartment. It didn't seem like she could do enough to help him on his marital reunion to Rachel. She never actually said, but when another woman is so quick to help set up a scenario for two people to kiss and make up, it means only one thing. She's got the hots for the boss, and Rachel is the obstacle. Women have a sixth sense on these things. She probably figures he and Rachel are doing the dirty. Yah, she's my get-out-of-jail-free card.

He couldn't predict how long before some detective on Rachel's case discovered he was a wanted man. You better keep your ears to the ground and stay alert, he told himself. Paying for the second round and gulping it down, he stepped into the cold night air to return to his apartment.

Chapter Seven

At County General Hospital one day is the same as the next; pain, suffering, and death never takes a day off. Sunday is the same as Wednesday—patients to bathe, bandages to change, and appointments to keep.

Aaron arrives just as Rachel's gurney is being loaded onto an elevator by two orderlies. Stanley was there and they watch as the door closes.

"Good morning, Stan."

"Hello, Aaron."

"How is she this morning?"

"It's been about twenty four hours, and she's stable, but still in a coma. She's no worse and only marginally better, but at least she's breathing on her own. They're taking her up for her oxygen treatment. Sue cried all night and didn't sleep very much and finally dozed off around six, so I left her sleeping. You care to go have some coffee?"

Taking a sip of coffee and leaning forward towards Aaron, Stanley said, "I just don't know what I'm going to do if my daughter dies. She and her mother are my whole life. I never envisioned anything like this would happen to her, especially after her divorce. I mean like she got a degree and then she went to work for you. She's always had only the best things to say about you."

"I think a lot of Rachel, too. She's worked beside me building this company, and I cannot imagine going on without her. We'll do everything we can to save her."

"Well, Sue and I certainly appreciate all you've done for us."

The hospital orderlies soundlessly lined up the gurney at the top of the big oxygen chamber. The sheet is pulled back and the HBOT nurse gently grasps Rachel's wrist, checking her pulse and writing down her vitals on the medical chart the orderlies had handed her. Dr. Gerhardt lifts her eyelids, examining the pupils with his diagnostic pen light, and tries an external rub, attempting to ascertain some level of consciousness.

"Doctor, I've finished prepping the patient and I've checked her IV. Here is her chart."

"Okay, Rose." He flips through the chart. Hmm, he thought, pregnant, but she is only in the embryonic stage, so that could be less problematic.

The nurse fluffs the pillow and does a second check of her IV and her heart monitor. "We are ready. Please slide her stretcher into the chamber."

Rachel's stretcher is slightly lifted on both sides by two hospital orderlies, engaging it with the rails of the big glass and metal cylinder chamber, sliding her into place. The latch closes, sealing the compartment. The doctor sits facing the stretcher and adjust the dials on the front of the unit.

"This treatment will run about one hour, and I'll call her nurse in ICU when she's ready for transport," Rose said. She watches the orderlies walk out, speaking to dispatch on their two-way radio and obtaining their next assignment.

After her treatment, Rachel is quickly whisked back to ICU and gently placed into her bed. When the nurse finishes taking her vitals, Susan pulls up a chair and sits beside her daughter. "Rachel, honey, I don't know if you can hear me, but your father, your Aunt Amelia, and your boss, Aaron Townsend are all here. Honey, we love you, and we know you're going to be fine. Mom is right here and I'm not going anywhere. We're all just taking turns as it's kind of crowded in here. You sure look better today. I would comb your hair sweetheart, but you know I'm not very good at styling hair." She places her hand on the blanket and touches her daughter's hand. "Honey, I love you. Please wake up."

She thought to carry a baby for nine months in the womb only to watch them die. Parents outliving their child isn't supposed to happen! For the first time she fully grasps what it must've been like for Rachel to lose Sara. Tears slip down her face and it's good her hour is up. She didn't want to be crying in front of Rachel, in case at some level she'd know she's crying.

Two orderlies walk into the room. "We're here to take Rachel to the radiology department for a scheduled test."

"When will she be brought back to ICU?"

"We aren't sure of the exact time, but we think it'll be somewhere around one p.m."

The afternoon trickles by, one person at a time sitting by her bedside. It was approaching two o'clock p.m. when Amelia gives Kenneth the signal it's his turn.

Smiling at Rachel's nurse, Kenneth said, "I just want you to know how much her family and I appreciate the care you're giving Rachel. I know you're all doing everything you can to save Rachel and our baby."

"Thank you, Mr. Hamilton we're doing our best."

Leaning over and looking down at her, he says, "Rachel, if you can you hear me baby, I love you."

Regret washes over him like a lava flow. Feeling his chest tighten and struggling to hold back tears, thinking, oh God, how could I have done this? I love her.

She would probably come out brain damaged, and wouldn't the simplest thing be for her to pass away. His inner voice responds—easier for who? Easier for you is what you mean. Oh, man, I just can't go back to prison. I'm never going; they'll have to kill me first. Wasn't he so dumb for missing the window of opportunity to hit the switch, shutting off her life support? You are crazy; you could've never gotten away with it. Besides, that beady-eyed nurse never lets anything escape her. Oh, well, stop dwelling on an expired approach, you have to focus on the here and now and the future.

When he had arrived this morning a guard stood near the ICU. Feeling a little uneasy he wonders how far along they are in the investigation. He imagines the net might be closing. Wasn't it just a matter of time before the detective assigned to her case would be back here nosing around? Probably wanting a DNA sample from people, specifically him. Maybe he shouldn't stay too long; after all, her parents and her boss would surely want to spend more time with her.

Checking his watch, it's three o'clock and his time slot was up anyway. Walking to the door he sees Stan in the hall, talking to the guard. What's he telling him?

"Excuse me Stan. I'm going to leave, if you want to go in to see Rachel, it's your turn."

Dr. Johnson, along with another MD approaches. "Good afternoon. I'd like to introduce you to Dr. Baumbaker, Rachel's neurologist. This is Stanley Goodrich, her father, and Kenneth Hamilton, her ex-husband."

"Nice to meet both of you," Dr. Baumbaker says. "We're going to examine Rachel, and it'll take about a half hour."

"I hope there's some improvement in my daughter."

"I was just leaving. I really appreciate anything you can do for her and our baby."

"Hey, Rachel, wake up! Rachel, wake up!" Dr. Baumbaker says as he touches her, trying to check for a level of consciousness. "There's no response. Bob, let's try noxious stimulation like an external rub." Closing his hand, he rubs across her sternum. He hears a short but really low groan. He then tries it again and notices the same result. "This is the first positive response we've seen. When was the ventilator removed?"

"Bill, that was done last night when her vital signs improved and she began normal breathing."

Dr. Baumbaker manually opens both her eyes. "Rachel, I'm going to be flashing my pen light into your eyes." They notice the pupils looking similar in size and the eyes were in a forward direction. "It looks like we have a sluggish response. Rachel, I'm moving your head from side to side." The eyes lagged behind and slowly caught up. "My opinion, Bob, is that we've got an intact brain stem."

"I concur with your determination, Bill." They continue the examination, making notes in her chart.

Walking into the hall the doctors find the family, along with Aaron Townsend, clustered just outside the ICU door. Each doctor carrying a silver, metal binder containing her medical chart, they usher the group into an empty office near the ICU.

"We've got some news of Rachel's condition," Dr. Johnson begins. "She was given a sixty-minute hyperbaric oxygen treatment this morning. We did a sixty-minute treatment instead of ninety minutes because of her pregnancy. While it's still too soon to expect a lot of improvement, we do see some lessening of the coma. She groaned when we tried external stimulation. Her pupils were similar in size and shape. When we were moving her head from side to side, her eyes lagged behind and then caught up. Dr. Baumbaker's opinion is that her brain stem is intact."

"Exactly!" Dr. Baumbaker said. "In addition, her heart rate and breathing has normalized, which is the reason she was taken off the ventilator last night."

"Does this mean she'll wake up and be okay?"

"We're hoping she will, Mrs. Goodrich, but sometimes these things are in the hands of God. We conducted a position emission tomography, or what we call a PET scan this afternoon. We believe she has some level of consciousness based on this imagery. The physical exam we completed supports the PET scan results."

"Thank you, Dr. Baumbaker; this is a really hopeful sign. Her father and I are grateful to both of you."

"Well, we are far from out of the woods. However, it does look promising," Dr. Johnson said, rising. "Now if you'll please excuse us we have a few more patients we must see."

Chapter Eight

With a pounding headache, Kenneth gropes for and finds the alarm clock and turns it off. It was Monday, eight o'clock a.m. Rolling over on his side, thinking of how he wishes he could rescript a play gone terribly wrong. Reality sinking in and tears falling on his pillow. He used to be a damn good cop and he wasn't such a bad guy. Was he? What goes on behind closed doors, well that's private business between a man and his woman. If someone died it would be murder, and yah, they should go to jail. But otherwise, it was just part of the monopoly game which probably has gone on since man graced the planet.

Thinking of Sara, and how he'd loved holding her. The smell of her baby powder and the soft feel of her skin. When he first held her at the hospital he had counted her little fingers and toes. Such a perfect little thing. When he came home sad about some encounter he had experienced at work, it gave him comfort just watching her sleeping in her crib. The rhythmic rise and fall of her chest had a calming effect on him. When she died it was like someone cut his heart out and stomped it into the ground. He hated Rachel, blaming her even though he knew somehow that she'd had nothing to do with it.

There was this seventeen-year-old girl named Jackie Lynne living on the streets of Lincoln. He and his partner picked her up for prostitution on numerous occasions. He tried in so many ways to help her get off the streets, but she was addicted to crack. They found her dead in an alley in downtown Lincoln from a drug overdose. Coming home, looking at his baby and thinking, you'll never know a life like that; I'll protect you my little darling. But he couldn't protect her from death in her own crib.

Debbie and scotch helped dull the pain of losing Sara. Drinking and partying it up with her was clearly a mistake. He could see it now, but no sense crying over spilt milk, as his mother use to say.

Showering and dressing he picked up the phone and dialed the number.

"Coffee Genie, may I help you?"

"Yah, I need to speak with Sandy."

"May I tell her who is calling?"

"Kenneth Hamilton."

"I'm sorry, she's unavailable."

"Tell her I'll be in touch with her boss if she doesn't speak with me."

"This is Sandy."

"I want you to meet me at Ma's Diner at eleven thirty."

"I'm sorry, but I've got other commitments."

"I think you might want to meet me; otherwise, your boss might find out we know each other. You know, he might not like that."

"Okay, fine."

"Do you want me to buzz by and pick you up?"

"God, no! It is only two blocks and I can walk."

"Okay, Sandy, but don't stand me up. It might not be in your best interest."

"I'll be there," she said and the phone clicked with nothing left but the buzzing dial tone.

Sliding into the booth across from him, "I'm here, so what do you want?"

"Well, I want you to know how much I appreciate what you've done for me, finding the apartment and helping with the rent. I've got a lot to feel grateful for getting that kind of help from someone I barely know."

"I didn't really do it for you. I did it for Rachel, because she's my friend. Like I know she's all by herself, and when you called me and told me how much you loved her. You said you cheated on her, which caused the divorce. I've been questioning my stupidity of meddling into her private business ever since. Well, I just have one question; did you do this to Rachel?"

"Hi, Sandy," the waiter said as he approached the table. "What would you like today?"

"Give me a cob salad with ranch and a black coffee."

"What can I get you, sir?"

"I'll have Ma's potatoes with two eggs over easy, a side of bacon, and coffee and cream."

"We'll get these right out to you."

"Well, about Rachel. Things went all wrong. She hit me first, what was I to do?"

"My God! Certainly not beat her half to death! Do you know how she is?"

"I left after the meeting with Dr. Johnson on Saturday. At that time she was unconscious, and she was still unconscious when I saw her on Sunday. Your boss was all hot to get her those oxygen treatments. Guess because he figures she's carrying his baby."

"Baby?"

"Yah, she's about six weeks pregnant the doc said. You didn't know?"

"No, of course I didn't."

"Thought you were one of her best friends. Don't most of you ladies gab about stuff like this?"

"I didn't know it; besides, how do you know its Aaron's?"

Raising his eyebrows, "What, you think it's mine?"

"Of course not! But it could be someone else's."

"Is that speculation or a lot of wishing?"

"Why would I care if it's Aaron's or not?"

"Come on baby, I'm a cop. I can read people like a ten cent novel."

"Don't call me baby. This conversation is finished! In fact, I'm finished with you, Kenneth! Believe me, it was a huge mistake to get involved with this. Do us both a favor and forget you ever met me!"

"Well, Sandy, it's just not that easy. Besides, I need you to help me get out of Dodge. I need twenty grand to make this go away."

"You've got to be kidding! Where do you think I'm going to get that kind of money?"

"Come on, Sandy. I need you to help me. I feel so alone in the world, and you know I'm praying for Rachel to recover. Surely you must know I never meant to hurt her. I love her! Have always loved her since we were high school sweethearts."

"No, I can't!"

"I'm just trying to be reasonable here. You don't want to leave me in a lurch do you?"

"I don't have that kind of money at my fingertips!"

"Okay. Maybe you don't understand you could be considered an accomplice. I mean like the police could figure out you're involved simply by the fact you gave me her address. Plus, your name is on the rental agreement of the apartment. The other tidbit is just how is that boss of yours going to take to the news his office manager divulged confidential information?"

"Are you blackmailing me?"

"Well, let's not call it blackmail. Call it helping a friend. Or paying to make it all go away—like a service. Kind of like a plumber fixing a slab leak. You know, something like that."

"Kenneth, you wouldn't do that! How could you put it in the same category as hiring a plumber?"

"I'm just using it as an example. What I'm saying is it all depends on your perspective."

"I can't believe you would implicate me in this!"

"Have you heard the saying, desperate people do desperate things? Besides, I'm just saying things could leak out. You help me, I help you. And I need the money by tomorrow."

"Tomorrow? You've got to be kidding!"

"I'm dead serious, and yes, I need it by two p.m. If you don't deliver, I'm going to let it slip to your boss, telling him how wonderful it was you helping me get in contact with Rachel and renting me an apartment. Think of how he'll take that piece of news."

"He'd fire me!"

"Exactly! Bingo, I think the lady's got it," he said snapping his fingers.

"Fine, I get the money and you'll leave town?"

"Yep, and my lips are sealed forever. I never renege on a business transaction. You can trust me. I was a cop. Yah, and another thing, I need you to wire six thousand dollars a day to three separate bank accounts and give me two thousand dollars in cash."

"Why are you doing it this way?"

"Simple baby, anything over ten grand the bank has to report it to authorities. It might get reported anyway, but it is less likely. Besides, they've got fifteen days to report it, but by then I will be long gone."

"Don't call me baby! I'm not your baby!"

"Fine. Whatever. But I'll call you sometime in the morning with the accounts where the money will be transferred to."

"Great, you make me feel like some kind of criminal!"

"Well, I guess in a way you kind of are."

Sandy plays with the lettuce on her plate and tries to swallow a few bites, but she feels she's being sucked into a whirlpool, wishing she'd never spoken to a man named Kenneth Hamilton. Signaling the waitress, she pays her bill. "Excuse me, Kenneth. I really have things to do and I've got to get back to the office."

"Sure, remember our little agreement—two o'clock p.m. tomorrow." He smiles as he watches her hurriedly put her billfold in her purse and at the sound of the bell as the door closes behind her. He sure hoped she'd follow through. He thought he hit a nerve with her, and he was pretty sure she'd come up with the bread. He was certain she had a thing for good ole Aaron.

He felt a little sorry he'd involved her in all of this, as she was just a kid. She couldn't be much more than twenty-five. Her help seemed sincere, but with underlying motives she might not even be aware of. He looked at her as inexperienced in the ways of the world. Why would she be interested in a man so much older than herself? Was it a father image thing? Or was she a gold digger, wanting his money? He could read people pretty well, and he didn't think she was the gold digger type. He wouldn't want to really get her into trouble with her boss, but then when a guy's back is pushed between a wall and a hard space, sometimes there're no other alternatives.

Chapter Nine

*B*ack at the Coffee Genie, Sandy tells the employees she doesn't want to be disturbed, and walking into her office she closes the door. For a couple of minutes she looks out of the window. Cars are breaking to a stop as pedestrians stream into the cross walk. Right now she'd give anything to be able to change places with one of them. Tears and mascara flow down her face as she thinks, my life is such a mess right now.

Kenneth had called out of the blue while Rachel and Aaron were in Denver asking to speak with Aaron Townsend's private secretary. He seemed like such a nice man, very friendly and conversational. He wanted information about Rachel. He'd been searching for Rachel for a few years and recently got a tip she might be employed at the Coffee Genie. She had said that she was unable to provide information regarding anyone who may or may not be employed. He told her how they were high school sweethearts and they split up after the death of their daughter. She didn't know that Rachel even had a daughter. Sure, she'd told her she'd been previously married, but she never said to whom. She was sad

Rachel had lost a child. Maybe there was just a lack of communication. Possibly their relationship was fixable. Kenneth complimented her on her caring attitude towards Rachel. In less than an hour she was sucked into helping him make a love connection with his ex-wife.

He'd called her a few times and they discussed ways to bring this about. He told her he was on temporary disability. He'd been shot when he and his partner had been dispatched to a robbery in progress at a small convenience store. It was then that she suggested they rent a studio apartment for him in downtown Seattle. This would allow him time to woo Rachel back into his life.

Kenneth was not supposed to come to Seattle for two more weeks, but he called her from Spearfish, South Dakota telling her he was on his way. He sounded depressed and said that he just couldn't wait any longer to see Rachel. He wanted to work things out with her. He was feeling suicidal and thought it would be better to just get on the road. Trying to comfort him, she assured him the apartment was available and it wouldn't be inconvenient for him to come out now. It was sad he'd been injured in that convenience store robbery. She felt certain Rachel would do the same for her if their situations were reversed.

Oh, brother, how could she possibly know he had violent tendencies and she'd be implicated in a crime? Oh, God! Why did she do that? That inner voice replies—you hate seeing Aaron and Rachel together! She couldn't be certain there was anything between them, but she thought Aaron looked at Rachel in a special way. If things had worked out Rachel would remarry Kenneth and then she might have a chance with Aaron. To add insult to injury, Kenneth said Rachel was pregnant. How could all this be happening?

She loves everything about Aaron. His laugh, his slightly greying sideburns, his tall, slender body, and the smell of his aftershave—a combination of orange, bergamot, and lemon scents. It reminded her of walking into a real man's barbershop. She loved his thoughtfulness of other people. His employees would sometimes confide in him when they were having problems. All those lonely nights in the apartment, playing that one country album over and over again. What were the words to that song? *You can call me.* Sobs stuck in her throat. Oh, pregnant, she's pregnant, and I'm losing him. The whole thing is ruined.

How many times did she fantasize his lips on hers? How she yearned for him to notice her. All he had to do was compliment her and she'd relive the moment over and over in her head. Wasn't that mean of Rachel to not tell her she and Aaron had something going. It allowed her to hope. Maybe she deserved what Kenneth did to her.

Pulling a tissue from the box on her desk, she wipes her eyes and blows her nose. Picking up the phone she quickly dials her financial planner. "Neal, this is Sandy, and I need you to sell some stock for me."

"Sandy, you sound like you've been crying. Is there something wrong?"

"No, of course not! I'm just having sinus problems this week. It must be all the moisture in the air."

"Sandy, as your advisor I must caution you about selling off your investments. Isn't there something else you could do, like get a bank loan?"

"Look, Neal, I know you mean well, but I need twenty thousand dollars by tomorrow, so I want you to sell that mutual fund that we bought last March. Also, I need the money direct deposited into my checking account by tomorrow morning."

"Wow, Sandy. I'll see what I can do. This is a short notice. Do you realize this nearly liquidates your account?"

"I know, but I really need your help, Neal. Please let me know when it's been deposited."

"All right, Sandy. But as your financial planner it's my job to point out all the pitfalls—like the tax ramifications. You do know you could talk to me if there's a problem, especially a financial one?"

"I know what you are saying, and I appreciate all of the past advice you've given me."

"The other problem, Sandy, is your account will be too low to retain me as your financial planner. If this is the only way you can manage whatever problem you're having, I'll have to reassign your account to one of our stock brokers."

"I'm sorry, Neal. I'm in a jam, and I've got to have the money. Just let me know when it's been deposited." Neal had never let her down, so she feels relieved to have reached him. Yes, if Kenneth would leave town, maybe Rachel will get well and this whole thing can blow over somehow.

Stacy buzzed her. "Aaron is on line two."

"Thanks."

"Sandy, I'm at the hospital and I've been going through my emails, and I need to know if we've cut a check to the supplier for that Sumatra coffee that we talked about?"

"I'll check, and if we haven't, I'll take care of it right away."

"Is there anything new at the office?"

"No, not really. Oh, we did have that detective Gerald Hershel here around nineish this morning. He interviewed me and our staff."

"Do you know if Rachel was seeing her ex-husband or dating anyone?"

"Aaron, she never mentioned it to me if she was seeing someone."

"She really never talked to me either about her personal life. I hope they find who did this and quickly."

"Me too. I'm really sad about what happened. I told the detective we'd had dinner together on Friday evening and she took the bus home from the restaurant. Is there anything I can do?"

"Sandy, I really can't think of anything. I'll be back in the office as soon as her condition improves. Do me a favor though, and call Hal in Denver and ask how things are going, and see if he needs anything."

"Okay, I'll call him."

"Your voice sounds funny; have you been crying?"

"No, I haven't been crying. You know how this damp weather affects my sinuses. I could be coming down with a cold, too."

"Thanks, Sandy. You can call me on my cell phone if you need anything. I really appreciate you, and I know I can count on you to keep things going."

"You're welcome," she said, hanging up the phone. Feeling sad, she'd let him down by getting involved with Kenneth and hoping this whole thing would go away.

Chapter Ten

*A*fter his lunch meeting with Sandy, Kenneth drove to County General and spent a couple of hours playing the role of a dedicated future husband and father. Rachel was in a vegetative state when he left. He needed to go home and make escape plans, should the need arise.

Opening the driver's side of his 2000 Honda Accord, Kenneth tosses his raincoat onto the front passenger seat as he climbs into the car. He starts the engine and fastens his seat belt. Taking time to fiddle with the dials on the car radio and selecting a soft rock station. Glancing out his rear view mirror, he slowly backs the car out of the parking spot on the fourth floor of the hospital garage, guiding the car as it descends to the bottom level. He pays the lady at the ticket booth and the big orange and white metal rod rises, allowing him to pass. Parking here might not be such a good idea, especially if he were being pursued by the cops. Man, you have to anticipate your every move; just one faulty decision could have disastrous consequences.

He enters the I-5 freeway, heading back to his apartment in Belltown. Thinking, what is he going to do? The problem with most criminals is they don't have a well thought out plan. They leave out the little details, or don't consider what could go wrong. Then the panic sets in and they act like their brains have gone missing. I'm different. Wasn't I one of the best strategists on the police force? I need to diagram this and figure a way out.

Around March of this year he'd read an article about the reduction of the capture of fugitives crossing state lines. Yes, murderers, rapists, robbers and criminals worse than himself were avoiding capture by simply going across state lines. If he could just manage things right, South Dakota would never come after him. After all, he didn't actually hit Debbie; he only damaged her car.

Wouldn't it be nice if he was someone else and was on his way home from work? To be just a regular Joe, with a wife and kids in the suburbs. Nothing seemed to go right. What are the options? Ending it all, going to the police station and just turning himself in? The thought of going back to prison was just untenable. Cross that one off, buddy. How about a simple bullet to the brain and end it all? Whitney Houston's song, *I have nothing*, played on the radio.

As he exited the freeway the song ended and the four o'clock news came on air. "Police still have no definitive answers on an early Saturday morning attack of a Seattle woman on Cherry Street. She is in stable but critical condition at County General Hospital and has been identified as Rachel Goodrich. Ms. Goodrich is employed at the Coffee Genie as an advisor to the Chief Executive Officer, Aaron Townsend. The police are examining the 911-operator tape for any clues. Anyone with any information regarding this crime is urged to contact the Seattle Police Department. There's a new storm brewing out there in the Pacific Ocean, so expect heavy rain in the next twenty-four to forty-eight hours. Now back to your favorite soft rock after these announcements."

Oh shit! My voice is on that 911-operator tape! Driving a few more blocks to his apartment, he parks the car and hurriedly races up the steps and enters the apartment. Opening the blinds and going into the small kitchen galley, he opens the refrigerator, surveying its contents. He prepares a sandwich made with sourdough bread and roast beef. He uncaps a beer, and carries his meal and places it on the coffee table. Sitting on the sofa, he reaches for a tablet and pen. For a moment he thinks of how Sandy had gone shopping for him and how she was such a nice kid. He's sorry he involved her in all of this. It's too late; he's got to consider what the possible outcomes are.

First, the emergency operator tape isn't a good thing, but really there's no need to panic. His voice doesn't have anything special about it that would single it out. Oh sure, a forensic voice identification expert would be able to determine it's his voice if they did a comparison. But first he'd have to be identified as a suspect. That tape is a complication, no doubt about it.

If Rachel lives, she'll either remember or not remember that night in her apartment. If she remembers, he's got to get out of there because it is just a matter of time before the cops know it, too. If she doesn't remember, it'll buy him some time. He can continue letting everyone think they are an item again and he'll keep saying the baby is his. Can amnesia last a long time? If it does, it'll give him time to get back into her pants and into her life.

If everything goes belly up he's got to get out of Seattle. He'll never be able to outdrive all the highway patrol and police, based on the fact they would most likely have helicopters in the air. How many times has this scenario played out on the television news, only to have some poor smuck run out of gas or run over one of those spike strips? Yah, that's a bloody waste of effort. Like you could be in a car chase but you better have some chartered jet on the runway fueled up. That's it! A charter jet. He needs to get that lined up!

If he charters a jet where will he go? Hmm—then the thought hits him. Detroit! That's it. Detroit, the city that is nearly bankrupt! They're probably the crime capital of the world. If they can't stop all those houses from being torched to the ground what are the chances they'd catch him? Probably slim to none. He could then easily cross over to Windsor, Canada. His mood lifts as he reaches for the phone book, flipping through the yellow pages.

After a few telephone calls he finds what he's looking for, a small company called Clyde's Jetway Jets.

"Clyde's Jetway Jets, this is Ellen. How may I direct your call?"

"My name is Jack Williams, and I'm interested in chartering a jet in the Seattle area."

"Please hold while I connect you to one of our reservationists"

"Good afternoon, Mr. Williams, I'm Jennifer. How can I help you?"

"I'm interested in chartering a jet one way from Seattle to Detroit, Michigan."

"Would that be nonstop?"

"Yes, and I'm looking for something I can have at a short notice."

"That's about a four hour and nineteen minute flight, sir, and that would have to be a Lear Jet forty, which is approximately twenty nine hundred dollars an hour. With a short notice to flight time we'd charge an additional twenty-five hundred dollars."

"That's fine, I'm a private detective. I need assurances of complete confidentiality because I'm working on a high profile case from Washington D.C. It's possible your company could be contacted by the media or other interested parties."

"We have strict confidentiality rules regarding our clients."

"Do I have to go through all that security screening stuff?"

"No, it's a very minimal screening process. We use a private airfield near Boeing."

"What do I need to do?"

"You'll need to wire the fee to us and sign a contract. Do you have an email address we can send you the contract and you can fax it back to us."

"Great!" He provided her his email address.

"Do you have an approximate time when you may want to fly?"

"It'll probably be later this week. That is the closest I can estimate my departure time. If something happens and my plan changes, how do I get my money back?"

"Well, Mr. Williams we're keeping a plane fueled up on the tarmac and two pilots available. Therefore, we charge a twenty-five percent cancellation fee. We'd mail you a check for the difference within three banking days."

"Wow, that's a pretty hefty cancelation fee."

"Yes sir, it is, and we'd recommend you enter into this contract when you're almost certain to need our services."

"In my line of business the only thing certain is death and taxes. Okay, send me the contract."

"Fine sir, thank you for contacting Clyde's Jetway Jets. We look forward to serving you."

Is chartering a jet really worth it? His inner voice answers—you know it is because if things are going to go wrong it'll be in the next few days. The longer you can keep the charade going, the better chance you have of ironing out all the wrinkles.

When he divorced Rachel, she cried and begged him not to leave her. It was never in his conscious realm of possibilities there'd be much resistance from her. Just how naïve was he to think he could waltz in with a bouquet of posies and that she'd go to bed with him all in the same night? He remembered her in the old days, and clearly, she'd changed. Well, he has to get back to the matter at hand.

Fishing through his brief case, finding the fake ID and checking the expiration date. It'll not expire until January of next year. Jack T. Williams, Danbury, Connecticut. He smiled, thinking hell, he'd never been there. Vice usually gave their undercover cops out-of-state identification cards. It was usually worked out with a unit within the Department of Motor Vehicles.

Okay, now if it goes down like a car chase, how will I handle that? It would be really hard to get away from those helicopters. Rent another car, have it somewhere out of view from the air. Keep a suitcase of clothes in there and a different colored wig. Then if things go right, he could make the switch unseen.

Surely Sandy will come through. But if she doesn't, what then? What about a bank heist? Oh, God, this goes from bad to worse! He better call her tomorrow morning bright and early and keep the heat on. Would she tell her boss? No, she wouldn't do that, he would fire her!

It's too early, but the next thing is to rent a car. Once he's gotten the information on the airport location, it'd be good to plan the route from the hospital and from the apartment to the airport. The maps on the internet will be really helpful, as he's not very familiar with Seattle. He's got to find a place to stash the car where people live in close proximity to businesses which are open into the evening hours. Also, it'll need to be a place without those pesky parking booths and metal arms.

Chapter Eleven

"Rachel dear, it's time to cross over. We'll escort you through the tunnel and into the light and Cookie will be right beside you. There's nothing to fear. Come with us into the light, a place of love."

Tears slide down her face and onto her gown. "Gram, I don't want to go. If my physical body's hanging on to life, why can't I decide not to die? Isn't part of death a soul's choice?"

"Honey, it's complicated, and a soul doesn't usually have enough insight to understand the whole cosmic consciousness. You're primarily governed by free will, but the ultimate decision to remain on earth is made by God. Only he and the God Council knows if there is further soul development you can achieve in this incarnation. It's not just about you, Rachel. Your staying could prevent another soul from experiencing some growth or personal awareness caused by your passing."

"I still don't see why God would take me home if it's not my will," Rachel said, brushing away tears with the sleeve of her robe. "I want this baby growing in my stomach. Shouldn't this baby be allowed to become, to dream, and to experience being in the world. I know it was just a one-night encounter, but this baby was created out of love on my part. I realize now I love Aaron even though he probably doesn't feel the same. We're at least close friends, and I can't believe he wouldn't want this baby."

"What your Gram is trying to tell you is life is like a play," Grandpa said. "Everything on earth is props allowing souls to progress towards Godness. It's all so intertwined, like a fine lace scarf, where the play and players are affected in some way by the most simplest of events. The slightest experience, like someone brushing past them, can have an effect on a soul. Sometimes when people transition it causes others to strive for greatness because of some insight they gained from the experience. So you can ask God to let you stay, but only he can decide."

"Honey, Grandpa is right. We must trust God, who sees the bigger picture and has the wisdom to know what's best. Many times people become attached to material or physical things and want to control their own destiny. Also, because someone crosses over doesn't mean they don't bring with them their character flaws as well as their good qualities. When we're willful and don't let go and let God, we cannot truly reflect the flame of the God consciousness. You know, when you were a little girl I used to say that to you sometimes about letting go and letting God. Rachel, this is one of those times when the transition of your soul is in the hands of God."

"I've got so much to give my baby and I don't feel ready to die. Maybe you are right; maybe it is my time. I cannot help but wish things had been different and Kenneth had not returned, but I can't change what happened. Thank you for helping me through this." She puts her arms around her grandmother. "I love you both." She then hugs her grandfather.

"We love you too, Sweetpea. Are you ready?"

She wishes she could live and realizes this may not be her destiny. "Yes." Rachel holds hands with her grandparents as they walk to the door entering into the hall. She felt the magnet pulling her to the light, and suddenly she felt an intense love surround her, like some glorious warm bubble that lifted her, floating and floating, as she neared the brilliant white light at the end of the darkness. Her soul was carried along to the sound of soft harp music.

As they neared the tunnel entrance colors swirled about her spirit and it was like the warm feeling after a glass of wine. She felt so relaxed, wondering if she'd ever felt this good.

She became aware of a window, and looking into the window, she sees herself in a hospital bed. She watches as she is cared for and sees the reaction of her parents. Aaron looks so sad; his eyes are red. She never knew making love could be as special as it was with Aaron. If only he really loved me. Maybe he does.

She felt really sad for Kenneth. Even though he'd hurt her, she wished she could've helped him in some way and always hoped things would get better for him. She always thought he was stuck in an angry little boy stage. It's a lot like having a splinter you can't get out and it festers and festers. He loved Sara so much, and he was so gentle with her. Wondering if Sara was the only goodness he'd felt he ever helped to create. Her parents only seemed to see his shortcomings. Yet she knew he has so many good qualities. She believed no one was totally bad.

Chapter Twelve

*R*achel experiences a sensation similar to the dentist's first tug extracting a tooth numbed with Novocain. She's looking at her body through the window of her life, feeling soft and light as air on a warm spring day. There it is again, another tug in conjunction with being sucked into an air pocket. It begins as a light spinning and intensifies until she blends into an invisible whirl. The feeling of a rapid descent similar to being in an elevator in the Seattle Space Needle or the Sears Tower in Chicago, where all floors between the top and bottom are skipped, the ride, ending in a rapid fall as gravity sucks downward. The bump as the body feels the impact of arriving on the ground floor. Several seconds later, a slight bounce as the stomach catches up with the rest of the body.

She thinks, where am I? This must be what hell feels like. Drifting off, not wanting to open her eyes, hoping to escape from whatever this place is. Did she protest too much about living, thus angering God? Did he kick her out of heaven straight to purgatory? Or was she an interloper into heaven only to be identified and sucked away by some giant vacuum cleaner straight into the bowels of hell. Falling lower and lower into a flaming nightmare. Dressed in navy blue shorts, white cotton sleeveless blouse, and sneakers. Her hair flowing behind her in the wind as she runs down an old, deserted two-lane highway. The valley floor is ablaze and she tries to dodge embers falling in the front and on both sides of her. Her inner voice screams at her—keep running; don't stop. The air is scorching. Her body is drenched in a smoky residue that drips from her face and arms. Adrenaline pumps throughout her body. A presence is behind her, ready to grasp her hair. She's running and choking from the smoke. Keep running; you have to get free! Crying out as an ember hits her right forearm. Telephone poles are catching fire and burning like matchsticks. She's screaming, but no sound comes from her throat.

Somewhere in the realm of her consciousness comes the realization of her soul slamming into her body and the awareness of exquisite pain from her head to her chest.

Rachel's face contorts and her arms begin thrashing in the air. "Rose, please get me some rubber restraints from the top shelf of the supply cabinet. We don't want her to hurt herself. Rachel! Rachel! Wake up!" Placing her arms to her sides the doctor secures the rubber restraints. "Rachel, wake up! I'm Dr. Gerhardt. We're going to give you another oxygen treatment this morning. My nurse is going to take your pulse and after we do our examination we'll place you in the chamber for more oxygen."

Opening her eyes and examining them with his pen light, he said, "Give me her blood pressure and pulse."

"Doctor, her blood pressure is one-thirty over eighty-five and pulse is one hundred fifteen."

Pressing his fingernail on the nail bed of the forefinger on her right hand, he notices her pulling away from him. "Rachel, Rachel wake up; this is Dr. Gerhardt." There's no response. "The patient appears to be regaining consciousness. Rachel, you're in the hospital and you're safe. No one is going to hurt you. We're ready; let's place her in the chamber and start the treatment."

Drifting into a lower state of consciousness, Rachel's alone in a deserted cabin with the howl of wild animals approaching from a short distance. It's late afternoon and the terrain is rocky and hilly with lots of sagebrush. The cabin is grimy and filled with grit from years of past dust storms. Old empty bottles and cans along with torn newspaper are scattered on the floor's broken linoleum. It's stifling hot and airless.

The hair on the back of her neck stands up as she looks out the window to see a pack of coyotes circling the cabin. Their coats are a dingy grey, and rib bones protrude from their thin bodies. They snarl with raised upper lips, exposing jagged teeth. There's a crazed, yellow sheen to their eyes. Whining with low growls they communicate to the pack: the hunt is on and there's meat to eat.

The wind begins to blow and the cabin shakes with each gust. A coyote jumps against the window and it shatters. He digs at the broken window, bloodying his paw, and yelps as he moves away. Another takes his place, pushing against the remaining glass fragments. His forearms go through part of the window and he lunges for her, snapping but not quite able to make it through the window. He's cut by glass on his upper torso and yelps away only to be replaced by the next coyote.

Another blast of air hits the cabin and a wall creaks as it collapses from the air pressure. The coyotes are now inside, encircling her, tearing at her clothes and knocking her to the ground. Flesh begins to tear as they begin to feast. She tries to scream but is unable to. The feeling of falling causes her to jerk as she regains consciousness.

Chapter Thirteen

*O*n the way to the hospital Kenneth stopped at three large banks, opening checking accounts and placing a few hundred dollars in each. Two accounts under his real name and one account under Jack T. Williams. He calls Sandy and provides her with the account numbers. He tells her to put the first six thousand dollars into the Jack T. Williams account. He really didn't want her to know his alias but he saw no way around it. He needed to reduce the likelihood of the bank reporting these financial transactions to the authorities.

"Sandy, do you understand what you're supposed to do?"

"I got it, Kenneth; starting today you want six thousand in each account over the next three days and you want two thousand in cash."

"That's it."

"And what if the bank asks me about moving this much money?"

"Tell them you've got a slab leak and you're fixing things at home."

"What's with this slab leak story you're always using? No, don't tell me; I don't want to know."

"Whatever you do Sandy, keep your mouth shut, because you've now stepped over the line from being canned by your boss to being an accomplice, and you could get jail time."

"Don't worry; I'm not going to say anything. But I fail to see how I can be an accomplice when I wasn't there at the time you nearly killed Rachel."

"Do the math baby; you rented the apartment for me, gave me confidential information, and now you're giving me cash, helping me to evade the authorities."

"Well, maybe it's time to stop the madness and just tell the authorities and Aaron."

"Trust me Sandy; you don't want to tell them. Remember, I know where you live!"

"I'm sorry; of course I'll not say anything." She felt trapped with no way out. She'd read somewhere that many police officers had sociopathic tendencies. Was Kenneth a sociopath? Tears stung her eyes and she wished she could get out of this situation.

"Great. I'll call you later."

Hoping all of his preparations were unnecessary, he still had to assume the worst. Tonight he'd go pick up the rental car at the dealership. He also needed to go to one of those drag queen places and get a wig. The kind of place where those cross dressers go. They're usually pretty discrete with their clientele. It could be kind of embarrassing to some people if the word gets out they're living an alternative life style.

Aaron sits in the waiting room, responding to business email while he waits for Rachel to return from her oxygen therapy, and for her family, who are having a late breakfast in the hospital cafeteria.

"Good morning, Mr. Townsend," Kenneth says as he enters the waiting room. "It seems you're here when I arrive and still here when I leave. You must be some dedicated boss."

"I do care about Rachel. We've been friends a long time."

"That's truly admirable, having a boss who cares so much. I did want to talk to you though. Sometimes her parents are too demanding and they don't stop to think people have other things to do. Like you for instance; you've got your big company to run. They shouldn't be imposing on you like this."

"They aren't imposing at all. Rachel would be here for me if I were the one in ICU."

"That's my girl Rachel; she's so thoughtful like that. I just think if I were you I'd go back to my office and not wrap myself up in other people's concerns."

"I don't know what you mean."

"Well, Rachel is some better and it looks like she may pull through, which believe me, I've been praying for. But what is the likelihood she'll be returning to work at the Coffee Genie?

"Sure, there's rehabilitation, but it's not out of the question she could return to work."

"I guess you don't get what I'm trying to say. So let me just say it. She's pregnant with my baby. We already lost a daughter and I'm not going to want her doing a lot of things while she's carrying my baby. In fact, she never worked when she was married to me."

"You sound like you're making a lot of decisions without first consulting Rachel and finding out what she wants."

"How can I do that when she's in a coma? Before this happened to us we were planning on remarrying. I guess she never told you she was going to give notice, as we planned to move to Denver to be near my brother and his family."

"She never mentioned it to me. In fact, her dad doesn't believe she'd take you back. He told me all about your marriage."

"Well it was a two way street you know. Rachel's far from perfect; it was half her fault, too."

"I think she's near perfect myself."

"You don't know her very well then. You have to be married to a woman before you get the full monty of what bitches they can be. Besides, man, you don't have to get huffy with me. I'm just trying to let you off the hook. I'm sure you've got much better things to do then sit in this stuffy hospital waiting room."

"Whether I'm on the hook or not is quite frankly none of your business! And in my presence don't ever call Rachel a bitch!"

"I wasn't exactly calling her a bitch; it was meant as a figure of speech. So don't get all defensive with me. That's my wife, so it's my business, and I want you to leave and let me take care of her!"

"Let's get this straight, she's your ex-wife and you really have very little to say about it. Do you remember I have her medical power of attorney?"

"You sound like a lawyer instead of some guy peddling coffee grounds."

"For your information, I was an attorney, and I'm staying until Rachel tells me to leave. So get used to it, pal."

"I'm just trying to simplify things for Rachel and the family. I always hate people who meddle in my family business."

"This conversation is over, Hamilton! I've got work to do."

"The more I know about you, the more I think you're just like her father."

"You're free to think what you like. Please excuse me; I'm busy. Oh, by the way, did her parents tell you that detective stopped by yesterday evening to check on Rachel and he was also looking for you. I guess you're the only one he hasn't interviewed yet."

"Me? Why me?"

"Well, you are her ex-husband, aren't you?"

"That's true, but she's pregnant with my baby; why would I have a reason to hurt her?"

"I have no idea, but you're a police officer, right? Don't you have to interview everyone that knew the victim?"

Lowering his eyes, he dismissed Kenneth Hamilton and began reading the next email from one of his contacts in Mexico, Javier Gonzales. It, like so many others, was sending a note of sympathy for Rachel. All the growers like Rachel. How could her ex-husband be trying to push him out of the picture? He's in love with her and wants to marry her. Is this really Hamilton's baby, or is it his? God, please give me a sign. He's wishing this was a nightmare and he'd wake up to find things the way they used to be before she got hurt.

Rachel is placed back in her bed and her nurse pulls up the sheet and blanket to her chest. A Velcro restraint belt is placed on her night table. Rose, the HBOT nurse, told

Rachel's nurse that they'd observed some thrashing about with her arms prior to her oxygen therapy.

Noticing Rachel's eyes opening, the nurse speaks. "Rachel, are you awake?" Her eyes closed again and she groans. "Rachel, if you're awake and can hear me, try to blink your eyes." Taking her chart she notes that the patient opened her eyes and emitted a groan but there was no response to directions.

Leaning over Rachel, Susan gently kissed her daughter on her hand. "Honey, it's a beautiful fall day today. I wish you were awake and we could go out and get some fresh air. You look much better today. I hope you know your father and I love you very much. Your Aunt Amelia loves you too, honey. Please wake up, sweetheart. I don't know if you knew you're going to have a baby. I want you to know I'm thrilled I'm going to be a grandma again. Rachel, come on, honey, please wake up." Looking at her daughter's face for a sign, she saw her eyes open and stare straight ahead. "Rachel, squeeze my hand if you can hear me." She felt a weak tensing of the muscles in her daughter's left hand. "Rachel, please squeeze my hand again." There's no response. "Nurse! Nurse!"

"Yes, Mrs. Goodrich?"

"My daughter opened her eyes and squeezed my hand when I instructed her to. She's awake."

"I don't want you to get your hopes up too high, Mrs. Goodrich. Sometimes comatose patients can have muscle reactions and it doesn't mean they're conscious."

"No! She opened her eyes! I know she squeezed my hand when I asked her to! Don't you see, she's coming out of it."

"You may be right. It doesn't hurt to hope."

"I've got to go tell everyone; they're all in the waiting room. I'll be right back!" Running out of the ICU and down the hall to the waiting room Susan bursts through the door "She's awake! Stan, our daughter's awake!"

"Can she talk?"

"No, Kenneth, she can't talk. The nurse said it could just be a muscle contraction of her hand, but her eyes opened, and I asked her to squeeze my hand if she's awake and she did! But then I asked her to do it again but she didn't. So the nurse doesn't really think she's awake. But she's my daughter, and I know she was awake even if it was just for a few seconds. I know my daughter!"

"Do you think I could go in and see her now, as I have some errands I need to run this afternoon?"

"Kenneth, go ahead, and let me know when you're leaving."

"Okay. I'll let you know."

"Rachel, sweetheart. You look better today. Can you hear me? We all want you to wake up. I want you to know how much I love you and I'm worried about you. Please wake up, darling. I want to talk to you about us, our future, and our baby." There's no response. The nurse's probably right; she isn't coming out of this. He doesn't know why he's so worried. In police work he'd seen enough brain damaged people to know getting information from them was nearly impossible. For a little while he sits by her bed watching her and begins thinking of the detective who wants to see him. Is he at the hospital right now? Maybe he shouldn't stay too long; he still has a few loose ends to tie up. She needs her mother at a time like this. He better leave for the day.

He tells her mother he's leaving and hurriedly walks out of the hospital.

Halfway across the street to where the car is parked at the Mexican restaurant he changes his mind. He'd been fuming since the conversation with Aaron Townsend and he needed to give him a hand's off Rachel message he might be able to understand. In the parking garage he locates Aaron's car and hangs out in the garage for nearly an hour, staying a few cars away.

Finally, he sees Townsend walking to his car and unlocking the driver's side door. When he opens the door, Kenneth walks over, swiftly grabbing the top of the door. Aaron was taken a little off guard. "I figure you're a bit of a hardhead; you can't just take a hint, so I'm prepared to deliver my message in a way maybe you can comprehend." Kenneth takes a swing at him. Aaron ducks just in time as the blow lightly grazes his ear. Doubling up his fist he belts Kenneth square in the mouth, reopening the cut on his lip. Kenneth loses his balance and falls on his back.

"Shit, that hurt!"

"What do you expect when you tried to deck me? Oh, I get it; you only hit women. You aren't used to someone fighting back."

"What would you know about it?"

"Stanley has told me enough. If I find out you did this to Rachel, I'll bash your brains in!"

"Just a lucky punch, big guy. She's my wife, but you seem to think you're calling all the shots." He stands up, eyeing Aaron as he brushes the dirt from his pants.

"As a matter of fact, I am calling the shots. I'm her medical power of attorney. You better get someone to look at that cut, like I said before."

"Shut the fuck up! I've a gun and I could blow your fucking brains out!"

"Try it, Hamilton, and you'll be eating your gun for dinner. Now get away from me!" He watched Kenneth walk out of the parking garage before getting into his car.

Crossing the street Kenneth gets into his car. How could he have let that Townsend jerk show him up? Don't worry; there'd be a chance to get even with him. Just you wait until payback time, Mr. Big Executive.

He had to let that little skirmish in the garage go. He had more important things to take care of. He'd seen a place downtown called Gigi's Wigs and Things. He needs to head over there and get a wig after he gets that two grand from Sandy. He better give her a call right now.

Sandy's phone rings. "Yes."

"You've a call on line three."

"Okay, fine."

"This is Sandy. How may I help you?"

"This is Kenneth, and I'm calling about the money."

"Well, there's a problem! I can only have twelve thousand right now and the other eight thousand minus expenses won't be available for three banking days."

"Sandy, you wouldn't be jerking me around, would you?"

"No! My broker can't get the other eight thousand for three days. They're going to deduct all the fees from this amount. So who knows what the final payoff will be."

"This ain't good. You owe me eight thousand dollars. Maybe you should go and refinance your car or something, because I want the money. I thought I would stop by and get the two grand from you at the Coffee Genie."

"God, don't do that!"

"What? You afraid your boss might see you?"

"Wouldn't you be if you were me? Besides, I have other reasons."

"How about you drag your little ass over to the apartment and give me the two grand. Maybe I could pick up a bottle of wine and we could toast our deal. Maybe you might want to go to bed with me. I could use a little snuggling right now, if you know what I mean."

"I'll meet you at Ma's Diner. I can't believe you're talking to me like this!"

"Like what?"

"That I'd have sex with you or want to toast your forcing me to give you money."

"Instead of day dreaming about your boss, I could show you how a real man handles a woman in the bedroom. I can't think of anything better than putting my hands all over your ass. You'd love it, too."

"You're disgusting!"

"No. I'm needing some loving up. Come on, you'd love it. I could introduce you to my friend. He's getting all hard just talking about it."

"You can go screw yourself! I'll be at Ma's in one hour, so be there Kenneth."

"Don't get your feathers all ruffled. You can't blame a guy for trying. What would be wrong with me checking out your boobs? I could make you really hot if you'd let me. Oh well, what a cold fish you are. I'll be there at two o'clock p.m.; just bring my money. Find out how you're going to come up with the rest of the bread."

After meeting Sandy and collecting the two thousand dollars, he gets back on the I-5 freeway and heads downtown.

Parking his car in the empty lot next to Gigi's Wigs and Things, he walks to the front door, stepping inside. The bell rang and a tall, Rubenesque black woman with kinky, shoulder length hair, wearing tights and stiletto heels walks up to him. He couldn't get over the length of her purple and red fingernails, wondering if those were real or fake. God, wouldn't you hate to meet her in a back alley somewhere.

"Can I help you?"

"Uh," he stammers, thinking, oh my God, that's a guy straight out of that show he'd seen on TV.

"Cat's got your tongue? Don't be shy."

"I need a wig," he says, slightly choking.

"That's all right. We've all had that first time experience of venturing out and buying something risqué for the first time. Are you a cross dresser?"

"Uh, no, not exactly."

"Relax honey, you've come to the right place. Your secret is safe with us. Lots of us have been first timers like you. The wigs are over here."

Kenneth selected a brown, shoulder length, silky wig, a pageboy style with relaxed layers and side-swept bangs.

"Do you want to try it on, honey?"

His eyes dart from side to side, looking for other customers. "I guess so."

"It'll look lovely on you, sweetheart." Patting the seat of a nearby chair, the salesperson says, "Sit right here and we'll try this on."

"Okay, but I'm kind of in a hurry."

"Sure you are, honey." The salesperson places a nylon wig stocking cap on his head and then placing the back of the wig on first, adjusts it on the side. With a pink wig brush, the hair is styled into place. Handing Kenneth a mirror, he said, "Well aren't you mister gorgeous pants!"

"I'll take it, along with a hair brush."

"Is that all you want, honey? We've got some really nice black brassieres in various sizes. I personally like these black net stockings, and maybe you might want to try a silky night gown?"

"Uh, no, this is so embarrassing."

Rolling his eyes, the long eyelashes coated heavily with mascara, he said, "Don't be embarrassed honey. This is fun; enjoy the ride."

Wondering how his eyelid muscles have the strength to hold up all that eye goo, Kenneth asked, "Are you sure? How much do I owe you?"

"Of course, I'm sure! Like I said, your little secret is safe here, so just relax! We've got celebrities, politicians, preachers, and all types of people coming here. That'll be a hundred and ninety-five dollars and thirty-nine cents. We'll give you a ten-dollar coupon off your next purchase. Would you like to open an account?"

"God, no! This is my only time to shop here."

Batting his eyes, the salesperson said, "Honey, that's what they all say. Trust me, you'll be back, wait and see. It's kind of like crack; you can never get enough."

The sales clerk hands him his package and he can't wait to get out of there. The smell of all the perfume makes him nauseous.

Kenneth drives several blocks from Gigi's to his apartment and drops off his car in the parking lot. Crossing the street, he catches the city bus and travels the four miles to the rental car agency. He knew he wouldn't get away with using his alias, as all his credit cards were under his real name. The agent had been helpful, and after signing on the dotted line, he's given the keys to a white 2013 Mazda that's parked in front of the agency.

Climbing into the driver's seat, he pulls the map to the little private airport out of his shirt pocket. He'd printed it off the internet earlier in the day. He studies the directions and notes the time. Backing the car out of the parking space and easing the car onto the street, he turns right on Western Avenue, turns left on Battery, taking a left on Elliot, and takes the ramp onto the Alaskan Way Viaduct. Continuing to follow the directions on the map, he arrives at the little airport. The trip took twenty-three minutes from downtown.

On his return to Belltown, he drove around some residential neighborhoods and business areas. He found exactly what he's looking for: a large hotel attached to a convention center with underground parking. This hotel is about halfway between the airport and Belltown. Walking through the convention center, he sees restaurants, beauty salons, a liquor store, and several department stores. Seeing the Big is Beautiful shop, he thought, hmm, maybe he should have a dress he can slip into quickly as part of his disguise if the cops are trying to catch him. He opens the glass door and steps inside.

"Yes, can I help you, sir?"

'Yah, I'm looking for a dress for my wife. She's in the hospital; she's had a cesarean section and I want a dress that buttons down the front."

"Do you know the size?"

"Not exactly. She was always a size ten before she got pregnant. She's lost one of the twins and also had to have her gall bladder removed. She's a little bloated, if you know what I mean."

"I'm so sorry!"

"Yah, it's been tough, but we need something not too constricting because she'll be breast feeding, too."

"I only have two possibilities right now. We've got a nice blue cotton midi, and it buttons all the way down the front. The other one is a maroon polyester fabric. The cotton we only have to a size fourteen but the other dress we've got lots of sizes."

"She's probably going to be in a wheel chair for a while; the polyester would probably be better. I'm not any good at ironing clothes."

"I know what you mean. I hate ironing, too. What size do you think?"

"Let me see the size fourteen." She hands him the fourteen and he thinks, no, that might not fit with clothes under it. "I guess the sixteen would be better. Wow, guess she'll have to join a gym when she gets well so she can get her figure back."

"Is that all, sir?"

"Yes."

"Please step over here and I'll ring you up. That'll be twenty-four dollars and ninety-five cents."

He pays the cashier. "Thanks for your help."

"You're most welcome and I hope your wife gets well real soon. The living twin, what sex is it and what's the name?"

"It's a boy and we named him Gerome."

"That's a nice name. Thank you, sir. Have a nice day."

Walking out of the store with his package, he resumes his inspection of the convention center.

Walking past a shoe store he thinks a pair of shoes for the dress might be a good idea. If the car breaks down on the freeway from, say a flat tire from one of those strips, wearing men's shoes might be a tip off. He needs something he can walk in. He opens the door and walks in.

"Can I help you?" said a male sales clerk appearing to be in his forties.

"Yes, I need some women's sneakers that are easy to walk in and are supportive. My wife's pregnant with triplets and her feet are swollen and she's having trouble walking."

"Wow, triplets."

"Yah, it runs in both of our families. I am kind of in a hurry because I need to get home and make her dinner."

"Sure. Actually, we've got some nice leather sneakers on sale."

He picks a pair of white sneakers in a size nine and pays the clerk.

"Congratulations on your babies, but I feel for you bud. You better sleep while you can."

"Yah, I know. This is our second set. The others are six now. My wife seems to have them in batches."

"Wow."

He checks out the location of all the restrooms and makes mental notes of the more secluded areas.

There were a couple of exits leading out of the parking structure. In addition, there were no parking booths to hinder a speedy exit. True, he'd be wise to come and move the car each day. He thought it unlikely the car would be spotted by security or at least not for a few days.

Parking the car, locking the doors and taking his packages, he walks a few blocks up the street to a seedy little place called the Alibi Lounge. He sits at the bar, ordering a beer and calls a taxi. This has been a busy day setting up those bank accounts, seeing Rachel, taking a swing at her boss, meeting Sandy, getting the rental, and finding a place to stash it. No wonder you're tired; this is harder than a full-time job, he thought.

Taking a sip of the cold beer, he thought about Aaron Townsend and how he just seemed to ooze with caring for his ex-wife. The nerve of that guy to punch him. Just bide your time; you can even the score later. That guy was as annoying as her dad. What about that detective? Didn't he say that guy wanted to talk to him? If they took his DNA they would have him right there. Brother, he needs to avoid that.

Chapter Fourteen

$\mathcal{K}$enneth looks at his watch. The time is nine fifteen a.m. as he steps into one of the hospital elevators. He takes a sniff of the mixed bouquet of flowers as he enters Rachel's room. Her father is sitting by her bed.

"Good morning, Stanley, and my beautiful lady. I hope you're feeling better today. I thought you might like some posies."

"Since you're here, I'll go get some coffee."

"Fine." Thinking, you can't stand to be in the same room with me, can you, Stan the man. What a dick.

Rachel looks at Kenneth but she is unable to create or verbalize words. It's like being an infant again and having to learn how to talk. Posies echo in her mind like some mysterious clue to a puzzle. She keeps repeating the word posies over and over again. It should mean something. It's so familiar, yet she can't quite reach that space in her mind where the meaning lurks.

Placing the flowers on her night table, he sits in the chair beside her bed. He takes her hand in his and scrutinizes her face for any sign or indication her memory of Friday night was returning.

Aaron walks to the door of her hospital room and observes Kenneth sitting beside Rachel, holding her hand.

"Rachel, we're all so thankful you've finally awakened. We're trying to find out what happened to you. I know you can't talk right now. Squeeze my hand once if you remember anything about your attacker and twice if you don't remember anything."

Rachel, unable to remember, weakly squeezes his hand twice.

"Okay. It's okay, honey. Squeeze my hand if you remember when I came to see you this past summer."

She couldn't remember seeing him this past summer or when exactly was the last time she saw him.

"Honey, I know you've been through a lot, and we're going to find out who did this to you. You know I'm a good cop and I can always find a criminal. I want you to rest so you can regain your strength. I love you, Rachie, and I'm so happy you're having my baby. We can get our life back together, but it'll take time. When you're better we can find us a nice little house near my brother in Denver. You always liked Rodger and Cathy."

Hearing those words, Aaron knew right then that Denver was just an accident, a one-night stand. That was enough for him. He'd been wrong; she's involved with her ex-husband. Rachel didn't love him. A lump began forming in his throat and it felt raw. It's as if he'd contracted strep. Hamilton's right; he's been meddling in their family business. It's time to get back to work. His fantasy is exploding like a hot air balloon crashing to earth. He wanted to stop existing, like a candle flame being blown out. Did he still love her? Of course he did. You can't turn real love off as easily as flipping the switch on a coffee maker, or at least he couldn't. Would he still help her? Yes! She's a great employee, and he wanted her to get well even though she probably wouldn't be returning to the Coffee Genie.

Sergeant Hershel approaches as Aaron turns to walk away. "Good morning, Mr. Townsend. I came by to check on Ms. Goodrich and I'm looking for her ex-husband."

"He's with Rachel right now."

Entering Rachel's room, the detective said, "Good morning, Mr. Hamilton. I keep missing you. If you could please come with me I need to ask you some questions regarding your ex-wife."

"I was hoping to see you as well, but this is not very convenient right now because I need to spend time with Rachel."

"Well, it shouldn't take long, but I do need to interview you. We're trying to find the person who assaulted Ms. Goodrich, and your cooperation is essential."

"Fine. I guess we can talk now."

"Aaron, if you want to see Rachel, I'll come back later."

"We can use the waiting room across the hall. I believe it's empty."

Walking in and sitting down across from each other, separated by a rattan coffee table cluttered with well-read magazines of nearly every genre between *Better Homes and Garden* to *Popular Mechanics*.

Opening his notebook, the detective says, "Now, Mr. Hamilton, when did you arrive in Seattle?"

"Call me Kenneth, and it was early Saturday afternoon."

"How did you get here and do you have some type of proof of when you arrived?"

"I drove here, and no, I don't really have any proof."

"Can I see your license and your vehicle registration?"

"My driver's license and auto registration are downstairs in my car. Man, you aren't arresting me for drunk driving; you're supposed to be trying to find out who hurt my Rachel. I was a police officer for eighteen years. How long have you been a policeman?"

"I've worked for Seattle PD for ten years, and this interview is not about me; it's about you. What kind of car do you have?"

"It's a blue 2010 Ford Taurus."

"How long have you and Ms. Goodrich been divorced?"

"About twelve years. I'm sure her father's told you all about me."

"I want to hear it from you."

"Well, I did a dumb thing, which any other guy might've done. Our daughter died of crib death, and I started having an affair with a police cadet I was training. We ended up getting a divorce and I remarried."

"Where's home?"

"Lincoln, Nebraska."

"Are you still married?"

"No, we divorced several years ago."

"Why are you in Seattle?"

"Rachel and I reconnected and were planning to remarry. She's pregnant with my baby, you know."

"Have you hit her in the past?"

"I'm an honest man and I'm not going to lie. When we were married I did slap her a few times. But she hit me, too; it's a two-way street, if you know what I mean. I took some anger management classes after our divorce and I developed better ways of coping with my anger."

"Were you angry with Ms. Goodrich lately?"

"Of course not! We were totally excited about our new baby. When Sara died we were both devastated."

"Do you know anyone who would want to harm her?"

"I can't think of a person. Oh, you might want to take a second look at her boss. He's always here when I arrive and I wonder myself if he isn't a bit possessive. You know, you wouldn't expect an employer to be that committed to an employee unless there was some type of attachment."

"Do you have any specific reason you suspect Mr. Townsend?"

"No. I didn't exactly say I suspected him. Just call it a cop's intuition."

"I'd like to get a DNA sample from you so I can eliminate you as a person of interest."

"I think that's an excellent idea! But I was on my way out, as I've got a dental appointment to fix this tooth that's killing me. Would you mind if I did it tomorrow? I'm going to be late for my appointment if I don't leave right now."

"It would just take a minute."

"Look, I want to fully cooperate with you, but I don't have even a minute. I can do it tomorrow. I think you should be out there pounding the bushes looking for the perpetrator that did this to Rachel, to her family, and me."

"I thought you said you wanted to spend time with Rachel?"

"Well, yes I do, but I didn't realize what time it was when I said that."

"I see, fine. Be here tomorrow morning at ten o'clock a.m. and we'll get the sample."

"I'll be here. In the meantime, will you please find out who did this to her!"

Chapter Fifteen

Kenneth, touching his jaw and grimacing with pain, walks out of the waiting room. He grabs an elevator heading for the lobby, telling himself to remain calm as his stomach is doing flip-flops. This is ratcheting up and it's probably going to get tough. He's got to get that money wired to Clyde's Jetway Jets today!

On the way to his apartment he notices his tank is nearly on empty and stops and fills the tank. Great work, buddy, having your car nearly on empty. He hits his steering wheel thinking, dumb, that was so careless. How are you going to get away from the cops on an empty gas tank? Brilliant, just brilliant!

What if that chick Sandy doesn't come through with the eight grand? He sure can't depend on getting it. What can he do? He doesn't have very much credit left on his cards. He needs the money and the only solution is to rob a bank. It might only get him a few thousand but he needs the cash. He's going to have to go back to Gigi's and get some female garments as a disguise. He needs to look like a woman. The guy with the stiletto heels should be able to show him how it's done.

Stopping at a mail center a few miles from the apartment, he faxes the contract back to Clyde's Jetway Jets with a note stating he'd be transferring the funds within the hour.

At home, he powers up his laptop and signs into his online bank account. Sandy had deposited the six thousand dollars this morning, which brought his checking account to eighty-seven hundred dollars. He transfers eight thousand to his Jack T. Williams account, which brings the Williams account up to fourteen thousand dollars. He takes a cash advance on one of his Master Cards, which gives him enough money to pay for the lease on the jet. He transfers the fees to Clyde's Jetway jets. Done! Cha ching!

The time is one fifteen p. m., and he's got to get over to Gigi's to get his disguise. He packs the car with his suitcase, laptop computer, and the disguise he purchased yesterday consisting of the wig, dress, and sneakers. He drives to Gigi's Wigs and Things and takes a deep breath as he enters the store. He's greeted by the guy in stiletto heels.

"Well, sugar, you're back! Didn't I tell you? Hmm?"

"Yah," he said looking at his feet.

"Ah, don't be bashful. What do we want today, some nice silk panties?"

"Uh, I want a dress and some of those socks you told me about."

"Socks?"

"Yah, black socks. What are they called?"

"Oh, you mean black lace stockings?"

"Yah, that's them."

"If you're going to get a dress you need a bra, honey."

"Okay, whatever."

"Honey, you just need to relax and not be so intense!"

"We've got some little black dresses on this rack. Let's see. You'd probably take a fourteen. We can try that. What's your bra size?"

"How would I know?"

"Well, do you want to be voluptuous?"

"Look, I'm in a hurry. Could you just dress me up? I met some crossers online, and I'm going to meet them in Bellvue for cocktails."

"Wow, you're stepping out, honey!"

The clerk gathers stockings, the dress, and a bra and directs him into a dressing room. The panty hose are a real struggle to get on but he gets them on and puts on the bra and the dress. He stands looking at his image, groaning.

"Come on out; let's see you. Oh, honey this'll never do. Your ass is too flat and your bra is caving in. Take the dress off. I've just what you need. I'll be right back."

"I don't have a lot of time!"

"It'll just take a sec—be right back."

A few minutes later he returns with silicone sticky adhesive butt pads and sticky breast pads. "Here let me help you, honey," and he begins to pull down the stockings.

"Uh, I don't want you touching my ass!"

"Relax. Do you want to look good or not?"

"Okay."

The clerk shapes the pads to his butt and puts the pads inside the bra. "Now put the dress back on and come out of the dressing room and let's see you. The other thing is you really should shave your legs—they're unsightly,"

Walking into the hallway and looking into the full-length mirror, he had to admire how those pads transformed his butt.

117

"You're hot, honey." The clerk whistles. "Let's see some bump and grind."

"Uh, nah. I don't want to do that. Do you have any cheap wigs?"

"I've got one that's about fifty-nine dollars. Do you want to go blonde?"

"Yah, sure, I guess that'd be okay. Do you think it'll look good on me?"

"Sure, you could wear blonde. This style is kind of curly and hasn't been too popular."

"Fine. It'll be fine."

"Wait, honey. You need a little lipstick, eye shadow, and some foundation. We've got some fake eyelashes. Would you like some?"

"Uh, how am I going to get all that off my face? I'm married with kids and I don't want them to know."

"Oh, no problem. "I'll sell you some makeup remover, and I'll throw in a few cotton balls. You dip the cotton balls in the makeup remover and it'll take it all off."

"Okay. That sounds easy enough."

He skillfully makes up Kenneth and styles his wig.

"Oh, look at you! Aren't you so hot! You need some earrings. We've got some nice clips. Let me see, let's try these dangly ones. Yes! That's you!" He spritzes him with some perfume. "Those shoes have to go."

"Christ, those earrings are pinching my ears!"

"Pretty soon you'll not even notice it. Okay, we don't have a big choice in shoes, but I have some black high heels that'll go with your little black dress."

"How am I going to walk in those?"

"It takes practice. Just watch your posture and pick your feet up. In no time you'll get it."

"Okay. How much is all this?"

The clerk tallies everything up. "That'll be three hundred fifty-three dollars and twenty-nine cents."

"God, that's a lot!"

"Well, honey, to dress for success doesn't come cheap."

"Success? You call this dress for success?"

"Well, darling, if you want to wear the panties, you've got to pay the price. Cross dressing is a feeling of success and satisfaction."

"Oh, I see. Ah, do you have any scarves?"

"Wow, you're going all out! This is truly exciting! Yes, they are seven dollars. What color do you want?"

"Black."

He pays the clerk and wants to get out of there and get out of all this mess, but first he has to go and rob a bank. The wig is as itchy as the stockings. If he were a dog, he'd fall on the floor to try and rub all that scent off him. Lips greasy with red lipstick, he thinks, how disgusting, all he needed to do now was get his period. Christ, he'd never want to be a woman! He remembered those times when Debbie tried to get him to go down the sanitary pad aisle and he refused to be seen there, let alone pay at the cashiers'. Why do wives always put their husbands in that situation? But look at him now! God, no! What if someone he knew saw him?

Throwing the bag with his clothes and make-up remover in the front seat, he needed to go to one of those fast food places and change clothes. He drives a few blocks and sees a taco place and pulls into the parking lot. Picking up the sack with the dress and sneakers he had bought yesterday, he hastily walks into the women's restroom and darts into a stall. He quickly puts his arms into the maroon dress, buttoning up the front. The heels are pinching his feet and he is relieved to switch to the sneakers.

The time was three fifteen p.m. and he decided the best place to rob was Bob and Delia's Discount Grocery. They've got a small bank branch in the front of the store with two tellers. He'd been there a few days ago, buying some orange juice.

He parks the car three blocks away from the store. He gets the note with an empty bag for the money along with the other sack containing the wig and shoes. His gun tucked into the left pocket of the dress, he's ready.

As he walks the three blocks, he practices breathing and reminds himself to stay calm. He opens the door to the supermarket and is relieved to see it isn't very busy. Quickly, he walks up to the two tellers and hands them the note which tells them that he has a gun, along with instructions to fill the bag with the money in their till. The tellers are really frightened and follow his instructions. He takes the note and the sacks he is carrying and hurriedly leaves the store.

He is afraid to look back and swiftly walks to the medical center in the next block. Just inside the door is a set of individual restrooms. He enters the women's, and locking the door, he removes the maroon dress and changes back to the high heel shoes. He changes his wig, styling it with his fingers. He places the maroon dress, sneakers, wig, and the money from the robbery into one bag. Stepping into the hallway in his little black dress, heels, and brown, shoulder length wig, he hobbles to his car.

The street is crawling with cops, and he hears more sirens in the distance. He backs out of his parking space and carefully makes his way out of the area.

He can't go back to the apartment looking like this. He has to find a place to change and get this crap off his face. The Mazda has to be moved and that would be a great place to change clothes.

He turns on the car radio and the soft rock music has a calming effect on him.

"This is breaking news. Around three forty-five p. m. the Seaview Bank and Trust located in Bob and Delia's discount grocery was held up at gunpoint. The robber is a woman appearing to be in her middle thirties to early forties approximately five feet ten inches tall, hazel eyes, with blonde, curly hair. She took undisclosed sums of money. If you have any information please contact the Seattle Police Department. Do not try to intercept this person, as she is armed and possibly dangerous. Now back to our regularly scheduled program."

Hmm, too bad. That's why all those cops are out there. Hope they catch her.

Arriving at the convention center, he pulls into the garage and parks several parking spaces away from the Mazda. He carries a sack with his change of clothes and the make-up remover and walks into the convention center. Finding a restroom near a deserted coffee kiosk, he quickly enters the men's restroom, rushing into a stall, hoping no one sees him. He'll deal with the itchy stockings back at the apartment. He steps out of the heels, shoves them in the bag and finishes removing the dress and all the padding. He sits on the toilet and applies the makeup remover to get the guck off his face. He cringes from pain when one of the fake lashes is torn off because he didn't apply enough remover. There's no mirror and he's unsure of how much makeup remains on his face. He puts his clothes and shoes on and bags everything up.

Hearing someone enter the restroom, he waits minutes for them to use the toilet and leave. Then he steps out of the stall and sees a blotchy looking face with rouge lipstick and smeared eyebrow liner. He quickly wets his face and applies more make-up remover, followed by more soap and water.

Finally, he's happy with himself and relieved to be a man once again. Time to go and transfer stuff to the Mazda and move the car to another level.

He leaves the wig, maroon dress, and sneakers in a sack on the front passenger side of the Mazda. He then puts his suitcase and laptop into the trunk. He moves the rental car to the bottom level.

Back at the apartment, he cannot wait to remove the panty hose. The robbery was not too successful, as he only got away with sixty-seven hundred dollars. Hardly worth the risk, but it'll help out if he has to go on the lam.

Chapter Sixteen

———————— ⟁ ————————

*G*erald Hershel sits in the waiting room, alone for a moment, thinking back to the pain he went through with his wisdom teeth. Poor guy, hope he gets out of pain soon. Touching his notebook, wondering if he'd stumbled onto an important piece of information on this case. Kenneth was a cop, one of them for a long time, and maybe he had a point. He had to admit, Aaron Townsend did seem a little more interested in Rachel Goodrich than what you'd expect an employer to be. Sure, he'd verified that Aaron was in Denver at the time of the attack. He has a lot of money; he could have hired someone to kill her because she was seeing her ex-husband. Was this a love triangle? Could she have been having an affair with both of them and her boss found out? It's hard to imagine that scenario, as Aaron Townsend's reputation was squeaky clean. In fact, he hadn't been able to find anyone who'd had anything negative to say about him. Well, this is an avenue he better explore.

Walking back into Rachel's room, the detective says, "Mr. Townsend I've got a few more questions I need to ask you."

"Do you want to talk to me now?"

"Yes, let's go into this waiting room across the hall. I was just in there and it's empty."

The two men enter the waiting room. "Have a seat, Mr. Townsend. Now about Rachel, you know sometimes things never go the way you want them to in life. One minute everything is copasetic and the next thing you find yourself embroiled in one of life's little turmoils."

"I'm not sure I understand what you're getting at."

"It's occurred to me that maybe Rachel was more than an employee; in fact, maybe you were having an affair and then her ex-husband comes on the scene and she's carrying on with both of you at the same time. You became jealous and enraged and you decided to have her killed. Isn't that exactly what happened?"

"I can't believe you'd talk about Rachel like that! She's not that kind of person!"

"Were you romantically involved with her?"

"Rachel's worked for me for seven years, and yes, the past three years we've traveled a lot and became close friends. About six weeks ago, I had sex with her in Denver one time. I realized she was much more special than a one-night stand and that I loved her. The next day I sent her back to Seattle because I needed some distance from the situation."

"Did you know she's seeing her ex?"

"No, I didn't know she was seeing him. To be honest, her family doesn't believe she's seeing him."

"Why not?"

"Rachel never really confided in me about her divorce. So I don't know much about her relationship, only what her father's said. I guess Hamilton was abusive to her.

"I bought an engagement ring and I was ready to ask her to marry me on Tuesday, but then this happened."

"Did you tell this to her parents?"

"No, her mom seems to be a little prudish and if Rachel and her ex are getting back together—well, I just saw no reason to complicate her life."

"Do you think the baby she's carrying is yours?"

"The timing seems right, and it's possible. Hamilton tells everyone who's willing to listen that she's having his baby."

"Can I get a DNA sample from you?"

"Look, you know I was in Denver when this happened, but if you want a DNA sample, that's fine with me. I have nothing to hide."

"I've no further questions. You're free to go."

Aaron, seething with rage, walks out of the room. He has to go find Rachel's family right now! By God, how could that detective suggest Rachel would carry on with him and her ex at the same time? True, she did let him make love to her in Denver when she might've been involved with Hamilton. But if she were involved with him, wasn't what happened in Denver just an accident? He was more to blame for it then she was. She's a good person! Why do they always have to sully the victim and paint them negatively? He saw that in the public defender's office and it's something in the legal field he never liked.

He sees them in the hallway walking towards Rachel's room. "Stanley, Susan, and Amelia, I need to talk to all of you right now. I think we should go down and get some coffee in the cafeteria."

Taking a sip of his coffee, facing the group, he says, "I just finished an interview with Gerald Hershel and there's something I want you to know. I want you to hear the facts from me. As you know, for the last three years Rachel and I have traveled a lot together, adding new coffee shops around the western part of the United States and visiting coffee growers outside of our country. During this time we've became very close friends.

"About six weeks ago our relationship became intimate in Denver, and I made love to her one time. I sent her back to Seattle because I knew she was a good woman and not a one-night stand. About fourteen years ago my wife, Meredith, and my ten-year-old son, Michael, were killed by a drunk driver in Los Angeles. It's been hard for me to get involved with anyone. I called Rachel last week and told her we needed to talk when I returned from Denver on Tuesday. I purchased an engagement ring, and I wanted to ask her to marry me. Then this horrible thing happened to her. I wanted you to know the facts. I don't want you, Mrs. Goodrich, to think badly about your daughter. She's a good person, and I love her. I'll always love her! I had no idea she was going back to her ex."

"Are you saying this might be your baby?"

"Susan, it's possible. I don't know. Hamilton keeps saying it's his. I just don't know what to believe anymore. But one thing I'll never believe is that Rachel would be involved with both of us at the same time. She's not that kind of person!"

"For what it's worth, Aaron, I never once believed she's back with that creep, Kenneth."

"I hope you're right, Stanley."

"I know my niece is a good girl," Amelia says. "She's thirty-eight and not a teenager. There's nothing wrong with what happened between the two of you."

"Amelia! They aren't married or even engaged!"

"Susan, this is not nineteen-fifty anymore. Relax! Stop being so stuffy."

"I need to take care of some things at my office, but I can call you later if you'd like to go out for dinner."

Everyone was in agreement they should go out for dinner and he leaves them sitting in the cafeteria.

Chapter Seventeen

*A*aron steps into the elevator, relieved to be the only passenger, and he pushes the garage level button. His eyes are burning and he knows he's about to have one of those gut wrenching moments, the kind real men aren't supposed to have. His father always said, real men don't cry, but when his son was alive he had never told him that nonsense.

He slides behind the wheel, sticking his key into the ignition and leans over the steering wheel as pent-up sobs escape from his body. He cries uncontrollably because she's obviously going back to that abusive jerk, cries because he's alone again, and cries for what might've been. Why did he send her back to Seattle? Oh God! Would it have been different if he'd popped the question right there? Well, you screwed up again and you're never going to know.

To add insult to injury the detective suggested she's having an affair with both of them and that he wanted to have her killed. This is one of the blackest days of his life.

He rubs his eyes on the sleeve of his suit jacket. His face and shirt were wet from crying. He thinks he better call Sandy, and fishes for his cell phone in his coat pocket.

"Stacy, this is Aaron put me through to Sandy."

"Yes, sir."

"Good morning, Aaron. Is there any news on Rachel?"

"She's unable to speak, but she's awake and doing better. I'm going to come into the office today, but I think I need to go for a drive and get some fresh air. I'll probably be in later this afternoon. I told her parents if they needed anything to call. If you hear anything you can reach me on my cell."

"Sure. Your voice sounds funny like you've got a cold. Are you all right?"

"I'm fine, really fine. I think it's just the connection. I'm in the parking garage at the hospital so the connection's probably distorted."

"Let me know if you need anything."

He closed the phone, placing it on the passenger seat. Backing out of the parking space, he pays the lady at the ticket booth. The sun is shining and it'd be a good day to go down to the pier. He's usually found tranquility watching the ocean waves. Spending some time on the pier and getting some fresh air sounds like what he's needing right now. He'd always enjoyed watching the fish mongers toss huge salmons in the air at Pikes Market.

He opens all four car windows and steps on the gas pedal, merging the car onto the freeway and edging it up to seventy miles an hour. The wind whips through his hair and beats and sucks against a dry cleaners bag hanging in the back seat. If only the wind could rip this pain away from him.

When she's out of the hospital maybe he'll take off a few weeks and go to Europe. He always wanted to cruise Italy but never seemed to have the time. He needed to get away from work and everyone.

He buys a bagel and a cup of coffee to go at Pikes Market and drives the six tenths of a mile to the Great Seattle Wheel on Alaskan Way. He sips on his coffee and sits on one of the benches facing Elliot Bay. The fishing boats are bobbing up and down on the ocean waves. Tourists are laughing and talking about their ride on the big enclosed Ferris wheel.

The day-to-day world is matterless to the ocean. People live and die, but the tides continue nonstop, rhythmically caressing the shore with the ebb and flow of waves, as they've done since the beginning of time. He enjoys the smell of salt in the air and the squawk of seagulls circling overhead. He tosses bagel pieces on the ground and five huge birds swoop down, flapping their wings voraciously, picking at the bread. They try to push the other birds away from the feast. Tourists are taking pictures of a white sailboat on the frothy, dark-blue water.

He and Meredith used to love to go canoeing and sailing when they were first married. Meredith's favorite was Balboa in Newport Beach, California. They'd pack a picnic on a Saturday and drive from the UCLA campus, hanging out on the sandy beach, working on their tans. The homework they brought was never touched. To be young again and to have her and Mike with him would be like heaven. He sniffles, remembering her laugh and the warmth of the California sun on her hair. She totally loved him, she was his and his only. Tears came to his eyes, and he rubs them, thinking why did you have to go? A love as great as theirs happens maybe once in a lifetime. For the time they had, he was so lucky.

A little girl asked her mother, "Why is the man crying?"

Taking her arm, the lady tells her to, "Never mind about that," and leads her farther down the sidewalk.

Thinking of Meredith in just such a moment when their son was small and inquisitive. Smiling, he thinks it seems the first words children learn are no and why. He'd hoped no one would notice him crying. Those old tapes from his father still played in his head, real men don't cry. His response is, yes, they do.

At forty-five it seemed life was passing him by. Rachel had filled an empty void in his life. It's over, and once again he's got to continue on life's path alone. He tosses the last piece of bagel and watches the flock of birds descend. He guesses he's a lot like them, swooping down, wanting Rachel in his life at the same time her ex-husband's always trying to push him to the side. Hamilton's favorite sentence is, she's having my baby. Wasn't that a title of a country song?

Drinking the final swig of his coffee, he tosses the used cup into a nearby receptacle. He thinks he'd better get back to the office. No sense sitting here wasting the day and feeling sorry for himself.

Driving the ten miles to the Coffee Genie, he's happy to see no one's parked in his parking space. Taking his laptop and briefcase out of the trunk and walking into the building, he pushes the elevator button. Thinking it feels like forever since he's been here. This is what he needs right now—work and a sense of normalcy.

Getting off on the fourth floor, he makes a right and opens the door to the Coffee Genie corporate office. Stacy is sitting at the reception desk and the waiting area is empty. Stacy's a petite five-foot-two-inch shorthaired blonde with blue eyes.

"Aaron, welcome back. It's so nice to see you!"

"Nice to see you, too, Stacy."

"How's Rachel?"

"She's looking much better, and I think she's back with the living."

"Wow, that's good. It's really awful what happened to her."

"Yes, it is."

Aaron walks into his office, closing his door. He places his briefcase on the chair by the side of his desk and lays his computer on top of the desk. Sitting in his big leather chair, he hears a short knock at the door.

"Come in."

"Welcome back, boss!" Sandy says.

"Thanks."

"Are you doing okay?"

"Yes, I'm fine. I'm not sure when Rachel will be well enough to return to work. We may need to hire someone temporarily to help out until we know what's going to happen with her."

"Do you think she might not come back to work because of the baby?"

Aaron pauses before speaking. "Sandy, how did you know about the baby?"

"I thought you mentioned to me that she's pregnant?"

"I don't remember telling you she's going to have a baby. Maybe I did and forgot it. The days and conversations just seem to blend into a big pile of mush."

"I'm sorry. I know how close you are to Rachel. We all care about her."

"I know. Well, if you'll please excuse me, Sandy, I need to get some things taken care of. Tell Kevin I'd like to see him in about an hour to talk about our website. I need to see the file on our Portland location. Get Hal on the phone for me. I need to speak with him about Denver."

The afternoon is melting away with one task after another. Looking up at the clock on the wall he notices the time is five-fifteen. Picking up the phone, he calls Stanley. "Hi. I called to check on Rachel."

"She can't talk, but she's awake. Dr. Johnson's going to have a speech therapist stop by tomorrow after her physical therapy treatment."

"That's really good. I thought I'd stop by and see her in about a half an hour. I'll take the three of you out to dinner as we discussed this morning."

"That sounds fine. Tomorrow Amelia needs to go home to San Francisco."

"Please tell Amelia I'd be happy to give her a lift to the airport."

"Thanks, Aaron. We'll be in Rachel's room when you get here."

"I'll be there as soon as I can. Goodbye."

Sandy and Stacy were putting on their coats when he walks out of his office. "Good night, ladies. I'll see you tomorrow."

"Do you want to go out for dinner with me, Aaron?"

"I'm sorry, Sandy. I'm on my way to the hospital to see Rachel and take her parents to dinner. They're so tired of the food at the hospital. Maybe we can do it another time."

"Sure, no problem. Tell Rachel we're all thinking of her."

"I will. I hope I don't run into her ex-husband, Kenneth Hamilton. He's a bit annoying to me—like a squeaky garage door."

"I know what you mean. You meet people and they just seem to grate on you even though you barely know them."

"Boy, isn't that the truth."

"Did you say Kenneth Hamilton?"

"Yes, Stacy. He's Rachel's ex-husband."

"Hmm, hasn't he called you several times Sandy?"

"No! You must be confused Stacy."

"No. Didn't he call you on Monday?"

"I don't remember a Kenneth Hamilton calling me."

"Yes, and you didn't want to talk to him. He said if you didn't talk to him he's going to call your boss."

"Stacy, I think you're confusing him with one of our customers. I get those kinds of calls all the time. People think just because they buy some coffee online or go to one of our coffee shops, they can get direct access to the boss."

"Well, you're probably right, Sandy. I'm sorry. The name just sounded so familiar."

"Sandy," Aaron says. "Why do I get the feeling you're hiding something from me?"

"I'm not hiding anything! Don't you trust me?"

"You wouldn't be my office manager if I didn't trust you. I hope you understand I don't like people keeping secrets from me, especially if it involves my company or my staff. You ladies have a good evening. I'll see you tomorrow morning after I stop by the hospital to check on Rachel."

They watch Aaron walk out of the door and the sound of the elevator door opening and closing. "Don't ever tell Aaron about my phone calls again!"

"Sorry, Sandy. I didn't think it mattered."

"You didn't think it mattered! You almost got me in trouble with Aaron."

"Sorry, I apologize."

"Just mind your own business and stop meddling into my personal affairs! Otherwise, you might be looking for a new job."

"I'm sorry, Sandy. I didn't mean anything. Good night."

"Goodnight, Stacy."

Rachel begins to doze off and she experiences a free fall through blackness, being sucked lower and lower, like an undertow. She struggles to regain her balance to stop the fall. A golden light appears below her seconds before she lands in a small, square room. The light glints against three white walls. On one wall are five symmetrical light-yellow pollen-colored doors shaped like diamonds. These doors are slightly curved and fanned. They ascend and descend in height from the center door, making the first and last the shortest and of the same height.

As she opens the doors strong floral scents of rose, carnation, alyssum, gardenia, and lily-of-the-valley are released, along with piano notes moving up the musical scale. Only the middle door offers an exit leading to a small, dimly lit room appearing to be in a hexagon shape. Venturing inside, the door slams shut behind her and she hears a waspy sound, reminding her of the word *posies*. Taking a few steps forward to better see the area, her foot hits something sticky and her nostrils are filled with the sweet smell of honey. Suddenly, the floor gives way.

Swimming in sticky, sweet honey, she grabs a piece of broken, waxy comb to help her stay afloat. The sound of buzzing becomes louder. To the side of her is a wall of honeycomb with perfect hexagonal-shaped cells. This wall separates her from angry, giant honeybees, larger than herself. She can see their huge, bulging eyes, antennae, and their oval, yellow and gold bodies. One bee works its way through a hole and slithers towards her. It buzzes, posies, posies, posies. She tries to scream but no sound comes. The bee harpoons her with its stinger through her abdomen. The venom travels through her bloodstream and she begins to feel paralyzed and whimpers as she feels antennae wrap around her, squeezing her body. Soon hundreds of bees form a ball on top of her and begin buzzing in unison, posies, posies, posies, as she loses consciousness. Rachel's an intruder and they're preparing her dead body for removal from their hive.

"Rachel, Rachel. Wake up, honey. You're having a bad dream. You're in the hospital. You're safe. Mom's right here." Stroking her daughter's hand and touching her shoulder, Susan thought that she heard her mumble something like posies, but she couldn't be sure.

The nurse enters the room. "Is she awake?"

"I tried to awaken her, as she's whimpering, and I'm not sure if she's in pain or having a nightmare."

"Bad dreams and hallucinations aren't uncommon for patients coming out of a coma. I brought some broth and some gelatin. Let's see if we can wake her up and try to feed her." Pushing the button on her bed she moves Rachel into a sitting position. "Rachel, wake up," the nurse says as she gently pushes on Rachel's shoulder.

Rachel's eyes open and she tries to focus. Relief washes over her when she realizes she's with her mother. She is grateful she's not drowning in honey and being crushed and being transported like garbage by bees.

The nurse feeds Rachel a few teaspoons of broth and she struggles to eat the gelatin. "Good girl, Rachel. Do you know what year it is?'

Rachel responds with slurred speech. The nurse asks her other questions and she struggles, trying to find the words.

"You're doing great. It'll get easier." The nurse lowers the bed and adjusts her pillow.

While driving back to the hospital Aaron thinks about the conversation he's just had with Stacy and Sandy. He has a feeling something's not quite right, and he plans to get to the bottom of it tomorrow. Why would Kenneth Hamilton call her—if he did? The other curious thing was that Sandy knew about the baby, and he honestly didn't remember telling her that Rachel's pregnant.

He stops and buys a bouquet of roses at a little flower shop a few blocks from the hospital. He chose a mixed assortment of colors along with baby breath. The sales clerk suggests a beautiful crystal vase, and he signs the card: From Aaron and all of the employees at the Coffee Genie.

Walking into the hospital room with the flowers, Aaron says, "Hello, everyone. I brought some roses for you, Rachel, from all of us at the Coffee Genie."

"Aaron, they're beautiful!" Amelia said as she sniffs them and takes the flowers. "I'll put them on your night table, dear."

"I'm glad you like them." Standing by the bed, touching her hand, Aaron says, "Hi, how are you this evening?"

"The nurse was able to feed her some broth."

"That's really good news, Susan. Rachel, everyone at the office misses you."

It's been a lot nicer since she's been moved out of ICU into a private room where there's enough space for visitors. Everyone's talking about how much better she looks when Dr. Johnson walks in to see her on his evening rounds.

"Let's go out to dinner so the doctor can examine Rachel."

"Aaron, that's a good idea. Let's go," Amelia says.

After her doctor leaves, Rachel begins to once again drift into a space where nightmares lurk in the inner brain.

It's a warm summer day and she's wearing a white strappy dress. Her straight hair hangs freely. She's barefoot and feels the damp meadow grasses beneath her feet. The sun warms her head and the smell of flowers and fresh cut grass causes her to relax with abandonment. She begins picking flowers for a bouquet and she thinks, posies, such beautiful posies. A shape crosses the sun, shadowing the meadow, and she looks up, realizing she's being watched. A cold breeze starts up and begins whipping her dress and tearing at her hair. She touches her arms to shield herself from the cold.

Terror grips her as the realization hits—something or someone is after her. In the corner of her eye she sees a middle-aged man wearing bib overalls, with blood splatters on the bottom of his faded blue denim pants. His boots are old, scuffed on the toes, and muddy. He's got a hedge trimmer and he's slicing through the air. Dropping the posies to the ground, some petals fall away from the stems. She begins to run, and she can hear the hedge trimmer close to her ear. She tells herself, run faster, run faster. The blades catch in her hair and large clumps of hair fall down her back to the ground. She screams and screams and screams.

The nurses hear her screams and rush in to find her wildly kicking and hitting her arms on the rails of her bed. They gently touch, shake her, and awaken her. She begins to cry. One of the nurses comforts her and remains with her until she falls asleep.

Chapter Eighteen

*T*he rain pelts the roof and crashes against his bedroom window with a vengeance, causing Aaron to awaken a few times during the night. It's like being a plate in a giant dishwasher, being scrubbed and rinsed. When it rained in the past he often found himself reflecting on his life or just life in general. A sense of peacefulness would often wash over him. This time was different. It felt more somber, like Mother Nature angrily trying to wash away the grime and filth created by living beings on the earth. He felt a sense of sorrow, similar to when his family died. Looking at the clock on his nightstand, he sees it's six o'clock a.m. He needs to get going, as he's promised to take Amelia to the airport. They're staying at Mary's Bed and Breakfast Inn, where they rented rooms after Rachel was moved from ICU.

He shaves and wonders what's going on at the office. His life feels like a laundry basket someone's just tipped upside down, jumbling everything up. It seems nothing has been left untouched by what's happened to Rachel. How could Gerald Herschel possibly think he'd be involved in a love triangle and try to have Rachel killed? He's not only lost Rachel but it seems his character's been maligned in the process. Now there's something haywire at the office and he can sense it.

Looking at himself in the mirror as he whips the necktie around his neck and ties it, he thinks, right now you just have to take one thing at a time. Putting on his suit coat, followed by his trench coat, he grabs his keys and brief case to begin another long day.

Backing out of his garage, feeling relieved that for the time being the rain has at least stopped. Approaching the little red stop sign at the end of his block, he notices a rainbow descending from the grey sky. The vivid colors of blues, purples, pale greens, and pink are pasted against the greyness. He sits at the corner admiring the rainbow. He's jerked back to the present when he hears the horn of an impatient driver behind him. Oh, sorry. Releasing his foot on the break, he steps on the gas.

The freeway's wet and slippery and some cars have spun out from driving too fast. A few cars are on the side of the road as drivers assess fender-bender damage and exchange information. The drive seemed to take twice the time he expected, and it's a good thing he started early.

At the bed and breakfast while loading Amelia's suitcase into the trunk of his car, he says, "Stanley, I'll be by the hospital right after work to see Rachel, and we can go for dinner if you and Susan would like."

"Thanks, Aaron. We can never repay you for all you've done for us."

"Pay is unnecessary; we all just want Rachel to get well."

"Amelia, are you ready?"

She hugs a teary-eyed Susan. "Yes. Susan, now you need to stay positive for your daughter. She's going to be just fine!"

"I will, and you have a safe trip home. Thanks so much for coming with us. I could've never made it through this without you."

"Thanks, Amelia, for everything. You are a gem of a sister-in-law."

"You're welcome, Stanley," she says as she hugs him and pats him on his shoulder. She again turns and hugs Susan. She climbs into the front passenger side of the car and Aaron closes the door.

After helping Amelia get her luggage checked at the airport, he hugs her goodbye and drives to the office.

Stepping into the door of the Coffee Genie, he sees Sandy conversing with Stacy, and she looks up at him.

"Oh, hi. I thought you'd be in later. Did you see Rachel?"

"No, I drove her aunt to the airport, so my plans changed. I thought I'd go see her after work instead of this morning. She looked much better when I saw her last night. I stopped and picked up some roses for her from all of us."

"That's nice. Do you want us to donate something for the flowers?"

"No. I got it this time. Stacy, I want to see you in my office."

Looking at Sandy, "Okay," she says, hesitatingly.

"Do you want both of us?"

"No, Sandy. Just Stacy for now."

Escorting Stacy into the office, he shuts the door, walks over to his chair and sits down. "Stacy, please sit down. I want to talk to you about Kenneth Hamilton."

Gulping and finding it hard to breathe, Stacy says, "Kenneth Hamilton?"

"Yes. You said he's called here several times."

"Oh, that. Sandy's right. I made a mistake, and I shouldn't have said he called."

Leaning over his desk and looking her straight in the eyes, Aaron says, "Honesty and integrity are very important to me. I could never keep an employee that's dishonest with me. I've always had an open door policy and my employees can come and talk to me about anything. So before you answer me, take a moment to think about what you're going to say. Now, I want the truth. Has Kenneth Hamilton called Sandy here at the office?"

"I can't discuss this. Sandy will fire me!"

"Look, this is my company, and if there's any firing, it'll be done by me! Now tell me the truth. Has he called here, or did you confuse him with someone else? I want the truth!"

Her eyes redden as she pushes back tears. "Yes. I'm certain he's called several times. What really stood out for me was on Monday when he called and she didn't want to talk to him. He told me to tell her if she didn't talk to him, he'd call her boss."

"Do you know how many times he's called here and when?"

"Well, no, I don't. But I know it's been several times. The first time might've been when you and Rachel were in Denver. But I'm not really certain. I think he's also called her on Tuesday and Wednesday of this week."

"Thank you for your honesty, Stacy. That's all I want. If Sandy says anything more about this to you, please let me know. Now you go tell Sandy I want her in here on the double!"

"Boss, Stacy said you needed to see me?"

"Yes, close the door and have a seat."

Leaning over his desk, narrowing his eyes, and looking her square in the face, Aaron says, "I want you to tell me about Kenneth Hamilton and what your connection to him is!"

"Aaron, that was simply Stacy misspeaking yesterday. I don't know anyone named Kenneth Hamilton."

"Sandy, he called you on Monday and you didn't want to talk to him, and he said he'd call your boss if you didn't speak to him. He's also called you yesterday and the day before that. Now you better tell me the truth and now!"

She collapses like a waffle cone on a hot July day under a pile of liquefying ice cream and lays her head on his desk. She weeps uncontrollably, tears puddling on the desk.

Walking around his desk with a box of tissues, he touches Sandy on her shoulder. "I know you're upset, but we need to talk about this. I want you to tell me everything."

Looking up at him with a face of makeup slipping like bad icing on a flopped cake, she says, "I got involved with him to help Rachel—and for us."

"Us?"

"Yes. I'm in love with you Aaron, and I thought maybe you'd notice me if Rachel went back to her ex-husband. But I didn't know the kind of person he really was."

"Sandy, you're young enough to be my daughter, and I'm sorry; I don't have feelings for you in a romantic way."

"I can't help it. I'm in love with you."

"I'm shocked, Sandy, and I apologize if I've ever done anything or said anything that would make you think I wanted a romantic relationship with you."

"No. I wished you would notice me but you never did. You only had eyes for Rachel! I dreamed of being the one for you!" She cried even harder.

Aaron walks to his window and looks out. This is such a mess! My God, how could she think he'd be interested in her? He never even thought about her in that way. After a few minutes he turns back to Sandy. "This might not be the best time, but I want you to start from the beginning and tell me what happened."

Blowing her nose, her eyes are swollen and red from crying. "You and Rachel were in Denver when he called. He told me he'd been looking for her for a few years. I told him we couldn't confirm or deny employment of any of our employees. He was really nice and told me they'd lost a daughter. I gave him her address and then I helped him get a studio apartment in Belltown. I didn't know he had violent tendencies or that he'd hurt Rachel. I'm so sorry, Aaron. I never wanted to hurt her. I just thought I was helping her get reconnected with her ex-husband—that it was some big misunderstanding. I guess she must've rejected him and he beat her up.

"He made me give him twenty thousand dollars out of my investment portfolio or he'd tell you I helped him. Neal called me yesterday and said he couldn't get the other eight thousand dollars for three banking days and I'd only get the balance after they deducted all of the fees. I told Kenneth that and he didn't care. He told me to come up with the eight thousand dollars and he recommended I refinance my car. If that wasn't bad enough, he asked me to go to bed with him and said disgusting things to me.

"Before you came in, I was able to refinance my car and get five thousand dollars. I called my Dad and he's going to wire three thousand dollars to me."

"Sandy, cancel refinancing your car. Tell your financial planner to nix selling your investments, and call your dad and tell him you don't need the money. Hamilton can go pound salt. If he calls you back, you transfer him to me! Sandy, right now we've got to call Gerald Hershel and you must tell him everything you know."

"Kenneth said I'd be considered an accomplice because I got the money to help him to evade authorities."

"What you did, Sandy, is unethical, but if you never intended harm to Rachel then it isn't likely it would be considered criminal."

Picking up the phone and punching Stacy's extension, Aaron says, "I want you to get Gerald Hershel on the phone. He's the detective working on Rachel's case. Call Seattle PD because I don't know his phone number. Ring me when you've got him on the phone." He hangs up and runs his hands through his hair, thinking what a big mess this is. He's going to have to fire her, but he can't deal with that now.

It seemed like forever but it's only been a few minutes when his intercom buzzes. "Gerald Hershel's on line one."

"Good morning, Mr. Hershel. I've discovered some information on Rachel's case, and I need you to come to my office. My office manager, Sandy Delray, has knowledge about her case."

"I can be there in twenty minutes."

"Sandy, Detective Hershel's on his way. When he gets here you need to tell him everything you know about Kenneth Hamilton. After he's finished interviewing you, I want you to take the week off. After that we'll meet, and I'll make a decision at that time whether I'll be terminating your employment here at the Coffee Genie. Right now we both need some space from this situation."

"You're going to fire me?"

"I'm not prepared to make that decision at this time."

"I did this all for you!"

"You didn't do this for me. Now, I don't want to talk to you about this any further, so please go to your office."

Gerald Hershel's escorted into Sandy's office and she offers him a seat.

"Ms. Delray, Mr. Townsend told me that you know something about Ms. Goodrich's case."

She reiterated the story she'd just told her boss while he scribbled down all the details.

"Do you know for a fact he did this to her?"

"Well, he said she hit him first and things got out of hand. So, yes I think by what he said, he beat her."

"Do you know what kind of car he's driving?"

"Yes, sir. He has a white 2000 Honda Accord."

"Where's he from?"

"He was from Lincoln, Nebraska, but he transferred to the Sioux Falls Police Department. I think a few years back. He told me he's on disability because he was injured when he went on a robbery call at a convenience store."

"Where's he currently staying?"

"He has an apartment in Belltown that I rented for him. He wanted to make up with Rachel and I felt sorry for him. I was only trying to help."

He asks her for his Belltown address and she provides it to him. "Do you have any other information?"

"No, sir. I don't. I never wanted to hurt Rachel."

He walked out of Sandy's office and spoke briefly to Aaron. "Thanks for the information."

"You're welcome. I need to contact her parents."

"Please wait an hour. We don't want to tip him off if he's at the hospital."

The detective walks into the hall and calls dispatch. He requests that a squad car be sent over to Kenneth's Belltown address and that if he is at home to bring him to the precinct for questioning. "I'm on my way to County General, but get someone over there in case he's already there. Larry Miller is stationed near her room to protect her. He'll need backup. Call Larry and tell him to meet the other officer, and tell them I'm on my way."

Chapter Nineteen

For the past twenty-four hours, Rachel's been experiencing fitful sleeps, dozing off only to be pulled into vivid and hellish nightmares. Her brain, the body's computer, is randomly rebooting itself, trying to reconnect its synapses and pushing bits and pieces of data to the surface. With each nightmare more and more data in her brain's being restored and reorganized for quicker recognition. When she awakens, the knowledge bursts into her conscious memory of the Friday night encounter with Kenneth.

Susan is tidying up the night table and picks up Kenneth's bouquet to add fresh water. Her daughter has tears glistening in her eyes. "Rachel, honey you're crying."

She looks at the bouquet and says, "posies."

"Why, yes, dear, your flowers."

Rachel, looking at Kenneth at the foot of her bed said, "You."

"Me what, Rachel?"

"H–u –r –t me"

"Rachie, I can't imagine what you're trying to say."

"Rachel, are you saying Kenneth is the one who hurt you?"

"Yes, he hurt me."

"For God's sake, Susan, you can't believe that! Didn't the nurse say sometimes when comatose patients regain consciousness they have hallucinations?"

"Well, yes, she did tell me that."

A couple of tears cascade down Rachel's cheeks, "Kenneth, you r-raped me."

"I can't believe you're talking like this. This is utter nonsense." He walks to the door, trying to calm down. The guard, along with another policeman, is walking down the hall towards Rachel's room. He begins to sweat, realizing his worst nightmare is about to come true. Susan is leaning over her daughter, and he swiftly crosses the room and grabs her by the wrist. "Come here!" He drags her, placing her on the other side of the bed facing the door and stands behind her.

"Kenneth, you're hurting me! What are you doing?"

"Don't move. I've got a gun, and I'll kill you and your daughter. Do exactly what I say and no one will get hurt."

"Kenneth, are you crazy? Let me go!"

Shoving the gun in her back "I'm dead serious."

"You're the one who did this to Rachel!"

"I didn't mean to. I love her, but she hit me first."

"I don't believe you!"

The police walk into the room. "Mr. Hamilton, we need you to come with us to the police station for questioning."

"I've got a gun and I'll shoot Susan and Rachel if you don't cooperate with me. Take your guns out and kick them over towards me, nice and easy. Do what I say, and no one's going to get hurt."

The policemen unholster there guns and kick them towards him. "You know you can't get away with this. You're only hurting yourself. We can talk about this calmly and we can help you."

"Guard, if I wanted your advice I'd ask for it. So shut the hell up!" Pointing at the other policeman, he says, "You sit in the chair over there in the corner." With one hand reaching for the restraint on the night table and handing it to Susan, he shoves her towards the policeman. "Put this around his shoulders and tie him into the chair. Make sure you do a good job or I'll kill your daughter." He moves near the head of the bed facing them; he glances at Rachel and points the gun at her head. Terror spreads across her face as Susan ties up the policeman. "Now get his hand cuffs." Pointing the gun at the guard, he says, "Move over by the bed and put your hands behind your back. Susan, put those handcuffs on the guard. Now take this medical tubing and tie the guard to the railing on the bed."

A nurse walks into the room to get Rachel ready for her oxygen therapy. "I've come to—" her voice trails off.

Switching the position of the gun, he aims it at the nurse's head. "You get into the bathroom and don't come out until I'm gone."

"But, Mr. Hamilton."

"Shut up and do what I say if you don't want to die."

"Now, Susan, get their guns and give them to me along with that police officer's handcuffs."

Susan cries hysterically "I can't. I just can't"

"I'll shoot your daughter if you don't, so do it now!"

She cringed, picking up each gun like it's a rattlesnake. Taking her as a hostage was going to be problematic. You can't control an emotional woman, especially her. Changing his mind about which hostage to take, he yells out, "Nurse, get your ass out here!"

"No, the door's locked and I'm not coming out."

"Come out now or everyone in this room dies. Do you want that on your conscience? I mean business. I've got nothing to lose, so believe me, I'm serious."

She steps out of the bathroom. "Please don't hurt us. I've got two little children who need me."

"Well, isn't that sweet. Do what I say and everyone makes it out alive. Now come here!" He shoves Susan against the wall. "Now stay there and shut up if you don't want this nurse killed!"

Grabbing the nurse's arm and pulling it behind her back. "Come with me!" They walk to the door and the hallway is clear. "Now, no funny business. We're going to go down the hall and grab an elevator. If you behave yourself, I'll let you go. Now move!"

Grabbing the next elevator, they get off at the lobby level and hurriedly exit the hospital, crossing the street to the parking lot of the Mexican restaurant.

"Mr. Hamilton, please let me go!"

"Shut up and you'll not get hurt," he says as he fastens the handcuffs on her hands and shoves her into the passenger side of his car. He can hear sirens in the distance and he knows the police are on their way.

"Mrs. Goodrich, you need to stop crying and help us. Mr. Hamilton's gone, but we need to catch him and find the nurse. Please come over here and remove this restraint."

She walks over to the policeman, undoing the restraint. He grabs his phone and calls dispatch "This is Bill One at County General. This is a code three. Suspect Kenneth

Hamilton has taken a female nurse hostage at gunpoint. I have Charlie two with me and the suspect has also stolen a set of handcuffs and both of our weapons."

The policeman frees Rachel's guard, Larry Miller, from the bed railing.

Two hospital orderlies walk into the room to take Rachel for her oxygen therapy.

Seconds later Gerald Hershel and his partner rush into the room. "Officer Miller, has Kenneth Hamilton been here yet?"

"Yes, we just finished calling in a code three as he's taken a nurse hostage at gunpoint no more than five minutes ago. He pulled a gun on us, taking our weapons and tying us up."

Leaning over the crying Rachel, Hershel says, "Miss Goodrich, you're safe and no one's going to harm you. The hospital staff is here to take you to your therapy and maybe it'd be good idea for you to go to your appointment. Would that be okay with you?"

Rachel nods okay, and another nurse comes in and helps the orderlies prepare her for transport.

When Rachel is moved out into the hallway, the detective turns to Mrs. Goodrich. "Please have a seat. I can see how distraught you are, but I need you to tell me what happened." A nurse walks into the room and he tells her, "I need you to go find Mr. Goodrich."

"Yes, sir."

"Now, Mrs. Goodrich, take a deep breath. That's it. Tell me what happened?"

"I was cleaning up Rachel's night table and I picked up a bouquet of flowers Kenneth had given her. She said, posies. And I said, yes, dear, your flowers. I thought she was crying.

So I asked her if she was. She looked at Kenneth and said, hurt. I then asked if Kenneth's the one who hurt her. She said Kenneth hurt her and raped her. Then Kenneth walked to the hall, and when he saw the policemen walking towards Rachel's room he pulled a gun on me." She begins sobbing.

"I know this is hard but then what happened?"

"He made those nice policemen drop their guns and kick them across the floor to him. It was just awful. He made me tie them up because he had a gun pointed at Rachel's head. Then he took that nurse with him. Oh, it's just awful!"

Stanley walks into the room. "What happened?"

Susan stands up and races into his arms, sobbing. "Kenneth almost killed all of us. He's the one who hurt Rachel. He then took a nurse hostage. Stanley, it's horrible."

"Mrs. Goodrich, that'll be all for now."

"That bastard! I knew he was the one all along! I just knew it! Are you okay?"

"Yes. I need a tissue."

He hands her one of his handkerchiefs. "What about our daughter? Where is she?"

"They took her for therapy, but she's okay. I'm sure she's frightened out of her wits. Poor thing. He held a gun to her head. It's so awful, Stanley!"

"Maybe we need to get a doctor to give you a sedative to calm you down."

"No! I don't want anything."

"That guy has always been a damn loser! If I could get my hands on him, I'd kill him myself! Are you sure you're okay, honey?"

"Yes. I wish Amelia was here."

"Well, she isn't, so you're going to have to be strong so we can get through this," he says stroking her shoulder.

Backing out of the parking lot and onto the street, Kenneth stops at the red light at the next corner and drives carefully, not to draw attention. It seems like forever but it's only been twenty minutes, and he's now merging on to the I-5 freeway. "What's your name?"

"Karen Wilson."

"Karen, I have no intention of hurting you and as long as you cooperate with me, I'll let you go. I really don't want to kill anyone. I just came out here to reconnect with my ex and everything has gone from bad to worse. I'm really not such a bad guy. I was a cop for eighteen years. Just remain calm because sniveling women make me edgy."

Leaning forward he turns on the radio just as the program is giving breaking news about a hostage taken from County General Hospital.

"We have breaking news of a nurse taken hostage at County General Hospital. Information is sketchy, but the suspect is Kenneth Hamilton, approximately forty years of age, six feet tall, hazel eyes, and black hair. It is believed he's driving a two thousand white Honda Accord. His hostage is a nurse dressed in nursing whites. Mr. Hamilton also has a prior warrant for his arrest in Sioux Falls, South Dakota for attempting to murder another ex-wife, Debbie Hamilton. If you have any information please contact the Seattle Police Department. He's armed and dangerous. Do not approach the suspect."

Looking out his rear view mirror he sees a police cruiser two car lengths behind him. He steps on the gas and switches lanes. The cruiser also switches lanes. He accelerates and he sees the flashing lights behind him. He swerves in and out of lanes to prevent the police cruiser from getting ahead of him. He's within five minutes of his exit. They're probably radioing in for back up. A couple of minutes later he hears a helicopter in the sky and he knows this is it. He's got to get to the other car and his disguise. A nail strip has been placed across the freeway ahead. He sees it and changing three lanes at a time, he steers the car onto the shoulder of the road, driving around the nail strip, just missing it by seconds. He and the nurse are jostled from side to side by the jerky car maneuvers. Back on the pavement, he steps on the gas pedal harder and the speedometer climbs to eighty-five miles an hour. He almost hits a car in front of him, swerving just in time to miss it. His tires squeal and he is at the off ramp.

Speeding forward, he makes a right at the next corner and knows he's got to lose the policemen who are behind him. He makes several quick turns and a bootlegger turn in the middle of the street. He has temporarily lost them, but he knows they're just minutes away, as the helicopter is still in pursuit. He drives to the convention center and parks three spaces away from the Mazda.

"I'm only going to say this once, so pay attention. Stay here and be a good girl. Don't try to do anything heroic. Just shut up and wait and you'll be safe. If you try to get out of the car, I'll kill you."

He jumps out of the car and races to the Mazda, almost getting hit by another car exiting the garage. He shakes as he opens the car door, grabbing the sack with the wig and dress. He throws the wig and brush on the passenger side and he puts his arms into the unbuttoned maroon dress and climbs into the car. He sticks the key into the ignition and turns it. The car engine makes a clicking sound. Oh crap, the damn thing isn't going to start. He pumps the gas pedal and tries again and the engine turns over. He grabs the wig, putting it on and not having time to brush it, he pats it down into place as best he can. Backing out of the parking space, he's now behind a line of other cars exiting the parking structure. He hears sirens and he knows he's got to remain calm. He buttons the front of his dress and waits for his turn to exit.

He is two cars from exiting the garage and traffic is backed up. He quickly speed dials Clyde's Jetway Jets. "This is Jack T. Williams I need to speak to the reservationist."

"Reservations. This is Janice. How may I help you?"

"This is Jack T. Williams. I reserved the jet and I am ready to go to Detroit."

"Yes, sir. It'll take about an hour to have the pilots there."

"Why so long?"

"There's some nut on the freeway with a nurse he's taken hostage from County General. The freeway's jammed up. But we'll get the pilots there as soon as possible."

"Oh, I didn't hear about that."

"Yes. I guess it's a domestic violence thing."

"Don't you just hate stuff like that?"

"Yes, I do. We'll get the pilots there as soon as possible. I apologize for the inconvenience."

"Your company should give me a discount for the delay." Thinking fuck! I'm fucking screwed! Then, stay calm. Look like a woman.

"Sir, I'm not authorized to do that. You can speak to my supervisor if you wish."

"I don't have time. Just get the pilots there."

Finally, it's his turn and he exits the parking garage and turns right. He's stuck at the stoplight, not more than a half of a block away. He's got to get out of there. He takes a deep breath when the light turns green and he drives away from the chaos. He reminds himself, don't make any traffic errors. He heads back to I-5 and proceeds to the airport.

Turning on the car radio and tuning it to a station, thinking any station will do. The station is talk radio and they are covering the car chase. It's the Slim and Jim show. He thought Slim and Dim sounded more appropriate.

"Can you believe Seattle PD has lost the suspect? The guy's simply vanished."

"Yah, leave it to Seattle PD to screw things up. What are we paying those guys for? We're getting new breaking information. The police have found the nurse unharmed in the parking garage of the Galleria Convention Center. They don't believe the suspect's on foot but has possibly changed automobiles. The police are searching the hotel and convention center at this time. If you live near the Galleria, we want to hear from you. "Denise, go ahead. What's it like where you are?"

"I was in the Galleria parking garage and some guy was running and nearly crashed into me and my little daughter. He matches the police's description. I didn't see if he got in a car or not. There are police everywhere and the sirens are blaring. I locked my car doors and got my daughter and myself out of there. You can't even go to the mall anymore without the fear of some waco threatening other people's safety."

"Glad you're safe. Jack, you're next. What do you have to say on the Slim and Jim show?"

"The traffic is backed up everywhere. It's terrible by the convention center. It took me fifteen minutes just to go one block. A friend of mine works there as a security guard and he thinks he's seen the suspect around the Galleria. He believes he's got a Mazda."

"Whoa! You better call Seattle PD with that information or get your friend to."

He has about a half hour before those pilots show up. You think you're incognito only to find out a million people have seen you, snooping into your personal affairs. He turns the radio off. He didn't need to hear it. What was his motto? If you can't hear it, see it, or feel it, it doesn't exist. He can do absolutely nothing about what the public does or doesn't know; all he can do is move forward to the goal. Yah, think of this as just another ice hockey game and the mission is to get to the goal. In his case, it is to blast off that tarmac.

Seeing the airport, he takes the exit and pulls over. He gets out, takes the dress and wig and shoves them under the seat. He does a couple of stretches and returns to his car to finish the drive to the airport. When he arrives at the little airport, he parks the car, taking his suitcase, briefcase, and laptop and walking into the small building.

"Hello. May I help you?"

"Yes, I'm Jack Williams. I'm supposed to be here to meet my pilots from Clyde's Jetway Jets."

"Yes, one of your pilots is here readying the airplane and the other pilot is only about fifteen minutes away."

"Great."

"While you're waiting, I need to see your picture identification card and ask you a few questions."

"That's fine," he said as he handed her his driver's license.

"Danbury. You're a long way from home."

"It's the nature of my job."

"What do you do?"

"I'm a private detective working on high profile cases for the government."

"Oh, that's impressive. Mr. Williams, do you have any explosives on you or in your luggage?"

"No. I don't."

"Has your luggage been in your possession at all times?"

"Yes."

"Do you have any weapons?"

"Yes. I've got a thirty-eight-caliber gun that's not loaded."

"You plan to put the gun in your luggage?"

"Yes. I did that before I came into the airport."

"I'll take your suitcase. Did you want to keep your laptop and briefcase?"

"Yes, thanks."

"I'll be just a minute." She takes the suitcase to the back of the airport so it can be loaded on to the airplane.

Returning moments later, she asks, "Would you like a cup of coffee while you wait?"

"Thanks. That'd be nice."

He sits sipping his coffee and can't stop glancing down at his wristwatch every few minutes. The hands just seem to creep by, and he wonders how long it'll be before the place is surrounded by cops.

The receptionist's phone rings, and from her side of the conversation it sounds like the pilot's arrived. "Mr. Williams, your jet is ready. Just go out this side door and you'll see the jet parked out on the tarmac behind us. Have a nice flight."

"Thank you."

Opening the door and stepping out, he feels a gust of cold, fall wind and hears the loud sound of a jet. It is a sleek, white jet with a sharp-pointed nose and Clyde's Jetway Jets emblazoned in red letters across the side. The hatch was open, ready to help him make his speedy getaway. At the doorway of the airplane is a stewardess dressed in navy blue slacks, white tailored blouse, and a jacket with Clyde's Jetway Jets logo on it. She has auburn, shoulder-length curly hair.

"Welcome aboard, Mr. Williams. I'm Judy Sanders." Stepping aside, allowing him to enter, she continues. "I'd like to introduce you to Captain Jim Rodgers and David Halliday. They're your pilots for today."

"Welcome aboard, Mr. Williams. We apologize for the delay. It seems as though Seattle has been in crisis mode over a hostage taken from County General Hospital."

"Your receptionist told me. Too bad."

"Yah, he's probably on drugs. You know they usually are."

"Captain Rodgers is a former police officer," Judy explained.

"I used to get these kinds of calls all the time," Kenneth says. "You're right; these situations often involve alcohol or drugs."

"I guess it's some kind of a family dispute, so let's get all of Seattle involved. Go figure. By the way, did you know you matched the description of that Kenneth Hamilton character?"

"No, I didn't. What does he look like?"

"They said about six feet tall, hazel eyes, and black or dark brown hair."

"You got me. I'm him. Why not? I've been compared to every six-foot Tom, Dick, and Harry that's on the planet," Kenneth says as he laughs, feeling his stomach bile coming up to his throat.

"That's a good one, Mr. Williams. I needed a good laugh. As soon as you're buckled up we're ready to leave. The flight plan's been filed and the tower's given us a runway."

"Fine."

The stewardess leads him further into the interior of the plane, which has cream-colored leather seats and red carpeting. The seating was certainly more spacious than those economy class seats on a commercial airliner. He sits and pulls the strap over his shoulder and locks it into place. The stewardess takes his laptop and briefcase, storing them in an overhead bin.

Nestling into his seat, he goes limp. It's the first time today he's been able to relax. Just get this buggy off the ground, he thinks. He vaguely hears the pilots talking to the tower, the engines rev up and the plane begins to move down the tarmac for the taxi. He's glad to be leaving the rainy weather behind him.

Chapter Twenty

*A*aron's intercom buzzes. "Yes, Stacy."

"Dan's on line two."

"Thanks. Dan, I was just going to call you. Where are you today?"

"I'm in our coffee shop in Olympia. But I had to call you. One of the employees had their radio on and some guy named Kenneth Hamilton has taken a nurse hostage at gunpoint. I guess he threatened to kill Rachel, her mother, and some police officers. They're looking for him, but right now they've lost him."

"Oh, my God! Did he hurt her?"

"No, apparently not. He fled from the hospital, taking a nurse as a hostage. They were chasing him on I-5, and now he's gotten off I-5. I forget exactly where they said. I think it may've been near the Galleria Convention Center. Even the police helicopters haven't been able to spot him."

"I need to get over to County General. Dan, I'm giving Sandy time off, and I need you to come in and fill in for her.

Since you're in Olympia today, come in tomorrow. I'll have Stacy take messages for today."

"Sure. I'll be there tomorrow. Kenneth Hamilton, who is he? How's he connected to Rachel?"

"Dan, it's a long story, but he's her ex and they've been divorced for about twelve years."

"Wow. I never knew she was ever married."

"Thanks for the information. I need to go."

Pushing Stacy's extension, Aaron says, "I've got to leave and go to the hospital, and I'm sending Sandy home. Dan will be in tomorrow. I need you to take messages. If something urgent comes up you can call either Dan or myself on our cell phones. You can also talk to Kevin. I'm counting on you to keep things running smoothly at the Genie."

"Yes, sir."

Aaron steps into Sandy's office. "Kenneth Hamilton took a nurse hostage at gun point and threatened to kill Rachel and her mother. I just thought I should tell you so you aren't shocked when you hear about it on the news. I'm going to the hospital. Please go home now and I'll call you next week."

"I'm so sorry."

He races to the elevator while he dials his cell phone. "Stanley. I'm on my way to the hospital. I just heard about what happened. Are Susan and Rachel okay?"

"Rachel just came back from her oxygen therapy. She and her mother are both upset, but things are better."

"I heard he took a nurse hostage."

"Yes. But they found her a few minutes ago in the parking garage at some place called the Galleria—unharmed. They've lost Kenneth. There were cops all over the hospital but things have pretty much settled down."

"I'm on my way."

163

"I'm leaving, Stacy. I hope you're happy with all the trouble you've caused me!"

"Sandy, I'm sorry you feel that way. I didn't have a choice. I had to tell Aaron what I knew. He would've fired me if I didn't."

"Well, if you would've just minded your own business and kept your mouth shut in the first place neither of us would be in this position. So great! You've saved your job but now I'm probably going to be fired."

"Look. It's not my fault you got involved with Kenneth Hamilton and almost got Rachel killed. So stop acting like the victim here when it's Rachel who's been harmed."

"I could still fire you for insubordination."

"No. You can't. Aaron said it's his company, and if I'm going to be fired he'd be the one to do it. I'm just glad I'm not you because I wouldn't be able to look at myself in the mirror if I did what you did to Rachel. Aaron's too decent to say it, but you should be ashamed of yourself. I've put up with you since Aaron hired you, but keep in mind, I've worked for Aaron from the first day he opened the Coffee Genie."

"Big deal! You're his receptionist, but I'm his office manager. Besides, if she had told me she was interested in Aaron none of this would've happened."

"Maybe so. But he and I go way back, and it doesn't matter if you were my superior. I fail to see how her being interested in him is any of your business!"

"I'm not gracing that with a response!" Sandy stormed out of the office, slamming the door, nearly breaking the glass window.

Aaron rushes into Rachel's hospital room to find Susan sitting in a chair, clutching a handkerchief. Stan's got his arm around her shoulders, trying to console her.

"Now, Sue. It's all over except for catching Kenneth, but the police will get him. Thank God, the nurse is safe. When Rachel comes back you need to be calm. Otherwise, you're no good to her or yourself."

"I know, Stanley. But I just can't get over how he could've killed all of us. You weren't here! What if he comes back?"

"Susan, the police are here, so don't worry, he isn't coming back. Do you want to go home to San Francisco?"

"No! I'm her mother. I can't go home!"

"Well, then you need to either calm yourself, love, or get some medication."

"I'll try."

"Oh, hi, Aaron, I didn't see you come in."

"Hi, Stanley." Walking over to Susan and leaning down in front of her, Aaron says, "I'm so sorry this has happened to you and Rachel. You've been through a terrible ordeal. Would you like me to take you to my house so you can rest? If you don't want to do that then we could take you to the bed and breakfast inn where you're staying and you could lie down for a little while?"

"Thank you, Aaron, but I really can't. I need to be here for my daughter."

"It would make me happy if you'd both come and stay at my house. I can loan you my car, Stanley, and I can drive my truck. I care very much for Rachel, and I want to help all of you through this difficult time."

"That's so kind of you, Aaron. We wouldn't want to impose."

"Stanley, it's no imposition at all. Where's Rachel and how's she doing?"

"Rachel's at physical therapy. They'd already scheduled it before this whole thing happened and the doctors felt it'd be best to keep her therapies on schedule."

"That sounds reasonable."

"I'm just so embarrassed about all of this! It makes our family look like trash."

"Susan, your daughter is a survivor of a crime perpetrated on her. None of this is her fault. No one ever deserves to have another person hit them or psychologically abuse them. There's nothing to be embarrassed about."

"You're right, I know. I just keep thinking how other people must view all of us."

"Susan, I seriously doubt if her doctors or anyone else is thinking much except about helping her recover and catching Kenneth Hamilton. We've got to all remain positive and focused on one thing—her recovery."

"You're right. I know you're right."

A nurse steps into the room. "The physical therapist just called me and they're bringing Rachel back to her room momentarily."

"Have you heard how the nurse that Kenneth took as a hostage is doing?"

"Mr. Goodrich, I haven't, but I'm sure Karen will be fine."

"Why don't you all take a short break while we assist the patient and take her vitals."

They were leaving her room when Dr. Johnson walked up to them. "I was hoping to see you, and I was wondering if we might have a word about Rachel?"

"Of course, Dr. Johnson."

They enter a small office and Dr. Johnson closes the door. "Please take a seat. Today has been pretty hectic around here, but I've got some really good news for you, and I think we could all use that."

"Doctor, I'm so sorry for what happened with Kenneth today," Susan said.

"Mrs. Goodrich, what Mr. Hamilton did has nothing to do with you and there's nothing for you to apologize for. We can only hope the police will catch him before he has a chance to harm anyone else. Your daughter's the victim here. She did absolutely nothing to warrant his abusive behavior. This has been a very traumatic experience for her and she's going to need a lot of love and support to help her get through this. You know, medicine can only do so much."

"Of course you're right, Dr. Johnson. We love our daughter and there's nothing her father and I wouldn't do for her."

"What's the status of her condition?" Aaron asks.

"The good news is the swelling in the brain has been eliminated. Partly due to the oxygen therapy she's been receiving these past several days. It's going to take a while for her wounds to totally heal. We believe there's a chance of nearly a full recovery for Rachel. Her speech is impacted right now, but even that's improving. I plan to release her in the next ten days to two weeks to a convalescent home to continue with her physical, speech, and psychological therapies. I wanted to talk to you now so you could decide where you'd want her placed."

"Can we take her home to Hayward?"

"You could do that Stanley, sure. However, she still needs to be in a care facility. I think it's important to include Rachel in the decision-making process. This will help to motivate and empower her to take charge of her life again. This is so important when someone has been victimized as she's been."

"Dr. Johnson, do you know of any holistic centers either here or in California we could contact?" Aaron asks.

"Aaron, I'm not entirely sure of what you mean by holistic."

"I'm thinking of someplace emphasizing the interdependence of all of the body. Alternative healing—like homeopathy, Ayurveda, naturopathic, and the best parts of the MD world. A center that looks as food as medicine and uses natural methods of healing. A place that practices total body wellness."

"Ah, I thought you meant something like that. No, I honestly don't. I know of antiaging clinics and the like, but all I really know about are the standard convalescent homes. Our hospital social worker will be happy to work with you to find a placement for Rachel, either here or in California. We really wouldn't want to consider homeopathy and all of that, as it's not a real science, you know. Rachel needs real medical care for her condition. Nutrition is really important, but to think of food as medicine, well, let's just say it's not very practical."

A grim expression crosses Aaron's face. "Well, Dr. Johnson, her parents and I can check on the options. We appreciate all the help you've given Rachel."

"That'll be fine, and I'll instruct Mrs. Simmons our social worker to contact you."

"Why don't we go and have something to drink at the cafeteria?"

"Aaron, that sounds like a good idea, and we can talk about what we're going to do for Rachel."

Aaron takes a sip of his iced tea and tries to formulate what he wants to say to her parents. "You might think me a little crazy for saying this but I'm not too much into western style medicine. I think I've been forever changed by the views of my wife Meredith and her father. They were always skeptical of standard medical care even though her father was an MD. Maybe it's not practical, but I'd love to see Rachel placed in a facility that embraces all aspects of healing, from natural foods to the best the MD world has to offer."

"That's not crazy at all. That's so San Franciscan!"

"Susan, I'm glad you don't think me crazy. Rachel's also pregnant, and I know when Meredith was expecting our son Michael, she told me this was the most critical time for good nutrition for the developing fetus. Our son was a very healthy child because of her."

"That must've been terrible for you when you lost them," Susan said touching his arm.

"Yes, it was." After all this time he still felt choked up when he talked about his wife and son.

"If there's such a place, wherever will we find it?"

"Stanley, let me start with Bernard, my pastry chef."

"A pastry chef?"

"Yes, Stanley. He's so much like Meredith sometimes I wonder if they're related. Did you know everything we sell at the Coffee Genie is organic and made the old world way?"

"No, we didn't"

"I started this business as a memorial to my wife Meredith and the nutritional values for which she lived by. The full name of the business is actually Meredith's Coffee Genie. Over the years our customers shortened the name and refer to it as the Coffee Genie. I've even heard people refer to it simply as the Genie."

"That's so sweet, Aaron. I can see why my daughter has always liked you and enjoyed working for you."

"Thank you, Susan."

"I don't know about all this hokus-pokus nutritional stuff, Aaron. I kind of prefer things with a strong scientific background."

"Well, Stanley, you might be surprised to know that modern medicine is the new science on the block and some of these natural approaches have been around for hundreds of centuries."

"All I'm saying is I'm a bit skeptical."

"Stanley, I agree with Aaron," Susan says. "I think we've got to have an open mind and do what works best for Rachel."

"I think the bottom line is to provide alternatives to Rachel and let her decide what's best for her."

Aaron says, "Why don't we go and see how she's doing and then we can all work on finding her a place for rehabilitation?"

"Let's go," Susan says.

Walking into Rachel's hospital room, they notice she's sitting up in a reclining geriatric chair, with a tray in front of her. She's focusing on papers in front of her. "Rachel, you're sitting up! That's wonderful! What are you doing?" Susan asks.

Rachel turns her head and smiles. Her speech therapist has given her some vocabulary words she's been practicing. She becomes flustered and her face turns red when she is unable to pronounce Aaron's name.

"Honey, Dr. Johnson told us you're doing really well and you might be transferred to a rehabilitation facility next week. Would you like to come home with your Dad and me to

Hayward? We could find a good place there close to our house."

"No, I want to stay in Sea—."

"Seattle," Aaron finishes.

"Yes." Tears spill down her face and she struggles to brush them away with unrefined motor skills, like a toddler. "I want to talk to Aaron."

"Aaron, we'll go to the little waiting room on the corner. Come and get us when you and Rachel are finished talking."

"I'll let you know, Stanley."

Stanley and Susan close the hospital door behind them to give them some privacy.

Aaron leans down in front of her and she tells him in choppy language "I'm so sorry about all of this." It was challenging but he finally understood her to say she "had not seen Kenneth in about twelve years until Friday night. He showed up at her doorstep, beating and raping her when she asked him to leave. She told him she'd died and started crossing over to the spiritual realm. She'd seen her dog, Cookie, her Grandma Emily, and Grandpa Henry. She came back because she's having a son. She didn't want him to feel responsible, but could she keep her job so she could support her baby. She's sorry for Kenneth but she's very afraid of him.

"Rachel there's a lot we need to talk about when you're better. I want you to know I love you, and you never have to worry about your job. This is my baby, too, and I'm thrilled. What's most important is for you to get well for the baby. I want to see you in a holistic place that will give you the best chance of full recovery and care for our baby. You know how picky Bernie and I are about our products at the Coffee

Genie. So if it's okay with you, I'll try to find something local for your rehabilitation."

She looks up at him and smiles.

"The other thing is I never want you to feel afraid again. If Kenneth ever comes back here he'll be dealing with me." He kisses her on her cheek through bandages. "I'll go get your parents, sweetheart."

Chapter Twenty-One

*I*t took a couple of hours before Kenneth's photo made it to mainstream media. Seattle's in a frenzy to find him. Social media's buzzing with news and opinions of the failure of the Seattle Police Department to catch him. Did they let him get away on purpose since he was a police officer? The injustice of it all! The escape was on the minds of many from the supermarket to the boardroom. It had become a topic of animated conversation and debate. Some said the detective and the chief of police should step down or be fired. How could anyone be so inept? There was no other rational explanation; they did this on purpose!

Seattle PD was inundated with hundreds of calls with tips and sightings. Trying to sort out the good leads from the bad was a daunting challenge. Right after the nurse was taken hostage they rechecked the National Crime Information Center with Kenneth Hamilton's correct state of residence. They found that Sioux Falls, South Dakota had a warrant out for his arrest for the attempted murder of his ex-wife, Debbie

Hamilton. This data had been previously overlooked, as it was believed he was from Lincoln, Nebraska.

Gerald Hershel begins to tack up pieces of credible information on the bulletin board in his workspace at the precinct. A security guard from the Galleria had called in, stating that a person matching Hamilton's description was seen during the last forty-eight hours around the convention center. He believed him to be driving a 2013 white Mazda. This is corroborated by a call from the car rental company, who provides the license number. He issues an all-points bulletin for Seattle and the surrounding areas and the information is released to the public.

A new tip comes in that the Mazda has been seen at the private airport close to Boeing, and a squad car is dispatched to the scene. A half an hour later the car has been identified. The police had spoken with the receptionist at the airport and they had no record of any Kenneth Hamilton. They refused to divulge any information about their flights unless they receive a court order.

"Fine. Get a God damn court order," Gerald Herschel said, fuming. "Those people out there who use that airport are a bunch of tea party types. We're just trying to catch a criminal, but, oh no, let's flaunt the constitution."

He's paged by police dispatch. "Gerald, you might want to talk to this guy on line two. He has information about Hamilton, or so he says."

"All right. Everybody has some information on him."

"This is Sergeant Herschel. With whom am I speaking?"

"I'm Gaylord Bismart."

"Spell your name for me."

"Sure, honey. G as in good, a as apple, y as in you, l as in love, o as in one, r—"

"No, just the Biz part. What did you say?"

"Honey, I said Bismart—B i s m a r t."

"Fine. So you've seen Kenneth Hamilton?"

"Yes, honey."

Ah, Christ! One of those gay types. "Look, don't call me honey. Only my wife can call me that."

"Well, I'm a salesman for Gigi's Wigs and Things, and this guy matching Kenneth Hamilton's description came into the store for a couple of days in a row. First, I sold him a wig. Then he came in yesterday, and I dressed him up and did his makeup. He said he was going to a crosser party. The funny thing is that when I went home and I saw the photo of the woman bank robber—well it looked just like him. Except he wasn't wearing the little black dress I sold him, but a maroon dress. I'd swear it's him."

He takes Gaylord's telephone number and address and thanks him for his assistance.

He gets in touch with the police officers who are dusting the car for fingerprints and searching the interior. They radio back that they found a maroon dress and a dark-brown, shoulder length wig.

Gerald Herschel thinks, Kenneth, you've been a busy boy trying to kill two ex-wives and robbing a bank. He contacts the detective working on the bank robbery and gives him the information he has, along with the contact information for Gaylord Bismart.

He makes a call to the Superior Court of King County, advising them he needs a search warrant for the airport and will be by in a half hour with an affidavit and will need to speak with the assigned judge. He has the request prepared and printed. It's nearly four p.m. when he rushes out of the precinct.

With the warrant signed off by the judge, he walks into the airport and presents it to the receptionist. She in turn calls her supervisor, a Mr. Joshua Denton. He's then provided access to the airport computer records. There's been seven flights from the airport this day, three of which he can dismiss because of the time frame. The other four are within the window of possibility. Two were small Cessnas; one went to Spokane and the other to Pasco. The third was a Beechcraft Air King, which flew to Bozeman, Montana. The fourth possibility was a Lear jet forty going to Detroit. He took the names and the contact information for the companies and left the airport.

After contacting the three airline companies, he's ruled out two of the flights. One was a church group, one was a medical supply place, and the other two flights were Clyde's Jetway Jet airplanes. Clyde Haskel, the owner of Clyde's Jetway Jets, told him to talk to his attorney. They weren't divulging anything without a proper search warrant. That guy was a staunch tea bagger for sure. He'd served his country as a bomber pilot in the Air Force, bombing Iraq. Gerald remembered he'd come home as a hero, one of Seattle's finest sons. But he also came home jaded and was totally against the government. He had no use for the police in general. He'd heard him and his type on talk radio plenty of times. He detested the new world order. However, he'd never known him to do anything illegal, but when you dealt with him it was all legal and by the book. The detective told him, fine, I'll have a search warrant signed off by the judge.

It was a long day and his shift was ending, so the duty officer assigned the task to another detective to follow up on getting a search warrant and obtaining the information.

Chapter Twenty-Two

*A*aron stretched out in his recliner, drinking a bottle of water. It'd been such a long day; he couldn't believe how so much could be packed into such a few hours. At the Coffee Genie he'd discovered his office manager's duplicitous behavior regarding this whole shabby incident with Kenneth Hamilton. Then, Kenneth Hamilton holding Rachel and her mother at gunpoint and taking a nurse hostage. It just seemed so surreal.

Her parents had declined his offer to stay at his house so they could be closer to the hospital, and he was sure they'd made the best decision for them. Her mother was a bit overwhelming at times, with her fastidious viewpoint on life. Everything with her was either right or wrong, no shades of grey in between. He wondered how Stanley survived with her all these years. Did he sound a bit irritable? He guessed he was. He had to admit he was just so tired of the whole situation.

He wasn't tired of Rachel, though. She's an amazing woman—all that she's lived through during her lifetime.

Would she ever be the same again? Would either of them be? So many questions and no real answers. Would she ever fully recover? He was sure about one thing, with standard American medical care, she wouldn't. She might not anyway, but in the MD world and all that toxic pharmaceutical crap, her chances were zilch. He was thinking of those ridiculous drug commercials he'd seen on TV, with the side effects sounding worse than the affliction. Why would anyone take some drug for a stuffy head if there was a chance it could result in a seizure? Only one percent, hmm, he wouldn't want to risk it. With his luck he'd have a grand mal seizure. Will the baby be okay after all she's been through? He could only hope.

Hamilton really had him convinced he was the father of this baby and that he'd been seeing her. It was all lies. The whole thing felt like a roller coaster ride. One minute you're in abject despair and the next minute you're up in the clouds. It was like always waiting for the next crash.

He was worried, too, about the company. It had been on autopilot for nearly a week. You can't run a company like that. He sighs, thinking, maybe it is not so important. Rachel is the most important thing to him. Anger swells up in his stomach like a tide. They should be planning their wedding right now and thinking of their baby. And now he's trying to keep hope alive and find a way to make her whole again. Thinking, Meredith if you're up there looking down on all of this, help me out, darling.

It's nine o'clock. He shouldn't disturb Bernie this late at night but he just needs to talk to him. He dials his home number and hears the phone ring a few times.

"Bon soir. This is Bernie."

"Bernie, this is Aaron. I'm so sorry to call you this late. I just needed to talk to you."

"Aaron, how's Rachel?"

"She's much better. I need to find a rehabilitation facility for her to go to maybe next week."

"Tres bon!"

"I want something more holistic, not your regular western medical care, which is so inferior to a holistic approach to wellness."

"Hmm, that's difficult, my friend. I can't think of any place like that off the top of my head. But I do have some contacts who might be able to suggest something."

"That's why I called you, Bernie, because if anyone would be able to find something like that it'd be you."

"Ah, you give me too much credit, my friend. I'll check around and see what I can find. I wanted to talk to you about an idea I've had for a new cookie."

"A new cookie?"

"There's much talk and news about how sugar causes inflammation in the body. I think we should test a new lower sugar cookie."

"Bernie, you aren't suggesting artificial sweeteners, are you?"

"No. Everyone who cares about their health doesn't eat that stuff. You know, aspartame turns into formaldehyde in the body and acts like wood alcohol."

"Whew! That's a relief. Now you sound like the Bernie I know," Aaron said, laughing.

"No, my friend. We'll cut half of the sugar out."

"Can that taste good? I mean like, wouldn't it taste like a dog biscuit?"

"Actually, I've tested a few batches and it's a good cookie, just not so sweet. We could make it with Acai berry and other flavors and give it some antioxidant properties."

"I don't know, Bernie. It sounds like a health food thing and we're running a coffee business."

"True enough, but our emphasis has always been to offer more healthful choices."

"You've got a good point. Why don't we do a local test of your cookie and see how it goes."

"Great! We'll call it the Rachel Wellness cookie."

"You make me laugh, Bernie. My friend, what would I do without you?"

"Dieu seul le sait!"

"You are so right God only knows. Goodnight, Bernie."

"Goodnight, and I'll see what I can find to help Rachel."

Wasn't he just the luckiest guy on the planet to have such good friends like Bernie? He's always on the cutting edge, not to mention that he is the best pastry chef around. Through the years other companies had offered him opportunities which exceeded what Aaron could offer, especially in the beginning. Bernie was loyal and stayed with the Coffee Genie. He really loved the team spirit his crew had. He wondered how he could have someone like Sandy working for him. He then thought, that's a bit harsh; she's really young. Firing people was his least favorite part about running the company. Sometimes it had to be done. Finishing his bottle of water, he's ready to call it a night.

Chapter Twenty-Three

*M*r. Williams, if you'll please buckle your seat belt, the Captain has advised me that momentarily we'll begin our descent into the Detroit area. The wind's really blowing, so it may be a bit bumpy going down."

"Thanks." Well, this was it. Welcome to what? Did they still call it Motor City? The home of slums, gangs, and house burners. He almost wished the plane would crash, better than being spit out into the bowels of the universe. If ever there was an underbelly of the United States this place has got to be it. He imagined there's lots of places a guy on the run could go to get lost here. No one cared if you lived or died. He'd heard Detroit's similar to the ruins of the Roman Empire. He'd seen those YouTube videos of trash heaped up four stories or more high and heard stories of abject poverty in the Detroit area. Yah, great, welcome to Detroit, the land of hopelessness. All too soon he'd be out there pounding the pavement looking for a place to stay among all those store cart pushers, druggies, alcoholics, panhandlers, and people with their teeth missing either from being rotted out or kicked out. Sure, he had some cash, around eight grand. After the money's gone, where would he be?

He could feel the plane circling and descending and the pilots speaking with the tower in their lingo of altimeters, all of it a foreign language he'd never paid much attention to. A gust of wind hit the plane and they dropped suddenly. He looks out of the window at the city lights below, the cabin lighting reflecting his ghostly image on the airplane window, which is reflecting back the blackness of the night. As they neared the runway the lights were turned off and he could see the illuminated blue directional arrows on the runway.

Cold and uninviting dirty patches of snow and ice lay in small, scattered clumps. He could see the plane lining up with the runway and then bump, there it was; they were on the ground and he could feel himself pushed forward as the pilots were braking to slow the plane.

They taxied to a spot on the tarmac and parked. He felt like he's being savagely ripped from his mother's womb. Clyde's Jetway Jets' sanctuary was coming to an end. They'd soon complete their contract and he would be given the kiss off. Above the clouds was a safe and warm space, an escape from reality. Soon he'd be making his way in the night through an ugly, unfriendly city—a dead city that really began dying in the nineteen sixties.

"Welcome to Detroit, Mr. Williams. Thank you for choosing Clyde's Jetway Jets. We hope you'll choose to fly with us again soon. The local time is now seven forty-five."

"Thank you. Can I just get my suitcase by the plane instead of having to go to baggage?"

"Certainly. This is one of the advantages of leasing a jet."

The pilots shook his hand and he gathered his belongings and headed for the terminal, feeling the cold blasts of air against his face and trying to avoid the icy patches on the tarmac. Christ, this is freezing, he thought, as a gust blew cold air down his neck.

His eyes were tearing from the cold by the time he made it inside the terminal. He needed to rent a car, so he made it past the baggage area to where all the car rental places were lined up along with public sources of transportation.

After signing his life away, verifying his address in Sioux Falls, he walked out with the keys to a blue 2012 Nissan. Finding the car, he places his suitcase, briefcase, and laptop in the trunk. Reaching into the suitcase, he takes out his thirty-eight-caliber gun and loads it. After all, this is Detroit—no man's land.

The night sky's black and it is freezing cold out. He locks the door and starts the car's engine and he fiddles with the buttons to get the heater going. His teeth are chattering and he's thinking, damn, this place is cold. He must find an economical hotel. He'd looked at some online but had thought he best not make reservations ahead of time just in case the cops were hot on his heels. The streetlights looked glary against the pitch-black night. There were probably thugs behind every corner.

He drove around downtown Detroit and finally selects a hotel not far from the bus terminal. He walked into the lobby to check on a vacancy and the cost of a room. There's bulletproof glass across the lobby check-in desk, and the bronze plating in the front of the counter is smudged. The furniture is clean but frayed. The tile floors hinted of a more elegant time. The clerk had a stern and unfriendly demeanor. Yes, they had a room, and he checked in for two days. Hopefully, by then he'd know what he wanted to do.

Walking to his room he catches a whiff of stale marijuana floating throughout the hallways. He smiles when he sees the panties and lingerie in a vending machine. Hmm, it's like buying a bag of chips or a Hostess Twinkie. He puts the key in the lock and gropes for the light. It's nothing fancy, but it looks clean enough. It's got a toilet, a bathtub-shower, bed, and TV. What more did he need?

His stomach is burning because he's hungry. He'd had very little to eat today. Sure, he'd been given some potato chips on the airplane and some coffee. He doubted a dump like this would have room service. But he looked around and on the desk he found a paper menu of a delivery place and ordered a pizza.

Devouring the pizza and sipping on some cola, he almost starts to cry when he thinks of the events of the last several days. What a mess everything is. Shoving the empty box in the trash, he's tired and he just doesn't want to think about it and climbs into bed.

The bed is lumpy; he'd have found a park bench more comfortable. He feels something crawling on him, flips on the lamp by the bed and sees that the bed is covered with bed bugs. One's crawling on his arm and two are on his face. Holy Crap!

He calls the front desk and they were so nonchalant about the whole thing. What did the guy say? Hey, buddy, bed bugs are a fact of life. We'll send someone up there with a can of pesticide.

After the hotel staff sprayed down the place he goes back to bed and dozes off. He's awakened in the early morning hours by the couple next door cursing at each other. He could hear things breaking and language that'd make a sailor blush. Pretty soon he's hearing other people shouting, shut the fuck up! He heard glass falling to the street below from what sounded like a chair being thrown at the woman and hitting the window. The cops finally show up and haul the man off to jail. He could hear him resisting arrest through the paper-thin walls.

Tomorrow he'd have to find another place to stay. It's like reliving his life again all in one night. Is this what he's like? He knew he was. Thinking he's just like all the other riff raff staying here. Maybe jail was not such a bad thing—three hots and a cot—as he dozed off to sleep.

He'd barely fallen back to sleep when he heard a guy screaming in the hallway. The ambulance was called to take him away as he was on a bad drug trip. Christ, they should pay their hotel guests to stay here. What would have given him the first clue this place would be like this? The bulletproof glass at the check-in desk or those panties in the vending machine?

Chapter Twenty-Four

When Kenneth awakens, the place is unfamiliar and it takes a couple of minutes for him to fully comprehend that he's in a flophouse in Detroit. Halfway across the country from Rachel and the fiasco in Seattle. By now, probably the whole country is looking for him. While showering, he notices the bed bug bites on his stomach and arms. He thinks, a hell of a lot of good that pesticide did.

He leaves, taking his laptop, briefcase and all of his money with him. If he left anything valuable in this room it'd be lifted before he came back. He'd drive around the city and try to find a better place to stay. He could pretend he was a tourist.

The city squalor is almost everywhere. Huge buildings stand empty and windowless, some with shards of glass hanging precariously by shreds of wire. He drives by building after building scarred with graffiti. Some of the drawings are quite artistic. The building's walls have become an artist's canvas, capturing a time, a feeling, and a sense of desperation.

He drives by a homeless man with long, dirty, stringy, blonde hair, who is peeing on the side of a redbrick building. He wonders when was the last time that guy had a bath. He turned his head in total disgust.

A couple of blocks later, there's an old woman with a shopping cart who's being hustled by a couple of boys who appeared to be in their early teens. Rolling down his window, he shouted, "Leave her alone or I'll come kick your butts."

The bigger one said, "Fuck you, whitie." They tromped off, not certain if he could or would carry out his threat. They decided they didn't want to chance it.

A church with a sweeping staircase was used as a ski slope. Kids had stacked up bricks along with other trash and laid boards in a sloping angle. Ice and snow had packed the area and kids wearing skis were jumping from a top balcony. They maneuvered the garbage slope with the skill of downhill skiers in competitions for medals. At least they aren't out doing drugs and robbing some old lady.

Elderly people with canes and walkers were out milling about on the snowy streets. One old lady, wearing a tattered coat, stood on the sidewalk midway in a block. Her cheeks, nose, and hands were bright red from the stinging cold. He pulled the car up to the curb and parked. He got out of his car and approached the woman, handing her a twenty-dollar bill.

She gave him a toothless smile. "Thank you."

"You're welcome, granny." He couldn't afford to do that, but he never liked seeing the elderly in a destitute situation, as they were easy targets for criminals. She'd probably be heading to the liquor store for a bottle of ripple, but at least he could feel good about trying to help someone out.

He didn't see any place he'd want to stay, so he'd leave Detroit tomorrow. He didn't want to be in a place like this where half the streetlights don't work, people doing drugs in plain sight and pissing on the sidewalk right there in front of God and the world. To be so reduced to non-humanness was more than even he could take. He thought he'd seen it all; well, maybe he hadn't.

Taking a break from driving, he stops for a coffee and a big mac. Coast to coast, you could get the same burger and it tastes identical no matter where you are. How do they do that?

He didn't want to go back to the hotel so he continued driving around. There were empty lots scattered throughout the sprawl, like a surgeon's knife trying to cut out lumps of cancer that has metastasized.

Call it an epiphany, an awakening, a realization, the ugliness of Detroit is a symbol of the dying of a city of a country. It's all around him. To die means something has had to have lived. Every building around him was at some point someone's dream, a concept, a blueprint—an excitement in the building and watching an idea materialize. Things new become old and die to be reborn again in some way.

The pain of growing, aging, dying, there's no escaping it even if one sits on their ass opting out; there is still no escaping it. We're all on the ride and going someplace, even if it seems one is standing still. What was that his partner in Lincoln use to say? You can always change your life, and you're never beyond hope until you die.

A tear slides down his cheek and he wants out of Detroit. The city mirrors the disaster of his own personal life. Rachel's the key to his happiness; if he could get her back everything would be good again. He had more right to her than that Aaron Townsend. He didn't know when she'd be released from the hospital but he's going back for her. Sure, she wouldn't come willingly, so he'd have to kidnap her. They'd go to Las Vegas and get married and he'd have her back either willing or unwilling. If they're married she wouldn't testify against him. He'd just appear when she least expects him. He'd do it right under the noses of Detective Hershel and all his cronies. Maybe this baby is Aaron Town-send's, but the next one would be his! Hello, Seattle.

He needs a scotch. He parks the car at the hotel and walks a block and a half to Mo's Bar and Grill. It was a dumpy little place. The tables are slick with grease, and used napkins and empty cracker wrappers remain on some of the tables. He walks up to the bartender, a black guy probably in his middle thirties, and orders a double scotch. He finds an empty booth in the corner by the men's room. As he sits there he realizes it might not be the best location because when the door opens the smell of urine wafts into the bar. The bar was just another example of Detroit, a city in decay.

A white woman with her front teeth missing leans over him, and he can smell the liquor on her breath layered with a smell of pus-infected gums from a lack of dental hygiene. That, along with strong body odor turned his stomach. Doesn't anyone in Detroit take baths?

"Hi, darling. How about some company?"

"No thanks."

"Ah, come on. We could talk. You could buy me a drink, and well, you never know where that could lead, if you know what I mean."

"Yah, a good case of the clap."

"I don't know what you mean by that."

"Ah, baby, like venereal disease. Ever heard of it?"

"You're an old sour puss. Come on, honey, buy me a drink."

"Listen bar fly, get lost; I'm not interested."

"Well, you don't have to be testy about it!"

A woman with a filthy and stained apron wrapped around her rotund hips sidles up to him. "Can I get you another drink or something to eat? "

"Do you have a menu?"

She steps away and comes back, handing him a paper menu with grease stains and what appears to be catsup or a tomato sauce blotch which has smeared some of the letters. The scent of stale garlic from the menu makes him nauseous. He would bet the kitchen is crawling with roaches, and he shudders at the thought. "Ah, give me another double scotch, and I'll try the barbecue pork rib sandwich with onion rings."

"You'll need to pay in advance."

"What? You're ordering it from some other joint?"

"No, you jerk, to make sure you pay."

"Fine. How much is it?"

"Hold on to your shorts; I haven't rung it up yet."

"Great. When you know, I'll pay. The other thing is, do you have some room freshener? The john stinks when the door's opened."

"This is Detroit; and no, we don't. If you don't like it, move to another table."

"Good idea." He moves to a table by the window, wondering when he'd last seen a person with such a chip on their shoulder.

After his sandwich and several scotches, he calls his brother. "Hello. Can I speak to Rodger?" he heard Rodger's son telling him that he thought it was Uncle Ken.

"Hello."

"Rodger, this is Kenneth, your brother."

"I know who you are. Where are you, and have you been drinking?

"I'm in Detroit, and yes, I've had a few," he says and he hiccups.

"Your parole officer called here looking for you. What the hell are you doing in Detroit of all places?"

"You didn't hear?"

"Hear what? That you took a shot at Debbie in her car? Yah, I heard about it."

"No. I had a fight with Rachel and almost killed her, and I robbed a bank in Seattle."

"How could you do that to her?"

"She started it. She hit me first, and I just lost my temper and belted her a few times. She was in a coma but she's getting better." He begins to cry. "I'm so sorry; I didn't mean to hurt her. I was low on money and I had to get out of Seattle, so I robbed a bank to get some money."

"To start with, I don't believe Rachel hit you, and God, man, you robbed a bank! What the hell do you expect me to do?"

"I went to see her and she was so unfriendly. I even took her posies and she was so rude. I just had to show her who was boss."

"What? It's been nearly twelve years and you expected she was going to open her arms and invite you into her bed the first time she sees you?"

"Something like that, I guess. Rodger, you're the strong one. You always had everything better than me."

"Don't give me that crap, Kenny! I took care of our old man when he was dying of prostate cancer and you never lifted a finger to help. I even helped our mother get a place to stay before she died of cirrhosis of the liver. So don't you sit there and tell me anything! Cathy and I picked you up and tried to help you when you went to prison. Well, I'm finished! Do you hear me? I'm finished with you. You're never going to change, never take responsibility for your lousy life. It's always someone else's fault, Kenny. Well, you're on your own with this one, buddy. You might try doing the right thing and turning yourself in, like a decent human being."

He hears his brother hang up on him with a thud. He was surprised; he couldn't think of a time when Rodger wasn't firm but empathetic. Just like this town, he's lost, totally lost.

He orders another drink and he notices some guys playing pool at the other end of the room, getting drunk and quite loud. They were mouthing off at the bartender. One was about his height and quite muscular. He had tattoos all over his arms and hands. He was wearing a baseball cap on backwards. The other one was about five-foot-six and was a scrawny built guy with a ring in his nose. The music had changed from Marvin Gaye to hard rap, and the boom, boom, boom gave him a headache. The muscular guy grabs the bartender by the shirt collar, choking him until his eyes are nearly popping out of their sockets.

"Leave him alone, God damn it!" Kenneth yells.

Shoving the bartender like a Raggedy Anne doll, Muscle Man walks over to Kenneth's table. "Hey, you fuckin white ass, you speaking to me, the dude?" He said placing his big hands on the table.

"The very one, asshole."

"I'll wipe your ass all over this bar."

"Not before I blow your fucking brains out," Kenneth said, pointing the thirty-eight-caliber gun at his head.

The guy, along with his buddies, storms out of the bar.

"Hey, man, let me buy you a drink," the bartender said. "You really shouldn't have involved yourself with this. He's called Sparkie, and he belongs to one of the meanest gangs in Detroit."

"Ah, I don't care who he is."

"I'm just telling you, you should!"

Kenneth's phone rings. "Yah, Rodger I never expected to hear from you again."

"Look, Cathy said I was too hard on you and I guess I was. I'm frustrated with you, Kenny, and your lifestyle. I just want to live a normal life. We couldn't help the way our parents were, but we can have the life we want to live. I'm thinking Cat and I could come to Detroit and we could go with you to the police. The only thing is our son has a game coming up, and well, I need to be here for my son."

He wept. "My life is such a mess and there's no way out. I need to just kill myself."

"Kenny, no!" Cathy said. She had picked up on a second phone line, concerned with Kenny's issues.

"Look. Why don't you get on the next Greyhound bus and come to Denver? We'll go with you to the police station so you can turn yourself in. When you get out of prison you can come live with us and we'll help you get on your feet."

"I don't want to go back to jail. I just want to die."

"Kenny, no honey; come on, let's work this out."

"Cathy, you're always so kind to me."

"You're Rodger's brother, and I care."

"Ken, stop drinking. Go back to your room and call me tomorrow. Let's work this out."

"All right, Rodger, goodnight." He thinks, hell I'm not turning myself in. This is all Rachel's fault. I'm going back to Seattle, and she'll either marry me or she'll be planted six feet deep, pushing up posies. I'm tired of women messing up my life! I'm heading back to Seattle. To hell with this freezing weather and all these Detroit losers.

Chapter Twenty-Five

*T*he past few days had flown by like a whirlwind. Aaron, along with Mr. and Mrs. Goodrich, had visited most of the nursing homes on Ms. Simmons list. Some of the ones they liked had no space. They're still at square one in trying to find a place for Rachel.

Rachel's made great strides, but the longer she's in the hospital the more dissatisfied Aaron is with her and his baby's care. Just yesterday the nurse came in to give her a shot, and he questioned what she was giving Rachel. She had nonchalantly said, "Why, it's the flu shot, Mr. Townsend. It is that time of the year."

"Stop, she doesn't need that."

"But it is doctor's orders," she argued.

"I don't care; don't do it!"

She tried to assure him that she's had the flu shot every year for years and it hasn't harmed her.

He had felt himself bristle. It was not like him to behave in this way but he told her, "If you want to shoot yourself full of aluminum, formalin, thimerosal, mercury and God only knows what else, be my guest. You're not doing that to Rachel." She'd stormed away in a huff to call the doctor.

Running his hands through his hair, he was remembering the conversation he'd had with Susan and Stanley earlier in the day. It involved the other irritating thing about the hospital staff, having to do with her psychiatrist. She wanted to put her on antidepressants. He told them, "There's another medical miracle for you. No, we aren't doing that to her!"

Her parents were falling right into step with her doctor. "What can it hurt Aaron? It might benefit Rachel," they'd said.

He'd responded, "I can think of lots of reasons not to. One, she's pregnant. Two, do you know how many people commit suicide from using antidepressants?"

"Well, no we hadn't heard that."

"Stanley, you might want to do some research on selective serotonin reuptake inhibitors. They can cause suicidal behavior. I think your daughter's been through enough hell! Let's not go there with her."

Susan had retorted, "Aaron, you're not a doctor."

He told her, "You're right Susan, I'm not. But I've done enough reading on health topics to have some knowledge. Bottom line, I'm her medical power of attorney, and I'm not going to stand for these doctors loading her up with unnecessary drugs. You shouldn't want that either!"

"Aaron, we're sorry. I know all of our nerves are frayed; it's been hard these last several days. Of course, you're probably right."

"I'm sorry, too, Susan. I didn't mean to come off sounding like a dictator."

He wished her parents were back in Hayward. They were nice people, but he's tired of the whole thing and he's trying to protect her and their baby.

He's exhausted and it's only nine p.m. so maybe he should go to bed and get some rest. He flips off the stereo when the phone rings. Wondering who could be calling him this time of night.

"Hello."

"My friend!"

"Bernie, how are you? I haven't talked to you in a couple of days."

"*Bon, tres bon.* I may have something for you. It is the only thing I could find. I've heard pros and cons but you might want to check it out. It's a residential clinic, Andersen's Total Body Wellness Center, and it's located on Mercer Island."

"What's it like?"

"It is nothing fancy, but it's run by a team of doctors, including a couple of MD's, a couple of naturopaths, a chiropractor, massage therapist, and a psychologist. They treat a lot of sports injuries and chronic illnesses."

"What do people say about it?"

"Well, some say it costs too much. I've heard it has changed lives, and yet others say it's all hype. It's definitely worth checking out."

"Okay, great Bernie. Let me get a pen and paper."

Sitting there, looking at the contact information and trying not to get his hopes up too high. This might be the place. Mercer Island's very beautiful and tranquil. He'd been there many times over the years. At one point he'd thought of buying real estate there but decided the commute to work would be too much

Chapter Twenty-Six

*A*aron had told Rachel the day before that he needed to go to the office, as his absence has created a backlog of work. He'd come by later in the afternoon after her therapies were completed for the day. Although she still had a long way to go, he's amazed at her ability to spring back after being in a coma.

At the office, he calls the Andersen Clinic, and a very cheery receptionist answers the telephone and transfers his call to Dr. Andersen.

"Good morning, Mr. Townsend. How may I be of assistance today?"

"I was given your phone number as a possible rehabilitation placement for my assistant, Rachel Goodrich."

"Was she the lady who was attacked in her home a few weeks ago?"

"Yes. She'll soon be discharged from County General, probably sometime next week. However, she still needs further rehabilitation and care."

"We have a small clinic along with a guesthouse on Mercer Island. We work with sports injuries and chronic illnesses. I'm not certain our clinic would be an ideal placement for Miss Goodrich, but I'm certainly willing to discuss it with you and entertain the idea."

"Her current doctors are pretty rooted into pharmaceutical drugs, and they've told me naturopathic medicine is unscientific. I was surprised when her doctor suggested Hyperbaric Oxygen Therapy. This treatment's been a miracle for her."

"We offer HBOT here at the clinic as well."

"I'm trying to find a treatment center with a more holistic approach to healing. In addition, she's about eight weeks pregnant."

"What's your experience or vision of holistic health care?"

"My father-in-law was a medical doctor who believed in treating the whole body, and he was skeptical of a lot of pharmaceutical drugs. His mother died of colon cancer, and I think he believed chemotherapy destroyed her immune system. He was also into antiaging medicine in its infancy."

"Who's your father-in-law?"

"Dwayne Turner. He had a private medical practice in Los Angeles."

"He didn't tell you that he's on our advisory board?"

"No. We haven't been in contact for about fourteen years. My wife and son were killed in a car accident in Los Angeles by a drunk driver. She was his only child, and he blamed me for not taking her and Mike to the soccer game in LA. I can't blame him. But we've never had contact again after the funeral."

"I'm truly sorry. Why don't you come over, and I'll give you a tour of our facility. If we can get a copy of her file we'll have a clearer picture as to what we might be able to offer."

"I'm her medical power of attorney, so I'll contact the hospital and get a copy of her medical file."

"That'd be great. Oh, one other thing. Please don't wear after shave or cologne, as some of our clients have allergies."

"What time can I stop by?"

"How would three o'clock be for you?"

"I'll be there." Aaron hung up the phone, hoping this could be the break Rachel needed.

Aaron drives down a tree-lined residential street, looking for addresses. He sees a sign carved into a grey cement retaining wall: Andersen's Total Body Wellness. The property had two houses on it, which were probably built in the nineteen fifties. There's a sign with a directional arrow for parking. He drives up the steep little incline curving around to the back of the property and parks his car. There are several old ponderosa pine trees standing over a hundred feet tall. He notices the reddish bark with deep lines running through it. He always loved the smell of the ponderosa pine; they reminded him of vanilla or butterscotch cookies.

He walks through double French doors into a small reception area. The old floor is a weathered oak. There's a small leather sofa and matching chairs, two mahogany end tables with ceramic lamps, and a matching coffee table scattered with magazines like *Prevention* and *Countryside*.

"May I help you?"

"Yes, I'm Aaron Townsend and I've an appointment with Dr. Andersen."

"Oh, yes. Please come with me," the receptionist said. "He's waiting for you."

Aaron followed her down a narrow hallway to an end office. Entering the little office he saw an antique cherry-wood desk along with a couple of matching straight back chairs, and a bookcase which took up one wall and was filled with leather-bound books. There were two oversized windows from which he could see grass, trees, and a few rose bushes.

"Dr. Andersen, this is Aaron Townsend."

"Thank you, Helen. Please come in and have a seat, Mr. Townsend."

"Thank you. Please just call me Aaron."

"Could I get you a cup of herbal tea or some filtered water?"

"No thank you. I'm fine. I've brought a file with Rachel's medical records."

The doctor puts on his glasses and flips through the pages. His hair is mostly white with a few streaks of black. He has a full beard and appears to be in his early sixties. His eyes are a beautiful blue and he's got a smile and a demeanor of pure gentleness. Aaron watches him flip through the forms, feeling like a small boy in the presence of a great wise man.

Looking up at Aaron, he speaks. "Her psychiatrist says she's suffering from depression and recommends she be given selective serotonin reuptake inhibitors. Have they initiated this treatment yet?"

"No! I'm totally against that! She may be depressed, but why wouldn't she be after what happened to her?"

"I couldn't agree with you more! Those are pretty nasty drugs. Her latest magnetic resolution imaging looks good. Those HBOT sessions have obviously stimulated healing."

Taking off his glasses, he leans over his desk looking at Aaron. "Our chiropractor uses cranial therapy, which may help Rachel. Can she walk?"

"Not yet, but she's been receiving some physical therapy at the hospital. Her motor skills still need work."

"Oh, yes, of course. I see that here. I see she's also receiving some speech therapy."

"Yes"

"Well, this is my theory, Aaron. Pharmaceutical drugs can have a limited place in the healing process some of the time. But the problem with western medicine is that we don't look for the root cause of disease; we aim to suppress symptoms. We manage disease and we don't really promote wellness. That's the problem I have with standard medical care. I think good medicine is to provide the body with optimal conditions and then get out of the way and allow the body to do what it's designed to do—bring the body back into homeostasis. At this clinic the cornerstone of our program is healthful eating, and I'm not talking about your Department of Agriculture food pyramid either. That food pyramid is what's wrong with our society today! No, I'm talking raw milk, organic fruits and vegetables, grass-fed meats, sauerkraut."

"Sauerkraut?"

"Yes. Lacto fermented sauerkraut and other vegetables to increase digestive enzymes."

"Oh, that sounds like the way my wife Meredith used to talk. I'm in complete agreement with you."

"We usually work with athletes and people with fibromyalgia and other chronic health conditions, as I told you on the phone. But I think we could help Rachel. However, our approach is not the standard and it's not endorsed by mainstream medicine. I think partly because they're afraid. Americans are tired of the prescription pad, of being treated like a number, mediocre results, and many have come to view doctors as limited. Which they are. You cannot take a body and treat it as separate parts. A body is like an orchestra; it can only make fine music if all parts are in tune with each other."

"This sounds like what I hoped we could find for Rachel."

"Insurance probably will cover very little of her treatment here, and I'll not beat around the bush with you, her stay here will be costly."

"I don't care if you can help her."

"Well, there aren't any guarantees. I wish there were. The other thing is if she were to come here, we only allow visitors on the weekends."

"Why?"

"Well, the therapy is intensive and we don't have the staff to deal with visitors. Plus, we have to consider all of our clients. Some are trying to recover from adrenal burnout, and we like to run a tranquil and restful place to stimulate adrenal healing."

"I see. That does make sense. Her parents are here from Hayward, California."

"Well, maybe they'd want to go home and have a break. She could still make calls whenever she wanted and they could call her during the evening before nine p.m. Let me have Helen give you a tour of the facilities."

"Thank you."

"I'll walk back with you to the waiting room. We can talk on Monday after you've had time to discuss things with Rachel and her parents."

Driving home he couldn't believe how uplifted he felt from meeting the staff and touring the clinic and the guesthouse. Everything, though simple, was spotlessly clean. Both the clinic and the guesthouse had hardwood oak floors throughout, along with wood paneling and vaulted ceilings with beautiful wood ceiling beams. The combination kitchen and dining room had five sets of oversized double windows through which the light flooded the whole kitchen and dining room. Helen told him the countertops throughout the guesthouse and clinic were quartz. She'd explained that although it's a partially manmade product, it's not porous, which prevents bacteria from seeping into the counters. She mentioned that Dr. Andersen was concerned about radon gas with granite. The living room was just off the kitchen and dining room. It had a marble fireplace which took up all of one wall. The windows ran all along the back wall as in the kitchen. The furniture was designed with hypoallergenic materials.

There were six bedrooms upstairs in the guesthouse and one downstairs. If Rachel comes here they'll place her in the room on the main floor. This bedroom had French double doors opening to a beautiful yard with a seven-foot high privacy wood fence. During the summer they have a garden and many of their clients enjoy the tranquility of the yard with the beautiful ponderosa pines, the green grass and flowers.

He hoped her parents would agree that this will be a great place for Rachel. He just couldn't imagine her getting the one-on-one therapy from a nursing home that she'd receive here. He briefly met Melody, the psychologist, who told him she preferred to use whatever methods best helped her clients. "Everyone is different. Some need behavior modi-fication, others require a more humanistic approach, and yet others benefit from Carl Jung dream analysis." She likes Gestalt psychology, something about the whole is greater than the sum of all the parts. Gestalt psychology tries to understand the laws of our ability to acquire and maintain meaningful perceptions in an apparently chaotic world. In other words, she had an eclectic approach to working with her clients. He knew that he didn't fully understand all the field of psychology. Some of it was foreign to him, even when Meredith used to try and explain Freud and his theories. He thought some of it is a little wacky. But he didn't have to understand psychology or even believe in it; if it helped Rachel get well that was good enough.

Chapter Twenty-Seven

⸻

*G*erald, with the help of the other detectives in his precinct, had assembled all the details on the Goodrich case. Suspect Hamilton on the night of September twenty-sixth had followed Ms. Goodrich from her transit stop to her apartment, where he battered and raped her. On October first, he robbed the Seacoast Bank and Trust, disguised as a woman. The suspect had fled Seattle on a chartered jet to Detroit, Michigan using an old police alias. Sioux Falls, South Dakota also had a warrant out for his arrest for the attempted murder of his ex-wife, Debbie Hamilton.

The public had been enraged over his escape, and trying to get him extradited from Detroit was going to be cumbersome at best. What was it that Captain Larry Thomas of Detroit PD told him? We're sorry, but we just don't have enough police officers to send them out looking for your suspect. We've got our own problems with murders every day here in Detroit. Bodies are stacking up in the morgue because the city is broke and can't afford to hire police officers and other staff. Every part of city government is stretched to the limit. If we pick him up, sure, we'll call you, but he's not a priority here because no one has died. Detroit had had a warrant for his arrest since yesterday, and all Seattle could do was wait and hope for his capture.

Aaron's pulling into the parking garage at the hospital when his cell phone rings. "Hello, Stacy."

"Aaron, Gerald Herschel just called and he needs you to call him back."

"Let me park so I can get his phone number from you. Is there anything else you need Stacy?"

"No. The afternoon's been pretty quiet. Oh, we did get a couple of calls from customers wanting to know if those test cookies Bernie is doing would be available in the supermarket like our coffee."

"Off the top of my head I'd say probably not, but I'd have to discuss that with Bernie."

He dials Gerald Hershel's phone number. "This is Aaron Townsend. I had a message to call you."

"Yes, we were informed Ms. Goodrich will be discharged soon from County General, and we need to know what the plans are so we can ensure she has police protection."

"Well, it really hasn't been finalized yet, but she may go to a place on Mercer Island."

"We've reason to believe Mr. Hamilton's out of state, but until he's captured she's not safe. My recommendation is once you know where she's going to be, it should be kept quiet, only providing the information to those who need to know. We'll arrange to have cruisers in the area where she'll be. The less people know, the easier it'll be to protect her."

"I thought for sure you'd have him by now."

"Sorry. I wish we'd been able to catch him."

"Okay, I'll talk to her parents and let you know when we have information on her placement. I don't think we should tell Rachel about her ex-husband, as it might have a detrimental effect on her recovery."

"I think you're probably right and there really isn't much she can do other than be afraid."

"Exactly."

"Give her and her parents my best. I hope you don't have any bad feelings towards me for suggesting you might have been the one who harmed Rachel."

"Well, I'm not going to lie; you did make me very angry. But I know you were just doing your job, trying to find out who did this to her. I appreciate the call and I'll tell her parents."

"Thanks."

Hanging up the phone he sits there a couple of minutes thinking he hadn't thought much about Hamilton lately, he'd been so focused on finding a place for her to continue her recovery. After all Hamilton did to Rachel, Aaron hadn't thought about him coming back to try to harm her. It made sense that Gerald Hershel would be concerned; after all, she'd be the star witness testifying against him. Just when he's so excited about Andersen's, he's yanked back to the fact that her life's still in danger. Would Andersen's accept her knowing Hamilton is still out there?

Before they go any further with the plans he needs to talk to Dr. Andersen, and he pulls his business card out of his billfold.

The phone rings and the receptionist answers. "Andersen's, how may I help you?"

"I'm Aaron Townsend. I was out there this afternoon. Could I possibly speak to Dr. Andersen?"

"I'm not sure if he's left for the day. Let me check."

"Aaron, this is Dr. Andersen."

"I just spoke with the detective working on Rachel's case. Her ex-husband's still at large and they believe him to be out of state. We never talked about it, but I wonder if that would be an issue at Andersen's."

"We have some pretty well known people who come to the center, so we do have a security company who patrols our area. We keep things confidential at Andersen's, so if you keep it quiet on your end where she's going we should be fine. Will the police have a presence in the area?"

"He said they'd have cruisers drive by."

"Okay. We'll see how it goes. Thanks for calling me on this."

"Thank you, Dr. Andersen. He hangs up, relieved that the center's still a possibility. He felt especially good about the clinic after learning that Dwayne, his father in law, is on their advisory board. He knew it had to be a good program for Dwayne to endorse it.

Walking into Rachel's room he greets her and tells Stanley and Susan he needed to speak with them for a moment. They went into a private waiting room and he advises them that Gerald Hershel had called him and said Hamilton hasn't yet been captured. "The detective indicated he might be out of state, and that when she's moved from County General her whereabouts should not be disclosed to anyone unless they need to know." He described his visit to the Andersen Wellness Clinic. Amelia had also found a nursing home within a mile of where her parents lived in

Hayward. They all agreed it would be best to let Rachel decide.

They returned to Rachel's room and Aaron said, "Rachel I know I've been kind of pushy lately, not wanting you to have that flu vaccine and not wanting you to take anti-depressants."

"Aaron, I've worked for you for a long time. Your and Bernie's attitudes about wellness have rubbed off on me. So I, too, don't want to take those pharmaceutical drugs. Especially not with my baby."

"Our baby, Rachel."

"Yes. Our baby."

"We've found two potential places for you to go to for your continued rehabilitation. One is a convalescent hospital your Aunt Amelia found, which is near your parents' home in Hayward. The second place was found by Bernie— Andersen's Total Body Wellness on Mercer Island."

The four of them discussed the pros and cons of both places. She could be close to her parents if she went to California. The care there would be standard and well defined within the scope of western medicine. The Andersen clinic would allow her to remain in the Seattle area, and the care would be tailored to her as the unique human being she is. Her health insurance would most likely cover her rehabil-itation in California, and in Washington State, very little would be covered. They felt she'd be more satisfied if she made the decision on what she'd want to do.

"I want very much to stay in Seattle and go back to work as soon as I can. But I can't afford the Andersen Clinic, so I think it'd be best for me to return to California."

"Rachel, I really don't want you to make the decision based on money. Either way you decide, I'll help you with expenses."

"Aaron, I can't let you do that."

"Rachel, please honey, if you want to go to California then fine, but don't make the choice based on money. If you're so worried about me paying the expenses then let me give you a loan and you can pay it yourself."

"Honey, if you want to go to Andersen's, your father and I'll help, too. We just want what's best for you."

"Then, okay, I'd like to go to Andersen's."

"Rachel, your parents and I'll make the arrangements. You've had a hard day; maybe you should get some rest."

"I do feel really tired. I think I'd like some time by myself, if you all don't mind."

"Fine, we'll be back tomorrow. Good night, honey."

"Goodnight, Dad."

In the hallway as they were leaving, Aaron said, "Stanley and Susan, if you'd like, I thought we might drive over to Mercer Island on Monday and take a tour of the clinic while Rachel is doing her therapies."

"Aaron, I'd really like to see the place. It might help me feel more confident about where she's going."

"I agree with Susan. It would be nice to have an idea of where she'd be. I have to be honest; I thought most of the nursing homes we visited were pretty depressing. On the other hand, I'm not sure of this alternative health stuff either."

"I do understand your concerns, and while I, too, have concerns, I just felt more at peace at the clinic and more uplifted than any place we've visited. The staff seemed like such a great team, and everyone's so positive."

"How do you know they don't act that way just because of the money?"

"Susan, I don't know that. But many times I've had to trust my gut feelings about stuff and it's often turned out to be right. We all want the best for Rachel, and working together and supporting her through this time will go a long way to help speed her recovery."

Chapter Twenty-Eight

On Monday morning around nine o'clock a.m. Aaron picks up Stanley and Susan at Mary's Bed and Breakfast Inn and drives to the northern portion of Seattle's south end. He takes the Lacey V Murrow Memorial Bridge I-90 to Mercer Island. He told them this bridge sank into Lake Washington in 1990 while repairs were being made.

He points out the bicycle path on the bridge. "Rachel and I were entertaining one of our Columbian coffee growers, Eduardo, last fall. We rented ten-speed bikes and rode across this bridge. Rachel and I were both sore for a week after riding this in both direction. Eduardo, well, he was more fit than us."

"The water looks so slate blue and beautiful."

"Yes, Susan. I've always loved Lake Washington and watching the boats in the summer. Right now, it's a bit foggy."

Crossing the bridge they drove through a winding tree-lined highway.

"This is like driving through a forest," Stanley said. "It looks so pretty how the leaves on a few of the trees have changed to gold and burnt orange. It reminds me a little of the time we took a bus tour of the New England states to see the fall colors. Of course, the trees back there were almost all changing to fall colors."

"That was such a wonderful trip," Susan said. "Aaron, have you ever been on one of those tours?"

"No. Afraid not. I've mostly been on the west coast, and with my business we've been as far as Denver, but I've not been back east."

They drive down a tree-lined street and Aaron enters the driveway.

"This is the place."

"It just looks like a couple of houses."

"Yes, Stanley, they've converted two residential homes into the clinic and the guesthouse."

Dr. Andersen meets with the three of them and Aaron watches the interaction with Rachel's parents and the staff. He toured the clinic with them but suggested he'd wait for them in the waiting room while they checked out the guesthouse. It was like being a realtor giving potential buyers their space to discuss the pros and cons. Susan's smiling and Stanley's asking questions. Aaron senses a complete change in their demeanor as pursed lips and wariness in the eyes seems to have dissipated like a winter storm.

Driving back to the hospital, each of them was thinking about Rachel and the place she'd be staying when she's discharged by her doctor at County General Hospital. Susan is the first to speak. "You know, I really like Dr. Andersen. I just felt so relaxed with him."

"Sue, honey, what I liked about him is he didn't make any fake promises. I was expecting something like a big sales job and promises for total recovery, and he wasn't like that. The guy seems to have integrity. He might be misguided though. But if our daughter wants this, I think it's worth a go. The worse thing is we'd have to move her somewhere else if she isn't improving. With the baby and all it might be better to be less intrusive with her care."

"I'm so glad you both like it. If it doesn't work out, we can always change."

"I wonder what kind of tea that was they served us?"

"Actually it's the Coffee Genie's organic acai berry tea."

"Your tea, Aaron?"

"Yes, the receptionist told me while you were touring the guesthouse."

While Susan and Stanley were touring the guesthouse, Aaron had watched the clients coming in and their interaction with the receptionist. He didn't notice the usual tension he'd seen in other doctors' offices he'd been to. Apparently, their clients included both walk-in appointments as well as residents of the guesthouse. He wondered how they seemed to keep the names straight and the schedule on time.

Dr. Andersen had given them a business card with a private ambulance service that would be able to transport Rachel when she was released by her doctor. He suggested they come to the clinic when she's transferred to see her settled in. Dr. Andersen would contact Dr. Johnson to advise that they'd be taking over her care when she's released.

It's a relief knowing a team of doctors would be managing her total care, and Aaron had presented him with the initial deposit. It seemed like there were so many forms to be signed, but it's now all done.

Rachel was sitting in a wheel chair, looking out the window of her hospital room, staring at the street below, oblivious to anything around her. It's hard to believe she's in this position where her body didn't do what she always took for granted and she's struggling to formulate what she wanted to say. She felt like a used dishrag, handled by so many people, feeling as if her life's under a microscope. Sometimes she just wanted to scream, "Leave me alone!" From the moment she remembered coming back to life, someone was poking, pressing her, drawing blood, and she's so tired of it.

She felt so ugly. How could Aaron ever want her if she didn't even sound like herself. He was a nice man, and there's no doubt she really loved him, but she didn't want some guy, especially him, to feel sorry for her. The only real good thing is the baby. She really wanted her baby. In the beginning she didn't remember being with Kenneth. She's truly relieved to learn the truth; she'd gotten pregnant before he raped her. She didn't want to have to tell her son his father drank too much and he hit women.

She'd tell her son all of the good things about Aaron, his father. It might be heartless, but when she recovers, she's decided to disappear, because it's best for Aaron. What she and Aaron had shared was special but too much has happened. She couldn't be sure he was with her for the right reasons. She's never going to settle again. Love with respect would be the only reason she'd commit to another man. She wanted to feel her man saw her as beautiful inside and out. She thinks her beauty days are behind her and she'll die an old unmarried woman, if Kenneth doesn't come back and kill her first. No one talks about him, so it must mean he is still out there, waiting for the opportunity to come back and kill her.

The other thing is that she's never told anyone, but her peripheral vision seems to be diminished.

Sometimes, especially after the oxygen tank treatment, she thought she could see better, but then her side vision would fade a little as the day wore on. Would she lose her sight? It was one fear she had among others.

She'd considered telling the psychiatrist about it, but she didn't really like her. She seemed to put words in her mouth and was out of step with how she really felt. There's something about her she didn't quite trust. She kind of wondered if she didn't think there's something mentally wrong with her. It was a certain look she gave her.

She didn't hear Aaron and her parents walk in.

"Hi, honey. We're back from visiting Andersen's, and we think you're going to love Mercer Island."

Irritably, she clipped back, "I've been there."

"To the clinic?"

"No, of course not! Why would I have gone there?"

"I'm sorry, honey. Are you having a bad day?"

She looked down at the floor. "I'm sorry, Mom. I'm just tired of this place—the food, my body, and so many people touching me and bugging me. Did you like the clinic?"

"Rachel, we all think you'll like it. It's a nice, homey feel, with big windows and lots of wood paneling and wood floors. But most of all, the people are so friendly and caring."

"Dad, that sounds good. I'm sorry. I don't mean to sound so snappy. I know you're all trying to help me. It's just that for the last twelve years I've been in total control of my own life and now I feel dependent. Things like walking and talking I always took for granted now requires so much effort. It's almost like being a one-year-old again."

"Rachel, I can see how frustrating this is for you," Aaron said. He walked over and put his hand on her shoulder. "I can see how hard you work at improving, and I believe you have the strength and ability within you to fully recover. I think that when you go to Andersen's you'll be able to rest better, and from the core of my being, I sense you'll receive new tools to speed your recovery. I need you, our baby needs you, and the Coffee Genie certainly needs you."

Looking up at him, she smiles. "How is it, Aaron Townsend, that you always seem to know the right things to say? You've been like that since I met you."

"Did I tell you Bernie's testing a new low-sugar cookie and he wants to call it the Rachel Wellness cookie?"

"No, you didn't. I just love Bernie and his half-French and half-English conversations. I never knew a lick of French until I met him. Now I can say a few things like *tres bon, Bon soir,* and even a couple of French curse words."

Aaron laughed. "Yes, Bernie's quite the guy. We're so lucky to have him as part of our team."

"That's the other thing I always liked about you, Aaron, the way you always looked at your employees as assets and part of a team and not just an employee. I haven't asked you, how is Sandy?"

"That's a topic for another time but I guess she's okay."

She'd seen that closed off look from Aaron before and she just knew the conversation was finished in that department. That's one thing she found a bit disconcerting about him was the way he could abruptly cut off a topic they were discussing. There's obviously some issue and she guessed he'd talk to her about it when he's ready. He was like that when he sent her back to Seattle. As much as she loved and admired him, sometimes she found him to be confusing. She found it hard not to personalize things because when she was married to Kenneth everything that wasn't perfect was always her fault.

They'd visited for a couple of hours, interrupted by her speech therapist and the nurse checking her vitals. Relaxation was in the air, and they're all talking about the future—her future, the baby. Her mother didn't see how Rachel could possibly know she's having a son, and she seemed skeptical when she told her of dying and seeing her grandparents.

Two orderlies came to take her to see her psychiatrist. She wished she didn't have to go; she just wanted to be here with her parents and Aaron.

Shortly after she left for her appointment, Dr. Johnson stepped into her room and summoned the three of them to an empty office. He wasn't smiling, and Aaron felt like they were little children who'd done something wrong, like breaking a window or tramping through old man Bench's garden when he was a small boy.

After seating themselves, Dr. Johnson spoke. "I received a call today from Dr. Andersen on Mercer Island. He advised me his clinic would be taking over Rachel's rehabilitation. I want you to know I only want the best for Rachel and I'm sure you do as well, but this plan you have is misguided. As her doctor, I just can't endorse it. Rachel has serious problems that must be addressed through proper medical care."

"Dr. Andersen is an MD."

"Mrs. Goodrich, I know, but his approach isn't endorsed by mainstream medicine. We aren't talking about a sprain from a sports injury or a simple emotional problem. Rachel's had a traumatic brain injury. She's made great strides, but improvement is going to require medication and the kind of therapy she's just not going to get there at Andersens. I offered to write him some prescriptions for when we dismiss her and do you know what he said?"

"No," Stanley said, looking down at the floor.

"He said that'd be unnecessary, that he'd prefer to evaluate her condition on his own and write prescriptions he determines to be appropriate."

"I fail to see what's wrong with that." Aaron said.

"I've taken care of Rachel from the beginning when she was brought here. I've been her primary care doctor for the past four years. I know her case better than anyone. Although I'm only one doctor, I'm part of a team of doctors who's helped Rachel make this wonderful progress."

"Dr. Johnson, we all appreciate what you've done for Rachel, believe me we do," Aaron said. "However, I fail to see what harm it'd do to have a fresh pair of eyes examine her. Maybe he'll have some skills to help her further."

"You're not a doctor, so you probably don't realize how important continuity of care is. You shouldn't go and radically change her treatment plan, as it could be detrimental to her progress. But Aaron, I can see you're determined to take Rachel in this direction. I do want to go on record and tell you I think this is quackery at its best."

"I'm sorry you think that way because I really liked Dr. Andersen when I met him today," Susan said. "I don't think it's very nice to talk about him in that way."

"I'm sorry, Mrs. Goodrich. I meant no offense. I just want the best for Rachel, too."

"What kind of prescriptions did you think Rachel should be given when she leaves here?"

"Stanley, I think she should be on some antibiotics because her wounds are still healing, I feel she should be on a cholesterol lowering drug as her cholesterol's a little high; she should probably have some pain medications, and maybe some sleeping pills to help her rest. I know her psychiatrist wants her to be on antidepressants. She's convinced she might have bipolar tendencies. But I do have to say that I never saw that or any psychological issues when she came to me for her regular checkups."

"What's all this stuff going to do to the baby?" Aaron asked.

"I know you'll think me insensitive, but in her case an abortion might not be a bad choice. It may allow her body to heal better and faster. We also don't know what kind of recovery we'll be getting with her. These types of injuries rarely result in a full total recovery. Statistics correlate with less recovery the longer a person's in a coma. Of course, there are always exceptions."

"An abortion! That's murder!" Susan's mouth blew open and her eyes widened. "What would people say? In the beginning you were considering the baby when you first started treating our daughter. So why have you changed your position?"

"At the time we first met to discuss her condition we didn't know how many days she'd be comatose or if she'd live. I'm just trying to be objective and suggest what may be in her best interest. Have you thought about what'll happen if she's unable to care for the baby? What if the baby's born with disabilities? You're all tired; you've been in a crisis mode for over two weeks. I get that. I wouldn't be doing a service to any of you if I didn't point out the possible pit falls."

"Aw, no. We couldn't tell our daughter to do that!" Stanley's face reddened as he tried to choke down his anger.

"God would never forgive us if we did that! If her baby's born, or however it's born, that's God's will. We need more people like the Sarah Palin's of this world! This would be a damn better place! She didn't kill her baby!"

"I'm sorry, Stanley. I didn't mean to upset you."

"I guess the final thing I want to know is when's Rachel going to be discharged from County General?"

"Aaron, I'd say tomorrow morning. But I'm reluctant to sign off on discharging her this early because I think you're all misguided in your desire to help her. Why don't we look at a few more convalescent hospitals, what do you say?"

"After that abortion comment, I say absolutely not! She's going to Andersen's. I was hesitant about it but not anymore. Aaron and Susan are absolutely right!"

"Again, I apologize if I offended you. You know we could have the attorney's at our hospital get a court order to stop you from moving her. After all, she really isn't in a condition to make her own choices. A ward of the court might be the best approach at this time."

"You just try it! I'll see you in court; her parents and I'll be owning this hospital!"

"I agree with Aaron, don't you try a bunch of legal games with us! Just get her paperwork ready. I want more for my daughter than you and this hospital."

"Okay, Mr. Goodrich."

Susan usually tried to tamp down Stanley's negative energy, but this time she thought he was right on. Wasn't that just disgraceful, suggesting an abortion. The baby deserved a chance to live even if it was illegitimate. She knew she never liked Dr. Johnson from day one!

The three of them walk out together and it felt like for the first time in a few days they were totally in agreement. It's going to be nice to turn the page, write a new chapter, forge ahead, and Dr. Johnson be damned, Aaron thinks. Maybe he never really fully got Meredith and Dwayne, but in that meeting it all became crystal clear what they'd both said more than a decade and a half ago. How could that doctor want to kill his unborn baby? Blurting out, he said. "You know, I don't think it'd be good to tell Rachel about this?"

"About what?"

"Susan, about Dr. Johnson suggesting she have an abortion."

"Aaron, I absolutely agree. I think it'd hurt Rachel and there's no sense in it."

"Thanks, Stanley, for your support on this one."

"Well, maybe we should tell her."

"No, Sue. Aaron's right."

"Yes. I guess you're right. I just don't like keeping things from her."

"Susan, this is just not the right time. She's got too much to deal with," Aaron said.

They walked back to her room in silence, wishing Rachel was out of here already.

It was about a half an hour before Rachel returned from seeing her psychiatrist, and during her absence they contacted the private ambulance to start the preparation for her transport.

"How was your session with your psychiatrist?"

"It was okay, Mom. I just don't feel very comfortable with her. I can't say why; I just feel nervous talking to her. I've got to be careful of every word I use. I feel like a cockroach under a microscope, waiting for her to pesticide spray me."

"Well, that's pretty dramatic." Aaron said with a laugh. "Did she spray you or did you scurry away?"

She couldn't help but smile and tried to stifle a laugh. "No, my time slot was up and the orderlies rescued me. With my body there's no scurrying anywhere." She thought it felt good to laugh. It did hurt her ribs, but they were into that free give-and-take she seemed to have with Aaron. For a minute it's like stepping back in time and none of this ever happened. She loved his sense of humor and the way he sometimes teased her. She thought of her grandmother's words, that was a passionate night in Denver. She felt her face blushing, thinking Rhett Butler. Her aunt was right.

"We aren't sure of the time but we think you're being discharged to go to Andersen's sometime tomorrow."

"Mom, that's really good news!"

Chapter Twenty-Nine

On Friday after Dr. Andersen's meeting with Aaron, he'd called an urgent telephone conference call of the advisory board for that evening, which included all of the doctors at the clinic, along with their attorney. He'd told them of his intention of accepting Rachel Goodrich, a trauma patient, as a client at Andersen's. This would be contingent on the board's approval and the family's decision to place Rachel in their care.

The advisory board and the staff were one of the most cohesive groups he'd ever worked with. In fact, you couldn't work at Andersen's or be on the board unless you had a passion to help others. Everyone spoke their mind at these meetings and he valued that. Even though they were only an advisory board, he rarely went against the majority. Just because Andersen's was his baby, he didn't always end up with board decisions supporting his views. The clinic had always progressed and went far beyond what he thought was possible.

Their attorneys, right off the bat, expressed what everyone thought—even himself. Taking this patient was unchartered water, and in this litigious society if something went wrong, it could be the end of the clinic. He'd reminded them he'd been a trauma doctor working for a large Boston hospital for ten years after he finished his residency. Dr. Kinsinger is one of the finest neurologists in the country. He believed that between the two of them, they had the expertise to care for Rachel.

It was really Dwayne Turner who made order out of chaos. He was a passionate man who motivated others, and he had a strong desire to help others. Dwayne also never hesitated to express his opinions, no matter who disagreed with him. "Wait just a minute here! Why was this clinic born in the first place? I'll tell you from the get go it has hung over our heads that we could be sued because we've always looked at the patient and not at medical protocol wanting to cookie cutter every patient we see. We love medicine and watching the results. Figuring out what makes individuals tick. We were all sick and tired of having so many patients coming through our doors like an assembly line. We didn't have time to really know our patients. Sure, we get patients we can't help, because half of it's the patient's responsibility to do their part to regain their health and follow directions. Many people are looking for a quick fix with no effort on their part. Anyway, enough of my rant. I'm firmly in Chet Andersen's corner on this one; just because we've never tried something it doesn't mean we shouldn't. Do I think we should try to become a convalescent hospital? Well, no, but we should never avoid something on the fear of being sued either!"

The call had lasted a few hours and it turned into an excitement of what they could try. The attorney wanted them to get a waiver and for the parents to understand there aren't any guarantees, and if at any time Andersen's believed their program wasn't of benefit to this patient, she'd be moved to another facility.

After the meeting with Rachel's parents, he received a call in the afternoon advising him Rachel would be released tomorrow. He told his secretary to notify all of the staff of a gathering-in-meeting tomorrow at eleven o'clock a.m. He expected everyone in the conference room at that time. Sometimes these meetings concerned some of the clients, but often the meetings were brainstorming sessions on improving services as well as a chance to express their feelings and concerns.

When the clinic was just a desire, a thought, a yearning for something greater, he'd decided there couldn't be an undercurrent of dissatisfied employees. He'd often seen that in other places he'd worked, and although a person might not say anything, it often spilled out in various ways in the work they performed. People became jaded, sometimes irritable; one patient became the same as the next. If you were like that, you couldn't work at his clinic. So if something was eating on you, whether it was in your personal life or something at the clinic, you'd better spill the beans or find another job.

The gathering-in-meeting was noisy, as usual, but when he gaveled them to silence, you could've heard a pin drop. "I've called this meeting on a short notice because we've decided to accept a client from County General Hospital who's experienced a traumatic brain injury. She was in a coma, so she has some speech and physical problems greater than some of our past clients. You may have heard of her; she's Rachel Goodrich."

"She's that lady who was beaten and raped by her ex-husband."

"Yes, and we're going to place her in the ground floor bedroom. I want to open the meeting to hear your concerns and your ideas."

His heart was touched by the caring, compassion, and excitement from his staff of her becoming a client of Andersen's. There was discussion of logistics of making things accessible. Karen, one of the nurses, recommended they place a baby monitor in her room, especially at night, so the nurse working the midnight-to-eight shift could observe her from a distance without waking her. They all knew the importance of the circadian rhythm, the body's internal clock, and sleep patterns' role in healing and wellness.

Sonia, the cook, chimed in. "That's a good point. Have you ever tried to sleep in a hospital? You just fall asleep and they wake you up to take your blood pressure. We need to give that woman some time to rest."

On the day of her arrival, the nurses working in the guesthouse would arrive thirty minutes before their shift started to help the other nurse with her care and bathing. Dr. Kinsinger would stop by to see her before he left for the day. He and Dr. Andersen would be on call on a weekly rotational basis and would provide the guesthouse nurses with an on-call schedule. Rachel would only have interaction with the necessary staff to administer her care on her first day.

A plan was created encompassing all that made Andersen's the beacon of futuristic medicine, including all aspects of treating the root cause of illness in the body. Everyone had their part to play, from Nick, the clinical exercise physiologist; Jennifer, the nutritionist; Melody, the psychologist; Stephen, the chiropractor; Fred, the naturopath;

right down to Sonia, the cook. Everyone had an important part to contribute, and for Rachel it would be no different than those clients who came before or after her, just a little different to embrace her unique individual needs, encompassing mind, body, and spirit.

Chapter Thirty

*Y*esterday, Rachel's mom and dad had cleaned her apartment, packing some things she'd need at the center. She and Stanley went shopping afterwards, purchasing a new bed ensemble for her apartment, some full-length night-gowns, and five women's active-wear sets. Susan felt a sadness of going home to Hayward without her daughter. But Rachel was thirty-eight, old enough to make her own decisions. Tomorrow night she'd be home in her own bed, Susan thought. It seemed like such a long time ago when they had left California. Yet it had been only a few weeks. The whole experience had aged her, and she felt ten years older. She could only hope things would improve for her daughter and the baby.

"You're sure quiet, Mom. Are you okay?"

"Yes. I was just thinking of how happy I am that you're better and how the last few weeks have seemed like such a long time."

"I thought so, too. When the ambulance pulled out of the hospital parking garage and we began driving down the street on our way to Andersen's, I felt like someone who's just been released from prison. I hope you know, Mom, how much I love you and Daddy. I know I've not always done what you wanted me to do, but all the same, I want you to know I'm very lucky to have you as my parents."

"Dear, I think sometimes you want the best for your children and you forget they have to live their own lives, make their own choices, good or bad. Sometimes I've wanted to live your life for you, thinking I knew what was best. I realize my little girl is a woman and I've got to let her make her own choices in life."

They held hands the rest of the way on the drive to the center, feeling a bond of love for one another in a way they never quite experienced before. A total acceptance of each other. It reminded Rachel of when she was dying and she had a powerful drive to be with her mother—an intense feeling of needing her mom. "You know, the way I feel right now reminds me of when I was dying and I felt driven to get to Hayward. All I could think was I had to get to you. It felt like the first day of kindergarten when you left me and I cried."

"Rachel, you never knew it but I cried, too. I didn't want to leave you at school, but I needed to let you grow up. I'm so touched you really wanted and needed me when you were in the coma."

"I know I've not always been the best daughter. I was pretty rebellious as a teenager."

"You think I wasn't?"

"Well, I guess I never thought about it."

"Let me tell you, your dad's mom was determined to have a nice Jewish girl for your father, and I didn't fit into her plans."

"I knew some of that, but I guess I never thought of you as the rebellious type."

"Well, in my own way I was."

It was nearly one thirty in the afternoon when the motorcade arrived, delivering Rachel to the next stage of her recovery plan. Aaron and Stanley had followed Rachel and her mother in the ambulance.

The ambulance parked in a handicap parking space, the attendants carefully placing the wheel chair on the asphalt and gently lifting Rachel from the gurney and sitting her in the chair. The group walked across the driveway to the guesthouse, trying to avoid water puddles that remained from the morning shower. The weatherman predicted heavy rain tomorrow, but for now the rain had stopped.

They were greeted by Karen, the nurse, and she directed the group to Rachel's bedroom while she stopped and signed some paperwork for the ambulance drivers. Susan began unpacking Rachel's suitcase, asking her where she'd want her to put her clothes and toiletries. Karen quickly took Rachel's blood pressure, temperature, and pulse while her mother finished unpacking.

The cook stepped into the bedroom after the drivers departed. "Hello. I'm Sonia, the cook. Could I make you all some tea or get you some filtered water?"

Everyone agreed some tea would be nice, and Karen suggested she serve the tea in the living room. Stanley pushed Rachel's wheel chair into the living room and placed her next to the coffee table. The cook served them some pomegranate tea along with a small, organic, mixed fruit plate with some cheese made from grass-fed cows. They spent an hour of small talk and trying to be cheerful. Everyone knew the pack of four would soon be going in different directions. It was an end of a stage, a beginning of change. They'd been through so much together these past weeks.

"Well, Rachel, your mother and I are going home to California, so we best get on the road. Now you take good care of yourself, you hear me. If you don't like this place, I'll be on the next plane to get you. Do you hear me?" He coughed, trying to clear a lump that formed in his throat.

"Yes, Daddy. I promise. I really love you."

"I love you, too!"

"Rachel, do you remember where I put your hair brush in that one little drawer on the top right side of the vanity? Oh, yes, and your nightgowns are in the middle drawer."

"Yes, Mom."

"I love you Rachel. You call me every day, do you hear?"

"Yes, Mom." Her tears were flowing and merging into her mother's as they hugged.

"Rachel, call me and keep me posted on your progress. I love you, too. If you need anything at all, please call me." Aaron's eyes were getting red, trying to hold back the tears, but they were seeping out, one at a time.

"Thank you, Aaron, for everything."

She watched them walk out the door, her face damp with tears, and for the first time in weeks she felt totally alone. She'd wanted space yesterday, but now she didn't want to be alone without them. Thoughts of Kenneth flickered across her mind, wondering where he is and worrying she might not have seen the last of him. She thought of that time when she tried to run away and he went and found her waiting to board a Greyhound bus to go home to California. He'd handcuffed her like a common criminal and threw her in the back of his squad car. He took her home and tied her to the bed, and when he was off duty, he took off his belt and beat her like a disobedient child. "You'll never be able to get away from me if I want you. I'm a cop, baby. And if you run away from me, I'll kill your parents because I've always hated them!"

Karen kneels down in front of her wheelchair and touches her arm. "Rachel, I'm glad you came to Andersen's. It was hard to see them leave, wasn't it?"

"Yes, it's just that my life's been whipped into a frenzy these past few weeks, and now, here I am in a new place, alone with people I don't even know."

"We're like family here and I hope you'll come to feel the same way. I think you've had a long day. How would you like to take a nice, relaxing bath and climb into your bed for a rest?"

"You mean like a real bath?"

"Yes, a nice, relaxing bath. We've got a walk-in bathtub and our other nurse, Alice, should arrive in a couple of minutes. We could wash your hair, too."

"If you think I could do it that sounds good. I've missed taking long showers or being able to soak in the tub."

"I'm sure. Have you ever heard of aromatherapy?"

"Vaguely."

"Well, it's the use of essential oils from herbs to create a sense of wellbeing—along with other benefits. We could try some and you can tell us if it's helpful."

She'd just finished her sentence when her coworker walked into the living room. "Hi, Karen."

"Hi, Alice. I'd like you to meet Rachel, our newest client."

"Welcome, Rachel. It's nice to meet you," Alice said, touching Rachel's shoulder.

The nurses took Rachel to her room, preparing her for her bath. Alice took out some vials of aromatherapy oils for Rachel to smell.

"Which did you like?"

"I like this orange-smelling one."

"The Neroli is a nice scent."

Rachel was placed in the bath and they allowed her a few minutes to soak and then turned the Jacuzzi jets to a soft swirl. They dimmed the lights and played Steven Halpern's album, *Music for Healing Mind, Body & Spirit*. The smell of the oranges, the soft dreamy music, and the gentle feel of the warm water swirling around her caused her to become limp. She didn't realize the tension she'd been carrying throughout her body until she felt the release. It felt good, and she felt so relaxed. The time flew by, maybe fifteen minutes, she didn't know. The lighting was slowly increased, and Alice, using a portable sprayer wet her hair, shampooing it and gently massaging her scalp. They said nothing, just skillfully helped her bathe.

She'd been placed in her bed only a few minutes when she saw a man in a white coat walk into her room. He had blonde hair with blue-green eyes, stood about five-foot-seven and was of average build.

"Hello, Rachel. I'm Dr. Kinsinger. I'm on my way home, but I wanted to stop and see you before I leave for the day. How do you feel?"

"I feel really relaxed. The nurses gave me a bath. I've had bad headaches since I got hurt, but the pain seems to have lessened."

"Was the hospital giving you something for the headache?"

"They offered me pain medication, but because I'm pregnant I only took them when the pain was more than I could stand."

"That's a wise decision," he said as he leaned over, taking his pen light and examining her eyes. "Do you have any other problems?" He listened to her heart with his stethoscope telling her to "Breathe in, hold it, and exhale."

"Outside of words not coming out right, not being able to walk very well, I can't think of anything else."

"Well, we'll get to work on all those things starting tomorrow. We need you to rest now because tomorrow is going to be a busy day for you."

Squeezing her hand, he said, "Welcome to Andersen's. I look forward to assisting you on your path to recovery."

She could hear the doctor talking to the nurse in the hall and then he was gone. Sonia walked in with a tray.

"Rachel, I brought you some sauerkraut and some bone broth to start."

"Sauerkraut?"

"Yes. This is lacto fermented, and it is loaded with enzymes to help you digest your food."

"I've never been fond of sauerkraut."

"Please give it a try. Think of it as part of your healing,"

She ate the sauerkraut and was glad it was only a few tablespoons. The broth tasted good. When those were finished she was brought her dinner, which consisted of raw whole milk, steamed green beans, pastured chicken, some roasted potatoes, and a small dish of blueberries. She was hungry and she couldn't remember when food tasted so good.

Aaron had taken her parents to the airport and it felt like closing a chapter in a book. His emotions were raw from the twists and turns of the whole experience of Rachel's attack. He wondered how much it would change her, if she'd be the same woman he made love to in Denver.

He'd never been able to feel emotionally attached to anyone after Meredith. It wasn't that he didn't want someone, but he always compared other women to her, his first love. With Rachel it was different; she didn't have to be anyone but herself. Sure, when you loved someone as much as he loved his wife, well maybe that first love feeling could never be replicated. He could go on to love someone else, and they would be special in their own way. When he made love to Rachel in Denver, he realized he was in love with her and had been for a long time. He wanted her in his life.

As he turned in for the night he hoped she'd get the help she needed and their lives could settle down. Before he could put this whole thing behind him he's got to fire Sandy Delray. He had no alternative because what she did was so egregious. There wasn't any disciplinary action for what she did. When trust is broken, especially in business, he wasn't willing to hope for a repair. Tomorrow's the day to get it over with.

Chapter Thirty-One

Stacy advised Aaron that Sandy had arrived, and he went to his office door, escorting her in. "Please have a seat, Sandy."

"Thank you."

Her appearance was stiff, and he sensed an air of defiance in her, but maybe he's just uncomfortable with the whole sordid deal. "Sandy, I called you this morning because I wanted to meet with you and discuss your future at the Coffee Genie. I've made the decision to terminate your employment with my company, and I've written you a check for sixty days of severance pay minus the taxes. In addition, you can file for unemployment, and I'll not contest it."

"I know what I did was wrong, but I don't think it's fair for you to terminate me!"

"You divulged confidential information about an employee which nearly resulted in her murder, and you don't see this as a serious problem?"

"Well, would you react so if it wasn't your precious Rachel?"

"I care about all my employees, and it'd make no difference to me which one this happened to."

"I never wanted to hurt Rachel. But none of this would have happened if she had told me you two were serious about each other. She never said anything, even when I told her I was really interested in you."

"My relationship with Rachel isn't the issue here. You provided confidential information about an employee of this company, and this is why I'm firing you."

Snatching up her purse and the check, Sandy said, "Well, I may sue you for wrongful termination, Mr. Townsend! What will you do if I say you came on to me and I said no? I could say you were sexually harassing me. You were having an affair with Rachel Goodrich; the court might believe you were harassing all your female employees."

"Miss Delray, as you know we always audio tape meetings with employees we are terminating. You could find yourself in serious trouble. I think I'm justified for firing you, and I'll win if it goes into litigation."

Aaron spent the afternoon having the locks changed at the office, removing her as signor at the bank, and meeting with his staff to discuss upcoming employee changes within the company.

The rain had been freezing and torrential all day. Big droplets of water smashed against the windows at Andersen's, and from the misty windows a view of the ponderosa pines showed them swaying wildly in the wind. Around eight-thirty in the morning there was a slight reprieve from the downpour, allowing the clinic staff to shuttle Rachel from the guesthouse to the clinic. Her wheelchair left a wet trail as she was pushed down the little hallway to a tiny elevator and taken to the second floor.

Her appointments had been nonstop since she arrived except for short intervals between clients coming and going. They'd taken hair clippings from the back of her neck, the sides and top for a test they called hair tissue mineral analysis. They explained her hair samples would go to a lab and they would receive a report of the levels of toxic metals along with the mineral levels in her body. Then there was the saliva test for adrenal function. As would be expected, they drew blood, and part of it was for an assay of the vitamins in her blood stream. The specific vitamins of interest are A, B, and D. A urine test was also taken to test her iodine level.

Rachel felt like a celebrity in a way because she wasn't sure if she'd ever had that kind of a thorough checkup. She spent time with the chiropractor, who checked the alignment of her spine and gave her a cranial therapy treatment.

She's not sure if it was the cranial therapy or the oxygen treatment, but she noticed a marked difference in the way she felt. Her brain felt less fuzzy and the pain in her head was barely noticeable.

Around noon she was wheeled into the staff's break room, where she, along with some of the staff, ate a wonderful vegetable soup with sourdough bread and the best butter she'd ever tasted. One of the receptionists told her the butter was raw cultured and made from grass-fed cows. At Andersen's, most lunch and dinner meals started with sauerkraut to provide the body with enzymes to digest the food.

Thirty minutes later she's whisked away for her appointment with the neurologist. This was the way her day went, moving from one appointment to the next. The least favorite experience was with Nick—that exercise—whatever he called it. He didn't understand how difficult it was for her. The other clients seemed to love him. She didn't! How could he insist she start using a walker a few hours a day? How insensitive was that?

The final appointment of the day was with Dr. Andersen. He examined her from head to toe. He left and the nurse helped her dress and wheeled her into his office.

"Rachel, how has the day been for you?"

"Okay, I guess."

"You guess?"

"Well, everyone is so nice, the place is beautiful, and to be honest, I'm not sure if I've ever eaten food as good as it is here. I do have a problem with the exercise part."

"What's your problem with the exercise portion of your therapy?"

"I think Nick doesn't understand I was in a coma and my body doesn't work right. He thinks I should use a walker a couple of hours a day. I just don't think I'm ready for that."

"Rachel, the thing is, if you want to heal your body you're going to have to challenge yourself to make progress. Otherwise, your results will not be to the level they could be. I always tell our clients fifty percent of the effort must come from the individual. It's normal you'd feel overwhelmed. Nick is one of the best exercise physiologist's in the state of Washington. Now, I've another question for you. When did you start noticing the problem with your peripheral vision?"

"How—how did you know about that?"

"Certainly not from reading your medical records. If we're going to help you it's going to require total honesty on all of our parts."

"I think it was a few days after I became conscious. It seemed to be better after the oxygen therapy, but then a few hours later it seemed to get fuzzy again. I was afraid I might lose my eyesight. It really depresses me to think of it. I was going to mention it to the psychiatrist because I wondered if I was just imagining it because it comes and goes."

"Why didn't you tell her?"

"I just didn't feel comfortable with her. She always acted like she knew what I was thinking and she didn't know me at all."

"I'm going to arrange for an ophthalmologist to see you. In head trauma it's not uncommon to have issues with vision and many times it just clears up over time. But we do want to keep track of that. Is there anything else you need to tell me?"

"I can't think of anything. Except I will say after I had that treatment with the chiropractor—or maybe it was the oxygen therapy—my headache is so much better."

"This is good news. While you're here and even when you go home, I would encourage you to ask yourself on a daily basis, how do I feel? People are so out of touch with their bodies and they ignore all the little warning signs along the way. So whenever you try a supplement, or anything really, you need to be aware of how it affects you as an individual. I like to think of the body as the soul's transportation to be and interact in the world. Think of your body like a car. You need to maintain it; otherwise, it breaks down and leaves you stranded on the road."

She smiled and laughed, "I never thought of me as a car."

"You might want to. Your case is a little different because you were injured. But many of our clients come here for chronic illness. The signs were there a long time; they just discounted them or took pharmaceutical drugs to suppress the signals. The body is this wondrous, living, breathing, mass of energy designed to maintain homeostasis. Well, enough of my lecture for the day. I'm going to take you back to our guesthouse. Oh, one final thing. How did you like the music you listened to when the nurses assisted you with your bath last night?"

"It's really relaxing, and I've never heard anything like it before."

"It's called music therapy and it helps in traumatic brain injuries. Music and motor controls share certain circuits in the brain; therefore, it's been shown to help the brain to heal. I will not go into all the details, only to say there's been a lot of great scientific research to support neurological music therapy. So we'll have to see if it's helpful to you individually."

"That's really fascinating, Dr. Andersen."

"I thought so, too. It's helped a lot of stroke patients and people who've got Parkinson's disease. Now let's get you home before the rain starts again."

The temperature dipped to forty degrees, but the rain had stopped and all that remained were puddles of water and trees dripping water from their saturated leaves.

Back at the guesthouse Rachel was helped by Karen and Alice into another Jacuzzi bath with aromatherapy and alpha music for brain healing and relaxation. They helped her into her nightgown and robe.

"Rachel, tonight we're going to wheel you down to the dining room for dinner. Around seven o'clock, I'll conduct a ninety-minute class. I do this almost every day on various health topics. I'm not sure if Dr. Andersen told you, but part of the plan at Andersen's is to teach people the proper care and nurturing of their human body."

"Alice, no one told me about it. Do I have a choice to participate?"

"Well, if you're feeling unwell, of course you don't have to attend the class. Otherwise, no. It's part of the requirement. Didn't Dr. Andersen have you sign a personal commitment agreement?"

"No, he didn't. What's that?"

"It's kind of like a goal where the client makes a commitment to participate fully in the programs at Andersen's and in return we give you our commitment we'll be available and do everything we can to help you achieve total wellness."

"Oh, this place feels a lot like the military. You have to exercise, you have to eat sauerkraut, you have to—I don't know. Everything."

"Don't you want to get well and keep yourself fit?"

"I'm sorry, of course I do. What's the class about tonight?"

"It's on the endocrine system, and how it all works together as one unit, not separate parts."

"We have a list of core topics we cover. When our clients go home we want them to have the skills, knowledge, and tools to take responsibility for their own health. We want them to be able to separate fact from fiction. I'm not sure if you ever watch the news when they come out with all those little studies and all they do is put out confusing little tidbits of information."

"I've noticed that, and often they conflict with another story, leaving one thinking, what's up with that?"

"Exactly."

Aaron went home and called Rachel around six-thirty p.m. "Hi, Rachel. I called to see how things are going?" When she spoke, there was irritation in her voice. The whole time she'd worked for him he didn't remember her being snappish.

"Fine. I've been running from dawn to dusk, and now I've got to go to some class in a half an hour."

"Well, tell them you don't feel like it."

"No. It's a requirement. Since I came back to life there's always a requirement, something I've got to do!"

"I'm sorry you're having a stressful day."

"No one understands what I've been through. They just don't give me a break."

"I'm sorry, honey. I know it's been really hard for you."

"Aaron, how could you possibly know how I feel? You weren't married, lost a baby, been beaten senseless by an ex-spouse, and not know if they're coming back to finish the job."

"Would you rather I not call right now?"

"No. I don't mean it that way. My feelings are all jumbled up. It's not about you. It's just me and my frustration with myself."

"I know it's difficult right now, but there'll come a time when your life gets back to normal."

"I know you're right. I need to go to my class. Goodnight, Aaron. Thanks for calling me." She hung up the phone and instead of ringing for the nurse to push her back into the dining room, she shakily stood up and holding onto the bed, she carefully walked a few steps, reaching for the walker. Straightening herself as Nick had demonstrated, she began to take laborious and measured steps to the dining room for the class. She mentally took each step like a baby learning to walk. They'd said there's nothing wrong with her legs; it's all about the brain and being able to make the connections.

She felt sweat forming in her armpits, and when she arrived in the dining room her housemates clapped and cheered for her like she'd just finished the Boston Marathon.

Alice helped her into her chair. "Good job, Rachel! Now ladies and gentleman, I want you to sit up straight, and we are going to do a little guided imagery exercise before we start our class on the endocrine system. Sit up straight in your chair, take a deep breath all the way down, hold it, and now exhale. Breathe in again, hold it, and exhale. Very good!" She took them through a visual imagery of being on a park bench in the summer, feeling the sun, hearing the sound of the birds, and enjoying the smell of fresh cut grass. Each thinking of something positive in their lives and not having a care in the world. Rachel thought of her baby and what his warm skin would feel like and she visualized her baby son. Others may have thought her near-death experience was drug induced, but she knew it was real.

Alice is a great teacher and she's so funny. Rachel found herself caught up in the subject and enjoying the class. She learned things about the adrenal glands and the immune system she never knew. The class ended with a quiz and a discussion. Everyone received handouts to put in their binders. Alice said she'd get a binder for Rachel tomorrow.

Aaron thought about Rachel after he hung up. Wow, she's so frustrated and snippy. He wondered if some of it might be because she's pregnant. He remembered Meredith would get a little on edge when she was pregnant with Mike. Sometimes he'd just look at her and she'd start crying. He looked at her the wrong way, she'd say. "What's the wrong way?" he'd ask her.

Crying, she'd said, "I don't know, the wrong way. You think I'm fat and ugly."

"No, I don't," he'd say. "I think you're pregnant and beautiful." She did get better after a time. He hoped Rachel's moodiness was caused by the pregnancy. He didn't doubt it was compounded by her neurological injuries.

The phone rings. "Hello."

"Bon soir, my friend."

"Bernie, I've left you messages. Didn't you get them?"

"Yes, my life's been crazy! Those cookies are *bon,* a real smashing success!"

"Great! Are we ready to offer them in all of our stores?"

"Bon tres bon. I wanted to suggest before we do that we do a publicity campaign to get customers asking for them. We could offer the cookie in all of our Seattle and surrounding areas stores and do it like a crowd kindness thing."

"Crowd kindness?"

"That's the name I've made up for it. For one day we donate the proceeds from the sale of these cookies to help Rachel with her medical expenses, say seventy percent, and the other thirty percent to charity."

"Bernie, you know that's not a bad idea. I think we should donate the thirty percent to domestic violence programs in the Seattle area."

"Bon tres bon. How's Rachel?"

"Better, but cranky."

"Condolences, my friend. Nothing worse than the wrath of a woman." Bernie laughed with a full belly laugh—"ha ha ha."

"That's not funny, Bernie." He couldn't help but smile. He was taking the whole thing too seriously with her. He needed to lighten up and not personalize her frustration. He'd probably be just as cantankerous were he in her situation.

"Well, not funny for you my friend."

"So when will we do this crowd thing—whatever you called it?"

"Crowd Kindness. Maybe in ten days."

"First, I need to talk to Rachel and see if she wants us to do this. If she does, we can get together and work on the publicity."

"Talk to Rachel and let me know, my friend."

Aaron hung up the phone, wondering how Rachel would feel about it. She didn't want Aaron to pay her expenses and he agreed to loan her the money, so this might be a way to help her financially.

Chapter Thirty-Two

*I*t's Saturday afternoon as Aaron parked at Andersen's. Rachel told him Sonia was teaching a class during the morning and all the clients at the guesthouse were required to be in attendance. Some of their walk-in clients were also taking this class. He smiled when she told him they were going to be learning about the health benefits of lacto fermentation and how to make sauerkraut. In addition, they'd be instructed on the proper care of grains, nuts, and seeds.

Rachel was sitting on the sofa in the living room when he walked in. She was in an animated conversation with some of the women and she didn't notice him at first.

"Wow! I had no idea that grains, nuts, and seeds should be soaked to remove anti-nutrients like phytic acid. I never heard of that. But then, I've got to admit that working in the kitchen is not part of my skill set. I took some cookies to an office Christmas party and Hank chipped his tooth on one of them. I was so embarrassed. Aaron, my boss, thought it was funny. I bet if it were his tooth he wouldn't have been laughing."

The group laughed, and one of the women said, "I think this place is going to change all of our lives for the good. I guess gone are some of the convenience foods I've always liked. I wouldn't be able to look at these foods in the same way knowing many of them are made with genetically modified ingredients and rancid vegetable oils."

Rachel looked up. "Oh, Aaron, hello! I want you to meet my roommates. This is Audrey, Helen, Denise, Allan, Jill, Maria, and this is my boss, Aaron Townsend, who owns the Coffee Genie"

"Nice to meet all of you. Rachel, I was wondering if you'd like to go out for a drive."

"That really sounds good. Could you please bring my walker to me? It's sitting by the fireplace."

"Sure." Aaron walks over, picking up the aluminum walker, carrying it to Rachel and placing it in front of her. He watched her grasp the top of the walker and slowly pull herself up, straightening her body. She had her hair pulled back at the nape of the neck with a gold clasp. Her black eyes were barely noticeable, just the slightest discoloration below the right eye. The other eye had completely healed. She was dressed in navy blue sports pants with a matching sweater with a pink stripe up the side of the legs and the sleeves. She said goodbye to the others as they carefully made their way outside and walked to his car. It's a clear day and the air smells so fresh.

He helped her in the car, closing her door and placing her walker in the trunk. He climbed into the driver's seat, fastening his belt, and noticing that she had fastened hers. He put the key in the ignition and started the car. "Let me know if you're cold. I had the heater running on the way over here, so it shouldn't take long to warm back up."

"I'm fine. Thanks for getting me out. It's nice to get out of the house for a break."

They'd driven a few blocks when he said, "Rachel, I wanted to talk to you about an idea Bernie had, and I do think it's a good one. But I prefer to let you decide if you think it's something we should do at the Genie. I'm not sure if you remember that Bernie created a low-sugar cookie we've been testing in a couple of stores?"

"Yes, I remember you told me something about it. He wanted to call it the Rachel Wellness cookie."

He laughed. "Yes, that's the one. Anyway, we're thinking of doing a fundraiser to help you with your medical expenses because you didn't want to accept money from me. Bernie suggested seventy percent could go towards your medical bills and thirty percent could go to a charity for domestic violence." Glancing at her he saw her face go white. She struggled to regain her composure and he could see her trying to formulate her words.

"Aaron, I'm so touched that you and Bernie would want to help me. I just want to put this whole incident with Kenneth behind me. I feel so ashamed of what happened. I don't think I'd like the publicity. Everyone talking about me and feeling sorry for me."

"Rachel, it's okay." He reaches over and touches her hand. "I'd never do something like this without considering your feelings and talking to you first. We don't need to do this. I guess I could tell you until the cows come home what happened to you was not your fault and there's nothing to be ashamed of. But until you believe it for yourself, it's meaningless. Domestic violence is a crime. Some people think what goes on behind closed doors is a private matter. It's not, because it hurts society in the long run. Children growing up in that kind of atmosphere often learn to cope with emotions in the same way as their parents and grow up to repeat the cycle. It can never be good to live in those conditions. Often women and sometimes men suffer in silence and blame themselves. I guess it's a lot like brain-washing."

"How do you know so much about it?"

"Before I started the Coffee Genie I was an attorney in California, and I worked as a public defender for three years and dealt with a lot of these types of cases."

"I never knew that."

"There's a lot I want to tell you, and I was going to talk to you but then Hamilton attacked you. Now, I want to wait until you're better."

He always had that tone in his voice, that certain look, signaling the end of the conversation. "You could talk to me now."

"I'd rather wait until you're better. So how have things been working out at Andersen's?"

"I'm better. Why wait to tell me? Are you going to tell me you're a Jack-the-Ripper type or about some sordid life before the Coffee Genie?" She looked at him, smiling, because if there's one thing she knew, he'd never do anything illegal or anything to hurt someone else or at least not intentionally.

"Nothing like that, little one."

"You never called me little one before."

"Well, you were always petite, but being pregnant you're thinner than you were before you got hurt. Better put some meat on those bones."

"You know, Aaron, let me think about the fundraiser before I say no. It'd be nice to help other women in my situation. I want to talk to Melody about it first."

"Melody?"

"She is the psychologist at Andersen's I've been talking to."

"Oh, yes. I met her. I forgot. Talk to her and let me know."

"How are things at the office?"

"A bit chaotic. I hired a couple of new employees in the corporate office."

She swallowed. "You've replaced me already?"

"Of course not! This might not be the best time to tell you, but I fired Sandy."

"Fired her! Why?"

"Hamilton saw us in Denver and found out about our company. He called Sandy and coaxed her into giving him your address. She also rented an apartment for him in Belltown. He turned around and blackmailed her for thousands of dollars that he used to lease a jet to go to Detroit. She also threatened Stacy, and Sandy didn't tell me about any of this until I pressed her. I can't keep an employee I can't trust."

"Why did you keep this from me?"

He could hear anger creep into her voice. "I thought I'd tell you when you were better. I thought you had too much to deal with right now. Besides Rachel, this is my company." He thought, where did that little bit of anger come from? Maybe because he'd been trying to straddle the fence and not make waves, struggling to guess the right thing to do or say and feeling it was wrong even when he thought it was right.

"I know it's your company! I just wonder is there anything else involving me you think I should not know?"

"Rachel. I'm sorry if I upset you. I was just trying to consider what would be best for you."

"Don't consider!" She knew she sounded sharp, and she knew he was right to wait to tell her. "I'm sorry. I didn't mean to be like that."

"It's all right. I'm sorry, too," he said, squeezing her hand. She didn't say anything for about five minutes. They just drove through the winding roads, looking at the trees and a few hikers they passed along the way.

"It must be really hard for you at work without Sandy."

"It's been challenging without you." He smiled. "You're like my left hand. All of the employees have stepped up and helped me keep things running. Rachel, I don't want you to think badly of Sandy. She thought she was helping you. She's young, and I think she was no match for Hamilton."

"Great. You sound like my parents, nothing but criticism for Kenneth."

"Well, there's not a lot of good things to say about him, is there?"

"How would you know? You never really knew him."

"You're right. I didn't! All I know is he tried to kill you!"

"Well, maybe it was my fault; after all, I knew what he was like and I shouldn't have made him mad."

"How can you believe that?"

"I think Sandy was attracted to you and maybe that's why she did it."

"Yes. She was attracted to me. She told me that and I was shocked, as I never looked at her in that way. I told her I was old enough to be her dad. She is so not my type."

"What's your type?"

"You."

"Me?"

He pulled to the side of the road, leaned close to her and kissed her. "Yes, you."

She felt his warm lips on hers and it was electric. She felt that kiss all the way down to the pit of her stomach and down to her toes. It was like a flame igniting within her. But after a brief kiss she pulled away. There was her inner voice. How could he love you? He is only doing all this because of the baby and he feels sorry for you. No guy would ever want you because you are damaged goods. She couldn't still her inner voice. His company, that's a warning sign, isn't it? How many times did Kenneth say the money coming into the house was his? How well did she really know Aaron? He could be like Kenneth, certainly to a lesser degree. But weren't all men that way?

Aaron felt her pull away. "I'm sorry, hon."

"No. It's okay. I'm just not ready for a relationship."

"I understand. It's all right. Do you want to get something to drink?"

"No. I'm a little tired. I think I want to go back to Andersen's."

"Okay." He drove her back to Andersen's and neither of them spoke during the remainder of the drive.

Aaron helped her into the house, leaned down and kissed her cheek. "I love you, Rachel. I'll call you tomorrow, and I'll come by next Saturday."

"Thank you, Aaron. I enjoyed the drive." A feeling of guilt crept over her for being so sharp with him. She loved him. Why did they snap at each other? She couldn't remember that happening in their past relationship. But then, he was her employer and they were just friends. It all became messy when they made love in Denver. She shrugged and decided she needed to lie down to ease her headache.

Aaron's glad to be on his way home. He didn't like the way their relationship was going, and he felt unsure of what to do about it. She sounded insecure about her job and he got that. Oh, well, no sense analyzing it to death. He would go to the gym and work out. He'd not been to a gym since Rachel's hospitalization.

It was all that racquetball he played with the guys at the gym that had prepared him for the interaction he'd had with Hamilton in the hospital parking garage. Hamilton tried to deck him and it was just like dodging one of those balls. Yes. He'd been feeling tense, and a nice workout would be good.

Chapter Thirty-Three

*T*he weekend had evaporated and it was Monday again, time for another round of therapy treatments. Rachel's dreading the appointment with Melody, to be reviewing and rehashing the same old issues in her life. Melody assists her into her office and she sits on the love seat, ready to spend another hour tackling her demons.

"Good morning, Rachel. How was your weekend?"

"Frustrating in a way because of my encounter with Aaron on Saturday. We always had such a nice friendship before I got injured."

"Rachel, I want you to close your eyes and take a deep breath in. Hold it; now exhale. Take another breath in and exhale slowly. Imagine that every negative feeling is being expelled with each breath." She softly talked her through a relaxation technique, tensing and relaxing the muscles from the top of her head to her toes. "Now open your eyes. Let's explore the interaction you had with Aaron. Tell me what happened and what your thoughts were."

"I was feeling great after the class Sonia gave us on lacto fermentation. Aaron came and took me for a drive and we talked. I was upset because he and Bernie were thinking about having a fundraiser to help me with my medical expenses and to raise money for domestic violence programs in the Seattle area. I was horrified my name would be dredged up and my story would be back in the public arena and being discussed everywhere, like it was when Kenneth attacked me."

"What's the feeling?"

"Shame and embarrassment."

They went into a role-play. Melody became Rachel and Rachel became Melody. They talked for nearly twenty minutes and the bad feelings dissipated.

"You must get tired of me covering the same old feelings and the same old topics."

"Not in the least. It takes what it takes and however long it takes. Some of these feelings you have are deep-seated and have been around for a very long time and resurfaced when Kenneth appeared on your doorstep. When you're ready to let go, you will. Have you thought about what your decision will be regarding the fundraiser?"

"I'm going to tell Aaron yes, if they'll do fifty percent to charity and the remaining fifty percent for my medical bills. My insurance covered most of my hospital bills but it didn't cover everything. It'll help a lot. I was thinking maybe I'm never going to get better if I don't accept my past and be willing to let others help me."

"Sometimes acceptance can be the first stage to recovery. I'm not sure if you ever heard of the serenity prayer in Alcoholics Anonymous, but part of the prayer is, God grant me the serenity to accept the things I cannot change, the courage to change the things I can, and the wisdom to know the difference. This could be a healing step for you.

"Well, Rachel our time is about up for today. I want you to start keeping a journal for yourself. You can write anything you like in it. It's for your eyes only. I started journaling when I was in graduate school. I call it my paper psychiatrist because it can really help you sort out what's going on in your life." Melody handed her a spiral notebook. "This is your assignment."

Rachel smiled. "Thank you for helping me. It seems everyone at Andersen's gives me homework assignments."

"That we do."

In between appointments Rachel called Aaron and told him she'd decided they could do the fundraiser if fifty percent would go to domestic violence as well as any money left over after covering her medical expenses. He'd been in a hurry but said he'd get with Bernie and set it up. She thanked him and told him she appreciated their help.

Chapter Thirty-Four

*T*en days had sped by and the Crowd Kindness Day had been advertised all over Seattle. The phone had been ringing off the hook at the Coffee Genie, and they'd hired extra staffing to help cover all of the coffee shops. But at last, it's all over.

Aaron's feet hurt and he wasn't sure when he'd worked so hard. The fundraiser for Rachel had been a tremendous success. They'd had balloons for the children and all of the Coffee Genie's in the Seattle area were overflowing with people. He traveled around to most of his coffee shops, helped make coffee and also rang people up at the register. Their cus-tomers were caring and some made donations in addition to buying the cookies. It would be a few days before all of the money raised could be tallied. The comments on the cookies were mixed, some really liked them yet others compared them to eating a dog biscuit. There were enough likes to make the cookie a permanent offering at the Coffee Genie.

Rachel seemed happy when he told her the turnout had been fantastic. Some of the regular customers also dropped off get well cards for her. She seemed touched by all the caring people who came to help.

He couldn't quite put his finger on it but their relationship seemed a bit strained. Maybe he was just tired, possibly working too hard, or trying to help her too much. He wasn't sure, but for some reason he felt walled out of her life. He reasoned, don't read too much into it; be careful about being pushy; back off; let her indicate where she wants the relationship to go.

He thought about the baby and wished things were different. He never dreamed he'd have the opportunity to be a dad again, and he really wanted this baby. But would he be a dad with visitation rights? Or one without any rights? He brushed tears from the corner of his eyes. Why didn't he ask her to marry him that night in Denver? He wondered why in relationships he seemed to regret things he did or things he didn't say? Was he destined to make the same kinds of mistakes over and over again?

Chapter Thirty-Five

When Alice arrived at work on the Monday of Thanksgiving week for her four-to-midnight shift, Karen asked to speak with her in the office the nurses shared on the second floor. Karen advised her that two of their clients went home on Saturday and two on Sunday, which she knew was the plan. Three of the clients were leaving tomorrow, and Rachel would be going to Aaron Townsend's home on Wednesday afternoon and return Sunday afternoon.

"The real item of concern, Alice, that you need to know about is that a car was seen slowly driving up and down the street and stopping in front of Andersen's. Celeste, the weekend four-to-midnight nurse, said she observed a suspicious car on Saturday night around eight p.m. At the time she was in the office, straightening the supplement cabinet and happened to be looking out the window. She noticed a car driving by very slowly and stopping in front of Andersen's. The car made several trips up and down the street."

"What did she do? Do you think it was Rachel's ex-husband?"

"No one knows if it has anything to do with Rachel or not. Celeste called Dr. Andersen and he called the security company, who in turn contacted the police department. Other neighbors had noticed it as well and also called the police."

"Did they find the person driving in front of our clinic?"

"No, when the police arrived the car had disappeared. Celeste said it happened again on Sunday night around seven p.m. One of the clients noticed it and told her. The police were contacted again. So the police will be patrolling the area more."

"Am I supposed to do anything special?"

"No, just be aware of anything unusual. Make sure all of the doors are locked and the alarm is set and that we don't have any open windows. I also wouldn't talk about it too much with the clients because we want to keep everyone safe but we don't want to instill fear or create stress for them."

"I agree. Thanks for the information, Karen."

Alice gave her class on vitamins and minerals and in which foods they can be found. She gave them spreadsheets showing the role of these nutrients in the body as well as the physical problems when there is a deficiency. The clients didn't know about Vitamin F and that a deficiency may cause eczema, hair loss, kidney, liver, and heart disease to name a few. This vitamin can be found in foods such as flax seed, walnuts, salmon, crude pumpkin oil, and many other foods. She gave them a match sheet and they worked as a group to complete the assignment. The clients were really interested in this class and they had some great discussions.

After the class, everyone had a cup of tea and talked about Thanksgiving and how nice it was going to be to be back with their friends and family. Around nine thirty, everyone went to their rooms to settle in for the night.

Alice made her rounds, checking that everything was locked up, setting the alarm system, and turning out lights. She needed to finish the inventory Celeste started on Saturday and prepare a list of supplies the guesthouse needed. She also had to prepare individualized vitamin packs for the clients leaving tomorrow.

The guesthouse was quiet and it was nearly eleven thirty p.m. She thought, where did the night go? In a half an hour Dawn would be here to take over.

Suddenly, she looked at the monitor on the desk and noticed that the silent alarm had been tripped. She sat down at the desk and started moving the screen around and realized that the sensor lights on the patio side had turned on.

She hit the button to connect with their security company. "I'm Alice Nielson, the four-to-midnight nurse at Andersen's. The silent alarm went off and the back patio lights have turned on. This is not a false alarm! Someone's out there!"

"Ms. Nielson, we've notified the police and they're on their way. Are your doors locked? Do you know if someone has gotten into the house?"

"This is a big house. I can't say for sure, but I didn't hear anything. Wait! One of our clients whose room is downstairs has pushed her call button. I need to get to her! Get someone over here now!"

"Just remain calm and stay on the line."

"I can't stay on the line; my client needs me."

She hangs up the phone and races down the stairs to find Rachel rolled up in a fetal position in her bed sobbing hysterically. "Rachel, Rachel, I'm here with you and you're safe!"

"The lights came on and someone's shadow moved past the window! I know it's Kenneth. He has come to kill me! I knew he would come back. It was just a matter of when!"

"The police have been called to investigate." Alice said as she put her arms around Rachel to sooth her. "You know we had this happen a couple of summers ago, and you know what it was?"

"No."

"It was a neighbor's Doberman Pinscher that had gotten out of his yard and came onto our patio. Turns out he had a passion for snow peas and he stole some out of our garden before the police busted him. It did scare us, but later we had a good laugh over it."

"Really?"

"Yes, really. The police will be here soon, so let's just wait and see what they find."

Rachel stopped crying and Alice brought her into the living room and was making her some chamomile tea when Dawn arrived, along with two squad cars.

The police did not find anyone and they looked at the recordings made by the cameras on the patio. The image appeared to be a man, but it was too fuzzy. They took the film back to the precinct to see if it could be enhanced.

The nurses talked to Rachel until she calmed down and then she returned to bed and slept for the remainder of the night.

Chapter Thirty-Six

Rachel found it hard to believe that she had been at Andersen's almost a month. The days seemed to blend one day into the next and evaporate. That is until that frightening experience on Monday night, and now the hours drag by and she wants to leave for the Thanksgiving holiday.

Two weeks ago, Saturday, Aaron came by to visit and picked up the rented wheelchair and returned it to the medical supply place. Last week the walker was also returned, as she's now only using a support cane. The black eyes, fractured ribs, and other wounds were completely healed. Her broken nose was a little askew and everyone said they barely noticed it. She noticed it, and she no longer felt pretty—if she ever did. She had felt attractive when Aaron had encouraged her to experiment with clothes and makeup. She sighed. That's a time of the past and she couldn't ever get it back.

The baby in her stomach was growing, and the obstetrician Andersen's took her to see seemed kind and positive. Dr. Andersen completely agreed with Dr. Ivan Ingram's choice of baby vitamins. The baby was the driving force to work with Nick. He wasn't a bad guy after all. It was harder in the beginning and her frustration and impatience spilled out easily.

Her emotions had not been fully resolved. She'd worked with Melody three days a week. She talked to Kenneth in empty chairs, beaten the sofa cushion, wrote letters and burned them in coffee cans, and she'd taken plenty of guided imagery trips. She'd walk out of Melody's office thinking today she'd experienced catharsis only later to see old feelings seeping back into her consciousness, like trying to rid a kitchen of a colony of ants. It seemed like the ant baits are working and there aren't any ants for a few days. Suddenly there they are, a surge of ants crawling up the cabinetry all over the counter tops. So it was with her feelings. Things were good and then a word or a thought and her feelings would swell up and she was back to the beginning like a never-ending loop.

Besides, working with Melody she'd learned so much about the body during her stay here. The health topics were fascinating. It surprised her to learn how much the gut influences the brain. Alice had said, "It's called the enteric system and it plays a role in serotonin regulation. Seventy percent of the immune system is connected with the gut bacteria-controlling invaders." She just never knew that much about her body. Maybe the major thing she learned was when she was entering puberty and the school showed the girls some videos and they were given a little booklet called *Now You are Ten.*

She'd have preferred to keep being battered and raped a private matter, but now everyone in Seattle probably knew about it. She loved Aaron and she'd always love him. It wouldn't be real love on his part. He could have any woman he wanted and someone without any emotional baggage from the past. He was sweet, caring, and so good-looking. She played it over in her mind many times what she'd do when she left Andersen's and she still wasn't sure. She's also afraid of Kenneth and it doesn't help that he's still at large. In fact, she is certain he was the one who was at the guesthouse on Monday night. The thought makes her shiver. Aaron would be there to get her within the hour, as Andersen's would be closing for the Thanksgiving holiday. She felt so safe with him, and she needed that. It is her first time in almost two months staying somewhere outside of a medical facility.

Aaron had invited her parents for the weekend. Bernie and his partner, Trae, were also spending the weekend. Bernie and Trae were preparing Thanksgiving dinner for everyone. Aaron said Stacy and her boyfriend, Dennis, would be alone for the holiday and Rachel agreed that Aaron should invite them for dinner. It felt good and reminded her of the times she and Aaron had entertained some of their coffee growers for a weekend.

Aaron insisted she call her parents and tell them that Bernie's gay. She knew it wasn't necessary to call her parents, but she did it to put Aaron at ease. He had this Victorian image of her mother, which was mostly right, but not totally. Her mother said, "How silly to call me about that. You know, your Dad and I look at people who are gay like a physical characteristic. Some people are fat, thin, tall, short, and some people are gay. We all have our own personal preferences. Some prefer blondes, some brunettes, and some prefer the same sex. Big deal. There are lots of gay people in San Francisco."

She told him what her mother said and her response made him happy. He's very close to Bernie and while he preferred the female gender, the fact that Bernie's gay was irrelevant to him. He really had an open viewpoint on people. He didn't care about the color of your skin, if you were fat, thin, disabled, or gay. If you had a positive attitude and a good work ethic, he'd hire you. There was no denying they had to make a profit to stay in business. He often told her, "The Coffee Genie, for me, was never really about making money so much as it's about people and spreading around some kindness and living right in the world."

The guesthouse was nearly empty when Aaron rang the doorbell. He came in and stooping, he kissed her on the cheek. She was sitting in the chair near the living room fireplace and looking out at the trees. She's thinking, what a beautiful house this is. Sometimes they lit the fireplace and it was so relaxing watching the flames dance and flicker. It has one of the biggest fireplaces she'd ever seen. It shares one entire wall with the door that enters into the dining room.

"Are you ready, Rachel?"

"Yes. My suitcase is in the bedroom. Could we go by my apartment so I can pick up my laptop and a few things?"

"Sure. I don't see why not. Trae offered to go and meet your parents at the airport, so we have plenty of time."

"That's great. Where's Bernie?"

"At my house making apple and pumpkin pie. He's all ecstatic because he got a great deal on some fresh organic leaf lard."

"I bet your house smells like heaven!"

"Yes. Anything Bernie bakes is good. We were able to get a pasture-raised turkey. We should all be able to eat ourselves silly."

They drove through downtown Seattle. "Can you believe they already have Christmas decorations up?"

"Yes. I was seeing Christmas decorations before Halloween."

They drove past supermarket parking lots packed with cars. Aaron remembered plenty of times he'd gone to the market the day before Thanksgiving, buying take out for a private celebration of the day with just himself and the television set. Especially when he first moved here and didn't know anyone. There's nothing like lonely during the holidays, when you see everyone running around planning for guests. Christmas's were equally dismal when he'd see things in the store windows he knew Mike or Meredith would like.

"A penny for your thoughts."

"Ah, me. I was just thinking how wonderful this Thanksgiving will be. I've got a house full of guests, and most importantly, you'll be there."

"It's so nice of you to invite me and my parents."

There was disappointment in her response. Why couldn't she say, Aaron, oh Aaron, I love you, and I'm so happy we're together with our future baby. "You're welcome, Rachel."

She bit her lip. What she said came off cold and distant. She saw his expression change to sadness and she was so sorry she hadn't found something better to say. She didn't want to lead him on. Let him think the wrong thing, that she'd be willing to marry him, work things out for the baby, or do the right thing. Behind it all, isn't that what he really thought.

"Will going into your apartment be traumatic for you? If you give me a list, I could get the things you want."

"I've thought about what my reaction would be. I think if I was attacked by a stranger it might be harder. What Kenneth did to me was kind of the same old, same old. Well, he never quite took it to that level. So I think I can handle it. At some point I've got to go there. I can't stay at Andersen's forever."

"I can't imagine what it must've been like living in a repressive environment the way you did. I'm sure Monday night was hard, too, when you thought he was trying to break into the guesthouse."

"I don't want to think about Monday. I still feel afraid. You know, after all these years it's still hard to talk about my life with Kenneth. I guess I played a role in it, allowing it to go on. What is it they say, hindsight is twenty-twenty. I should've left him the first time he pushed me. I just got all wrapped up in what Melody called random reinforcement. Battering is a cycle. There's the honeymoon phase where he's all apologetic and then things escalate, ending in abuse. The cycle repeats over and over again. Each time the abuse is a little worse and the duration between attacks becomes shorter. We'd never have divorced if he hadn't forced me to sign the papers."

"I'm sorry that happened to you. I hope you know not all men are like your ex-husband. Sure, there are a lot of his type out there. I hope you know I'm not in that category. I also want you to feel safe with me."

"I know you aren't the type. I admire you for the kind of person you are. This sounds so depressing, and it is Thanksgiving. Why don't we talk about something upbeat?" She smiled. "Sometimes talking to you is like talking to my therapist."

"I'm in no way a therapist. I'm your friend, and I'd like to be more if you'd let me." He saw her turn her head, watching the traffic and he knew that once again he'd gone too far. They finished the drive to the apartment, neither saying anything else. Parking close to the curb and getting out and opening her car door, he asked, "Do you want me to go with you?"

"I don't think so. Oh, do you have my keys?"

"Yes, I nearly forgot." He'd been picking up her mail and checking her apartment after her parents returned to Hayward.

"I'll just be a minute."

"Okay." He stands by the car, waiting for her.

She went up the stairs and into the building. She stopped and took a deep breath, unlocking the door and walking in. All the evidence of her Friday night with Kenneth had been erased from the scene. The table stood empty where the lamp once sat. Walking across the living room into the bedroom she saw that the bed was made up with a new ensemble. The place was spotlessly clean. Bits and pieces of the night flashed in her mind and tears formed in her eyes. This had been her retreat and it would never be the same again.

Grabbing a small weekender bag from the bottom of her closet, she picked out a blue dress and some black, flat shoes. She wasn't ready for heels. She laid these items on her bed and unzipping the suitcase, she places the dress and shoes inside. She opened the dresser drawer, found a bra that worked with the dress, a slip, and some panty hose. She hadn't worn her favorite chocolate perfume since that fateful Friday, so she threw some into her cosmetic bag, along with foundation and a few things. She turns back to the bed and leans over, adding these items on top of the others.

As she added the last item, her cosmetics, she was startled by the feel of a hand on her shoulder. She straighten-ed and turned, seeing Kenneth in his police uniform. He is young, like when he was a new rookie on the Lincoln Police Force. He looked so tall and slender and his smile was alluring. She felt faint as terror spread across her face. She blinked, and he was gone. Did she imagine it? Maybe this was just too much for her. She grabbed her suitcase and laptop; she had to get out of there!

Aaron rushed up the stairs to take her bag and help her down the steps. She's doing so well. He wondered if the outcome would've been the same in a convalescent home. He doubted it. They were meticulous with her diet. She could've never gotten this kind of help somewhere else. When he got closer he noticed the color seemed to have drained from her face. "You look pale like you just saw a ghost. Are you feeling okay?"

"It felt like I did see a ghost. I thought I saw Kenneth but then he vanished. I guess going to the apartment was a little more traumatic then I thought it would be."

"This is your first time back at the apartment, so it is understandable you could have an emotional reaction. Are you ready?"

"Yes."

Looking at his watch, he said, "Trae should be at the airport right about now and Bernie should be up to his hips in cooking."

For the remainder of the drive they talked about places they'd been to, about the business, and they laughed about some of their experiences. Some were not funny but developed a humorous aspect over time, similar to the aging of a great wine. "Do you remember when we were trying to kill time in Chiapas, Mexico when we were going to try some food from a street vendor?" Aaron asked. "You'd just touched a tortilla to your lips when we finally comprehended that the filling was made up of giant ants. You almost wretched right there on the spot."

"Yes. You bent over laughing and I was just sick." She laughed. "I'm not sure we ever bought anything else from a street vendor again. You paid anyway and you were so diplomatic. We walked away with our food and chucked it once we were out of sight of the vendor."

Aaron chuckled. "I thought you would turn green, you looked so sick. You never quite trusted the food in Mexico again, did you?"

"Well, I did, but let's say cautiously."

"Admit it, you didn't. When we were in Mexico I saw the way you always played and picked at your food."

"Well, I'm just squeamish about insects and quite grossed out at the idea of eating them."

"They're a delicacy in many parts of the world. What's the word your Aunt uses a lot? Oh yes, stuffy. Don't be stuffy." He laughed.

She laughed, too, It was like the way they were before the attack. She loved the way he teased her. It's so comfortable the way they could just talk about anything. Why did this whole thing with Kenneth have to happen and ruin it for her? Stuffy, yah; she gets that from Gram. Gram was always, "this is stuffy, that's stuffy."

"I kind of thought it might be part of the family DNA, although I can't say I've ever heard you use the stuffy word very much."

"I guess I don't. Maybe I should start."

"No. Don't change anything about you. I love you just as you are."

They didn't say anything for a few minutes.

"Aaron, do you remember when we rented that Harley motorcycle to drive out to see one of the growers in Mexico."

"Sure do. It seemed like my mouth was gritty from the dirt for a week."

"I was nervous, but I rode on the back of the bike and you know when we took that drive I just felt so safe with you. It was a dirty ride, but wasn't the scenery so beautiful. Remember how we stopped on the way back just to look at the sunset."

"It was nice, wasn't it? The way things are in Mexico, I no longer feel comfortable going there. It's nice to invite some of the coffee growers or brokers here."

He turned down his street and parked the car in the driveway. "Rachel, I'll get your suitcase. I thought you could have the bedroom across from mine on the main floor. I'm putting your parents upstairs, along with Bernie and Trae. I thought it'd be easier so you wouldn't have to go up a lot of steps."

"Sure. That sounds fine."

"I'm sure Bernie's in the kitchen if you want to go and see him."

Bernie stood over the kitchen stove with his big white hat and one of the biggest whisks she'd ever seen. "Hi, Bernie. What are you making?"

Pushing the double boiler from the burner he turns and stretches out his arms. "Rachel, *cela fait plaisir de te voir!*"

"Bernie, it's nice to see you, too! I've missed you! What are you making?"

"Crème brûlée—your favorite."

"It is, and I especially love the burnt sugar on top."

Bernie turned back to the stove and returned the double boiler to the burner, whisking the contents in the pot.

Aaron came into the kitchen after leaving Rachel's things in her bedroom. "Bernie, this is going to be the best Thanksgiving."

"My friend, it will be. But you are probably going to have dishpan hands because a fine chef like me doesn't do dishes." He laughed.

"No problem, Bernie. I can keep up; just try me."

Bernie continued preparations for the evening and the Thanksgiving meal while Rachel and Aaron sat at the breakfast bar, talking to him and watching him. The aroma of baked apple pie with cinnamon permeated the house. He'd also made pumpkin, which looked almost too beautiful to eat. The crust on both was a beautiful, golden brown with fancy crimped edges. He gave Rachel a small demitasse cup of crème brûlée. He and Aaron sipped on red wine.

They hear a car pull up in the driveway and park. Aaron and Rachel walk outside to greet Trae and her parents. The luggage is carried upstairs while Rachel walks her parents into the kitchen, talking non-stop. "How was your flight?"

"Choppy, but good."

"Rachel, honey, you look wonderful!" her dad said as he hugs her.

Her mom kisses her on her cheek. "You look radiant and pregnant. Wow! This place smells yummy."

Bernie pours her parents a glass of wine and offers them some hors d'oeuvres—little pastries made with brie cheese, some sliced strawberries, and a plate with small pieces of homemade French bread and liver pate.

The weekend was relaxed and dreamy. It was as if Stanley and Susan had known Bernie and Trae all of their lives. Aaron fussed over everyone, asking to refill their glasses or if he could get them something else. The place emanated with warmth, caring, love, and laughter. The outside world didn't exist for them and they opted to not watch any news, just to be here now, in this space, in this time.

Wednesday night everyone felt so full from snacking, and Bernie had made the right decision to serve spinach quiche, steamed broccoli, a tossed salad, and berries for desert.

Thanksgiving afternoon Stacy and Dennis came to dinner and brought a plate of cookies and a bottle of wine. They, too, melded right into the group.

They sat down to Thanksgiving dinner at around three-thirty in the afternoon. Trae had decorated the table with tall, red candles in crystal holders and a white lace tablecloth. A floral arrangement of fall foliage was in the center of the table with miniature pumpkins and orange carnations. The bone china was Royal Dalton Country Roses, which had belonged to Aaron's mother. The plates were stunning, with the gold edging and a deep red rose pattern contrasting with the white and gold trim. Stanley said grace. White and red wines were uncorked, swirled, and sniffed. Trae poured each guest a glass of their choice, except Rachel, who he handed a wine glass of cranberry juice. The table was pretty quiet as they feasted on turkey, stuffing, mashed potatoes, steamed asparagus and apple salad. Everyone agreed it was the best meal they'd remembered having.

Towards the end of the meal Aaron suggested they go around the table and everyone share a few things they are thankful for. Aaron started giving thanks for Rachel's recovery, her wonderful parents, and the best staff on the planet. Everyone expressed thankfulness for Rachel's improvement. Bernie was thankful that most people didn't look at his Rachel Wellness cookies as tasting like dog biscuits. Although he thought he might be able to make a dog biscuit for people who brought their dogs to the Coffee Genie. Aaron laughed and said no dogs at the Coffee Genie. Can you just imagine what the health department would do with that one. They all laughed. Dennis was thankful for Stacy and lifted her hand to show off her engagement ring, as he'd recently popped the question. Trae was thankful for Bernie. Rachel's parents were thankful for their future grandbaby. Rachel was thankful for them all and for their help and love.

Bernie served desert and coffee a couple of hours later. The final cleanup was completed and Trae brought out a stack of poker chips and asked if anyone would like to play poker. Everyone agreed and gathered around the dining room table, and by popular vote they played Texas Hold'em. The blind bid was made prior to dealing each player their two cards. They had laughed and challenged each other. Stanley beat the pants off of all of them, pulling all of the chips in the middle toward him, which was then converted to forty-two dollars in cash. Dennis yawned. It's nearly midnight and he needed to get Stacy home before he fell asleep at the wheel.

Stacy hugged Rachel goodbye. "We miss you at the office. I'm so glad you're better."

"Thank you, Stacy. I miss everyone at work, too. You and Dennis drive safely home."

Stacy yawned. "I'll keep him awake."

She hugged the other house guests goodnight and they went upstairs to their rooms.

Aaron patted the sofa cushion beside him. "Would you like to just talk for a few minutes before turning in?"

"Hmm, that sounds good. I love your fireplace and the marble mantle."

"Thank you. I think looking at a burning fire is so relaxing. Did you have a nice time, Rachel?"

"It was wonderful. It seems you and I always have such nice times when we're together. I don't think Kenneth and I ever shared a Thanksgiving like this with my parents. It's so wonderful—and Bernie, I just love him."

"Yes. I think a lot of Bernie. His cooking is just over the top." He put his arm around her. She turned her head, seeing the contentment in his eyes.

He kissed her on the cheek and then her lips. "You look so pretty in that blue dress."

"Thank you. It's the first dress I've worn in a couple of months."

He kisses her again and pulls her closer to him. "I love you, Rachel." He felt her stiffen. "Rachel, I need to talk to you about me and my life and we need to talk about us."

She pulled away. "Don't spoil the day, Aaron. I know a lot about you, and well, I think too many things have happened for us to be together."

He moved away from her like being burned by a match. "Rachel, please tell me why you always seem to pull away from me."

"In Denver, well, that was an accident and you realized it yourself; that's why you sent me back to Seattle. And now, well, I'm disfigured."

"You couldn't be more wrong about Denver. I've just been waiting for the right time when you're better to talk to you about it. How can you say you're disfigured?"

"Aaron, I love you, and you're the best man I've ever known, but I'm just not ready to be in a relationship. You could have any woman you wanted. Why would you want someone whose nose is not straight and who has scarring?"

"I don't care about that; I love you and our baby."

"No. You think you do, but you don't," she snapped. "I'm tired and I want to go to bed."

"Rachel, I'm sorry."

"We've been having such a wonderful time; let's not talk about us and ruin it."

"Okay, I'm sorry."

She softened. "Look, I adore you but I'm just not ready." She stood up and reached over and hugged him. "Come on. Put out the fire and let's go to bed." She took his hand and he got up out of his chair. They hugged goodnight and she went to her room.

He extinguished the fire and pledged he'd give her the space she needed and to keep the holiday experience from being tarnished by her rejection of him. He hoped things could work out. He felt like she had all of the power and he was willing to jump through any hurdle if she let him know what she wanted. Maybe the more you run after someone, the more they keep running away.

On black Friday they all decided to play a few rounds of golf instead of being part of the mobs at the stores. After golf, they went to a seafood restaurant at Pike's Market. They had a nice table with a view of the bay.

Too soon the weekend was coming to a close and they each had to face the world again. But because of their time together, they decided it was a much nicer place to be alive in.

Sunday afternoon the excess food was boxed for Trae and Bernie to deliver to a homeless shelter for veterans.

Aaron and Rachel dropped her parents at the airport and then he drove her to Mercer Island to begin another week at Andersen's.

Chapter Thirty-Seven

*R*achel continued to progress, and she'd be leaving Andersen's in two more weeks. What did she want to do with the rest of her life? Aaron hadn't mentioned the word love since Thanksgiving night, and he respected her space and kept their conversations courteous, friendly and polite.

She wanted a fresh start to move some place where no one knows her and where Kenneth couldn't find her. A nice little community where she could raise her son.

Thanks to the fundraiser almost all of her medical expenses had been covered, allowing her to keep her savings and roll it over. Aaron had continued to deposit her salary all these weeks. He told her it was her unused sick and annual leave. But she knew that should've run out a few weeks back.

Anyone else would've snatched the moment and married him, no matter what his intentions were. The last twelve years she'd been her own person. She made the bed if she wanted to; she went out to eat if she didn't want to cook; she could watch whatever she wanted to on TV. There was a part of her that liked being free and not being responsible to anyone. Her money was her money to spend as she pleased. She could buy a new dress if she wanted one. It would be hard to give up her independence, especially if she wasn't the most special woman on the planet to her mate. There wasn't any doubt she loved him, but she knew he couldn't possibly feel the same. She envisioned when their son was two they'd start having disagreements and fighting with each other.

She called her mother. "Hi, Mom. How are you and Daddy doing?"

"We're fine, honey. Your dad is out playing golf with some of his friends and I just finished repotting some of my African violets. How are you and your therapies going?"

"My therapies are going well. I rode a mile on the stationary bike. Those balancing exercises that I do with Nick has really helped my equilibrium. I'll be leaving Andersen's in two weeks, and I wanted to tell you I've decided to move to Boulder, Colorado."

"Rachel, are you sure? I thought you'd go back to work for Aaron."

"It's complicated Mom. I think Aaron probably wants to marry me. He hasn't actually said that, but he keeps saying he loves me, and well, I just don't want that."

"I'm surprised, Rachel. I thought you were quite fond of him."

"I do love him, and if all this hadn't happened with Kenneth—well, who knows. But I'm not convinced he loves me in the way I love him. He's a decent man and I think he'd offer to marry me for the baby or because he felt sorry for me."

"I think you've got it all wrong about him. I think he loves you very much, honey, and I think you should talk to him and let him tell you about his life."

"His life?"

"Well, I just think there's a lot you don't know about him and it might change your mind if you did."

"What do you know about Aaron?"

"I'm just saying you should talk to him. Besides, Rachel, if you're going to leave Seattle, why don't you come home?"

"Mom, I know you and Daddy would let me come home, but I'm thirty-eight, and I need to be on my own."

"But Rachel, what do you know about Boulder? Why would you go there?"

"When we were opening one of Aaron's coffee shops in Denver, we drove around the area. I loved Boulder. It's in the foothills of the Rocky Mountains. The sun shines about three hundred days out of the year. They have a university and their schools are some of the top in the nation. They have hiking and biking trails. The other thing is a lot of high tech jobs are located in the area."

"That sounds nice, honey, but you'll be so far away. You don't want to be trying to settle into a new location when you're pregnant."

"I thought about it, Mom, but I think it'd be easier before the baby's born and while I'm not too far along in my pregnancy."

"When you were in the hospital I realized maybe none of this would have happened to you if we had not tried to keep you and Kenneth apart when you were kids. I vowed I'd let you live your own life and not meddle in your affairs. Honey, I just think you need to reconsider this idea. Do you want this baby to grow up without a father?"

"I've thought about that; I honestly have. I just keep coming back to a child needs a stable environment with two loving parents. If the parents don't get along, then it's just as bad for a child. Look what happened to Kenneth."

"I think Aaron seems like a very stable guy, and I can't imagine him not getting along with you."

"Well, maybe he is, but you never really know a person until you marry them. I don't want to start out in a marriage where I'm pregnant and he's trying to do the moral right thing. Love's important to me."

"I think you should at least talk to him before you make all these plans."

"Mom, I almost feel like you're on his side."

"I'm not taking sides. But it isn't nice moving halfway across the country and preventing him from seeing his baby."

"He could have any woman he wanted; haven't you noticed how drop dead handsome he is?"

"Yes. He is good looking, but dear, he doesn't want just any woman, he wants you!"

"Mom, I'm not pretty enough for him. No, he would only come to resent me and I don't want a relationship like that. After Kenneth, I never trusted my ability to select the right man to be in a relationship with. That's why I've been single all these years. I never trusted men."

"You don't trust Aaron?"

"Well, of course I do! He's different! I'm not moving away because I don't trust him. I'm doing it because it is the best thing to do for him."

"Rachel, that doesn't make sense to me. On the one hand you love and you trust him, but on the other hand you don't know if he'd change if you were married. Do you see what a conflict that is?"

"I think you don't understand me."

"I don't think you understand yourself. Right now, you don't feel attractive. Maybe it's hard to feel attractive when you're pregnant or when you've been through what you've been through. I've seen the way Aaron looks at you, and it isn't pity. Are you crying?"

"Hold on, I need to find a tissue." She came back on the phone. "I love you, Mom. I just have to do what's right for me and for my baby."

"I know that, honey. Do you need some money?"

"No. I have a reasonable amount in savings to help me until I get established. Like I said, they've got a lot of high tech jobs in Boulder. I'm sure I could find something, and I've been looking online."

"Why don't you wait until after the Chanukkah and the Christmas holidays?"

"I want to get settled before I'm too far along in my pregnancy. But I'll come and stay with you and Daddy for the holidays."

"That'd be nice. All I ask, honey, is that you think about it and at least talk to Aaron."

"I've got to go Mom. It's time to see my chiropractor."

"All right, honey. Call me later, okay?"

"I love you, Mom."

"I love you, too."

Chapter Thirty-Eight

Aaron was sitting at his desk, checking his agenda for the day, when Stacy buzzes him, telling him he has a call on line one from Gerald Herschel.

"This is Aaron Townsend."

"Hi, Aaron. I thought you'd be the best person to contact. We'll be closing Rachel's case. A detective in Detroit called me about twenty minutes ago. Kenneth Hamilton was found murdered in Detroit, and they've finally identified his body through his dental records."

"What on earth happened to him?"

"Well, you know the money he blackmailed your office manager for was used to lease a Lear jet to fly to Detroit. He was also the one who robbed Seacoast Bank and Trust."

"Yes, I'd heard about that."

"So who murdered him?"

"He was in some bar in downtown Detroit the night after he left Seattle. A gang member by the name of Sparkie was choking the bartender and he went to his defense and pulled out his thirty-eight-caliber gun. He was pretty drunk when he left the bar and they were waiting for him. I guess he did manage to kill Sparkie and another one of the gang members. The detective from Detroit told me Sparkie was extremely violent. They found them in the alley behind the bar the next day. Hamilton was partially burned and all of his identification had been removed."

"That's awful. Why did it take so long for the police to identify him?"

"Well, Detroit's bankrupt, and they don't have enough forensic specialists to handle all of the cases. They had to keep the body in cold storage while they waited for the information to come back and for his case to come up for review. Detroit is contacting his next of kin, which is his brother. Rachel's never going to have to be afraid of him again."

"I know, but no one would've wanted to see this happen either. She had a child with him, and no matter what he did, I don't imagine this is going to be easy for her."

"Maybe not, but at least she's not going to be dragged through a trial either."

"Give her and her parents my best."

"Thanks."

Hanging up the phone, he sits there a couple of minutes, thinking how awful that must've been for Hamilton. He had died violently, the same way he had treated Rachel. He did want him punished but he'd never have wished for him to be killed. How was he going to tell her?

Aaron called her mother, and she thought it was best for her to call Melody, Rachel's psychologist, and for the two of them to tell Rachel about his death. Her mom had told him, "Even though Rachel has been divorced from Kenneth for twelve years, there is no denying they had a history together.

They lost a daughter and probably knew some of the most private and intimate things about each other. I have no doubt it will be hard for her to hear of his death."

"Rachel, I called you into my office because I have your mother on the telephone and we have some information about your ex-husband. Mrs. Goodrich, your daughter is here with me if you would like to continue."

"Darling, Kenneth was murdered in Detroit the day after he left Seattle. Detroit is backlogged on cases and they had to get his dental records to identify him."

"No! That can't be what happened?"

"Honey, he was at a bar and was intoxicated. A gang member was choking a bartender and he defended the man. When he went outside they were waiting for him and they killed him."

"No! You've got to be mistaken!"

"No, honey. Gerald Hershel called Aaron about a half hour ago."

"Why didn't they take his fingerprints instead of the dental records? Dental records always take longer."

"Rachel, I'm sorry to have to say this. He was partially burned."

Sobs wracked her body and tears flowed like a dam bursting. "It's my fault. All my fault!"

"No, it isn't," her mom said. "He did a heroic thing helping that bartender, but Kenneth was his own worst enemy."

"No, if I would've been nicer to him maybe he wouldn't have attacked me and all of this would've never happened!"

"Rachel, you did absolutely nothing wrong!" her mother said.

"I know you and Daddy never liked him. You didn't know about the good things about him. I—I just want some time by myself if you don't mind," she said, sobbing.

"I understand. But if you want to talk to me, honey, please call me."

Melody asked the receptionist to reschedule appointments with their residential clients and to advise her three o'clock appointment that she might be a little late. She stayed with Rachel, trying to help her process her ex-husband's death.

Chapter Thirty-Nine

*K*enneth had been hovering near the refrigerated drawer in the Detroit Morgue where his remains were housed. It seemed he would be trapped in this space for an eternity. Sure, if someone on the physical plane would think of him, he would be teleported to the person for a close-up view to experience thoughts and feelings involving him. He was called before the council of twelve and his spiritual guide. Heck, he never even remembered he had a spiritual guide, let alone one who was assigned to him for the past six incarnations. Anyway, they reviewed him right down to the very last intimate detail. Where he improved, where he failed, people he helped, people he hurt, and ultimately, they decided he would exist on the physical plane until his body was placed in its final resting place. While karma is usually rolled over to the next incarnation, he would be provided an opportunity to learn and make some atonement for wrong-doing in this lifetime. If his remorse or actions were deemed as improvements, he would hear a bell ring and the tarnish on his soul would diminish. He hung his head as they dismissed him and he was dispatched from heaven.

One day is the same as the next on the astral plane, especially if your soul is tethered to the physical plane as his is. He was grateful for a change of scenery when he was thought of and could then be teleported to that person who was thinking of him.

He thought of the night he was murdered, and he wasn't sure if he had ever felt so frightened. Although he was pretty drunk, he managed to kill a couple of them before they killed him. He was surprised when he felt himself rising and something silvery, almost luminescent, break away from his physical body. He took his last labored breath and flew from the open mouth of his cadaver. He knew the body was gone, but he was still alive. He became an energy spark against the night sky. He hovered, watching as gang members burned his body, stealing his money and identification.

He became conscious of a strong, sweet smell like posies, and that was when he saw her, a young girl in her middle teens. She flipped between looking like his infant, Sara, and back to the young girl. Like, whoosh, a soft whisper, "Daddy." She had his eyes and Rachel's nose and hair. Sara had come to escort him through the valley of death to cross the veil and return to the Father. When she died, he had stopped believing in God, if he ever did believe He existed. Sara's spirit twirled about him, enveloping him with an incredible feeling of love and light he never remembered experiencing. She took his hand, guiding him into the light. Love was everywhere in heaven.

But alas, here he is, whiling away the days in the morgue. He tried to tell the workers who he was, but like everyone on the physical plane, they couldn't hear him. He wondered how many times he never really heard or listened to Rachel and Debbie. Isn't it so ironic that he now felt like a non-entity? Maybe it was karmic justice.

He thought about those nurses at that clinic where Rachel is and how they were wondering if he was the one doing the drive by the clinic. No, he wasn't the one, but when they thought of him, he was zapped into that car on the second trip up the block. It was a young kid named Terrance, probably seventeen, he guessed. He could have been him. He listened to his emotional rants about hating Andersen's and blaming them for his parents' divorce. He had tried to hack into their computer system, but was unsuccessful, and filled with rage, he decided he is going to smash that place up! Terrance figured the Thanksgiving holiday coming up would be the perfect time. He wanted to get the lay of the land. Kenneth tried to tell him, "Look kid, this is crazy. You have to take responsibility for your life." The kid never heard him. Just as he'd never listened to Rodger when he tried to tell him those same words.

After trying several ways to communicate with the boy on the second night of his driving by Andersen's, he knew he needed to do something drastic. Besides, what if someone got hurt—like Rachel. He had to protect her. He thought of how much he loved her and how he had hurt her. On Terrance's final trip up the street, Kenneth decided he was going to give that boy a ride to remember. Kenneth pushes Terrence's foot harder on the gas pedal, and taking control of the steering wheel, he skillfully maneuvers the car out of the area to a dark, curving two-lane road. The boy is frightened as he tries to take his foot off the gas and turn the wheel, but Kenneth has complete control. As they round a corner on the left side there is a cliff highlighted by the headlights of the car as it comes within centimeters of going over the edge. Terrance saw himself going over the edge and closed his eyes and when he reopened them he was right on the edge. Kenneth put the car in reverse and makes a sharp turn, bringing the car back to the highway. He saw the terror on the boy's face, and he pats him on the shoulder, telling him to stay away from Andersen's and to change your life, son. For some unknown reason, the boy saw him, felt him, and heard his words. Kenneth zipped out of there, back to the morgue, leaving that young man quaking in his boots. He smiled, thinking, damn I was always good at maneuvering cars. He hears a bell ring.

A couple of nights later, Kenneth returned to Andersen's, when a faulty wire tripped the alarm and turned on the patio lights. The nurse was thinking of him, and when he walked across the patio, inspecting the place, his shadow was captured by the camera. He stood in Rachel's room, watching the nurse trying to comfort her as she lay curled up on her side, crying and afraid that he had returned to hurt her. He tried to tell her he was not there to hurt her and he loved her, but they never even knew he was there. He felt powerless and ashamed for all the things he did to her. His remorse was deep and genuine, and he heard a bell ring. He felt as if a weight was lifted from him.

Thanksgiving weekend he had popped in and out when Aaron and Rachel talked about him. He was sorry he came between them and realized they may never become a couple and her baby could be fatherless. He never wanted that. He tried to counsel them, but they never heard him. He felt sad for their baby. He heard a bell ring. He noticed his soul was changing—like a jawbreaker going from grey to white.

He continued to spend his days in the Detroit Morgue, and as time passed people thought of him less. He was wanting to progress; maybe being in hell would be better than here. But then suddenly; his soul was zipping from place to place as the news of his death spread. He saw Gerald Herschel telling Townsend. He was surprised to see Townsend's reaction to the news, like he had caring for the guy who tried to belt him. He wished he'd been more like him and he couldn't think of a better guy for Rachel. He saw Melody try to help Rachel and the sorrow that she felt. He saw his brother crying. Rachel later called Rodger, and he and Cat told her they loved her and she would always be family to them. If she ever needed help she could call them. That was so sweet. He felt grateful to Rodger and Cathy. A bell rang and he felt lifted.

Rodger arranged for his ashes to be placed in the mausoleum in Lincoln with his daughter's. Rodger was so right; that is what he wanted. There was a small service; a police chaplain and some of his former coworkers were there. People shared memories of his life. One talked about the little girl who died of a crack cocaine overdose and how much he had cared about her. There were so many kind things said about him; his soul felt steamy with emotion. Several had commented on his sense of humor and how he just didn't care what he said and how he loved leading people on to burst out laughing because they believed him.

The final prayer was said and in an instant, he was transported to heaven for rest and a subsequent meeting with the group of twelve representatives of the God Council.

This was Rachel's final night at Andersen's and there was a sadness about leaving. During her nine-week stay she'd seen lots of people come and go at the guesthouse. Some stayed a week, some two. Even though the various classes she attended were repetitive, she seemed to learn something new each time. Maybe it was just that there was so much to grasp, kind of like watching a good movie, like how you pick up different nuances each time you watch it. But this was it her last night. She'd wanted to go home since she came here and now she's sad because she'll be leaving.

She even came to adore Nick, who she didn't like in the beginning. Because of him she was walking and had regained her strength. She loved Dr. Andersen and his gentleness, along with his unwavering honesty. He wasn't afraid to confront you if he thought you were doing something to impede your progress. At the same time, he understood human weaknesses and he oozed with compassion. Everyone really felt like family.

At lunchtime they'd surprised her with a baby shower, and she received so many things, including glass bottles to avoid Bisphenol-A (BPA) and other toxins found in plastics, organic blankets and knitted booties. For herself, she received some Steven Halpern CD's, a couple of cookbooks, a few vials of aromatherapy scents and organic toiletries. She cried, and everyone hugged her. Leaving was not as easy as she had thought it would be.

Tears fell on her pillow. She knew Aaron would marry her for the baby, but she still couldn't believe he really loved her for her. She didn't want to be married to someone who settled. Marriage had never been a particularly positive and happy experience. She guessed she was afraid of it. Turning out the light, she tries to make her mind go blank.

Aaron sat in his recliner, sipping a glass of wine. Tomorrow Rachel was being discharged and he's picking her up after lunch. Everything would finally come to a head. He'd buy her a couple of long-stemmed red roses and he'd take her to his special place by the giant wheel. They'd finally have the talk about Denver and he'd tell her about Meredith and Mike. He's going to pop the question. If she says yes, he'll be the happiest man on the planet.

There was that little nagging doubt within him that she might not say yes. If she didn't, he'd have to accept it. But he was certain he'd at least be in the baby's life. She's just too sweet and caring of a person to not allow him to be in the baby's life.

She'd been through hell and sometimes people change and they can't recover. The wounds might heal up but something on the inside cracks and only time and a lot of work can heal something so deep inside.

When he moved to Seattle he practiced being optimistic, and in the beginning it was like learning to walk, pretending and inching along. He built this company from one little coffee shop, and he amassed a team of employees most any company would be proud of. Many times bigger companies than his had tried to steal his pastry chef and some of his key staff. But they all remained loyal and stayed at the Coffee Genie.

After breakfast, Rachel packed her things and called a taxi.

"We thought Aaron was going to come and pick you up? One of us could drive you home."

"Karen, that's totally unnecessary, and I appreciate the thought. I'll call Aaron and tell him not to come. He's very busy you know."

"Are you sure you don't want us to take you home?"

"No, my ride will be here any minute. I want to thank all of you for everything."

"It was nice having you as a client, Rachel. I wish the very best for you and your baby."

"Thank you."

Many of the staff came and hugged her goodbye as the taxi driver loaded all of her things.

The flowers lay in the back of the car, wrapped in green tissue paper. The ring, a two-carrot, blue-white diamond was centered between their birthstones—a pearl and a purple amethyst. The ring was tucked safely into his suit jacket pocket. He felt like a teenager picking his date up for the prom. He actually had butterflies in his stomach. He hummed along with soft rock playing on the radio all the way over to Mercer Island. This is the beginning of something wonderful!

He rang the doorbell and Sonia came to the door. She opened the door and began wiping her hands on her apron, which was splotched with flour.

"Aaron, Rachel left this morning. Didn't she call you?"

"No, she didn't—I'm sure she must've forgotten."

"Yes. She took a taxi. We offered to give her a lift but she didn't want it."

"Thanks. I'm sure it is just a little miscommunication. Maybe she called the office when I was out."

"Sorry you had to drive all this way."

"No problem, really. I love Mercer Island."

A sinking feeling in his gut came over him as he turned away, returning to his car. He picked his cell phone up from the passenger seat and turned it on. Flipping through several text messages, he finds the message from Rachel, sent at eleven thirty a.m. It said, Aaron, I went home early and I don't need a ride. I'll contact you later. He thought they'd agreed he'd come and get her. How many times had she pushed back when he tried to get close to her? Was he as bad as Hamilton, not respecting her space? His inner voice had tried to warn him, but he just rationalized all the little signals. He had known something was not right between them for weeks. After Thanksgiving, he'd backed off and given her space, being extra careful not to mention the love word or upset her again.

What did this mean? He had to go see her, talk it out with her, and then if she didn't want a relationship with him he'd have to accept the situation. He could respect boundaries, what he couldn't respect was not having an adult-to-adult communication. It was partly his fault for allowing this to drag on. It was just that—what? He's afraid she'd think lesser of him in some way because he put his job first instead of driving them to the soccer game. Wow! All these years and you still haven't been able to let go of what happened to Meredith and Mike. Who's the one who needs therapy?

A sense of melancholy enveloped her, because not only did she leave Andersen's, she is leaving Seattle. She felt sad not telling Aaron, but she'd been working on a goodbye letter to him and still hadn't yet perfected it.

All the plans were in motion for Jim's Moving and Storage Company to deliver boxes to her apartment at ten thirty a.m. and come back for her things at two p.m. She guessed it shouldn't take longer than that. The apartment had been furnished when she rented it. She didn't have all that much in the kitchen. She had her electronic passport on American to fly in to Denver, and she had her hotel reservations in Boulder. The moving company would ship her things when she had an address.

Back at her apartment she begins packing the kitchen—a four-piece set of stoneware dishes, some jelly glasses, a couple of wine glasses, a basic set of Teflon cookware, and other items in the kitchen. She was surprised how much time it took. It was twelve-thirty by the time she finished the kitchen and began packing her clothes.

A knock on the door causes her to jump. She thought the movers would be here at two. Checking the time it, she saw that it was one thirty. It couldn't be Aaron; she'd sent him a text message that she'd contact him later. She wasn't quite ready, but she's close. She opened the door and Aaron stood there, taking it all in. She watched as the recognition hit him and the blood drained from his face.

"What are you doing?" he seemed to choke on the words.

"I'm leaving Seattle and the movers should be here any minute."

"You were going to leave and not even tell me!"

"I've been working on a letter, but it is not finished yet. Aaron, I know this seems insensitive on my part, but I'm doing this for you."

"For me! You're giving me a Dear John letter, and that's for me?"

"I don't want you to feel forced to marry me because I'm pregnant. I don't want you to feel obligated to me in any way. I've not had the best experience in relationships, but one thing I do know is I want someone to be married to me because they love me. Well, that's not possible anymore. I'm not pretty anymore; who'd want me? Just look at me. My nose is crooked because it was broken, and I have these scars near my ear. No. I hate to go, but it is the right thing to do for you! You'd only resent me later."

"My God, Rachel, I'm in love with you! What more could I possibly do to prove it to you?"

"You say that. But you're so caring and decent, I think you don't know your own mind. Besides, you couldn't really understand what I've been through in my life. I'm a battered woman and my baby died."

"Let me tell you something! You don't have a patent on grief and suffering! Kenneth attacked you and everything's been upside down for you ever since. I've bent over backwards trying to do the right thing, considering your feelings and trying to help you! Well, let me tell you something. I sent you back to Seattle when we were in Denver because I realized I was in love with you and that you weren't a one-night stand. That scared me a little because I've never been able to become attached to women I've dated since my wife and son died. See, you aren't the only one who's lost a child. My son was ten. He lived ten times longer than your daughter. I taught him to ride a bike, took him hiking and camping, we shared nine Christmases, his first tooth, and lots of things dads experience with their children. My wife, Meredith, and our son were killed by a drunk driver in Los Angeles. I was a new attorney in a private practice, and I argued with my wife because I needed to work on Saturday and she wanted me to take them to the soccer game. I've regretted my decision all of these years! There's not a day that goes by that I've not regretted the decision to work instead of being with them."

Looking down at her feet, Rachel says, "I'm sorry. I didn't know."

"There is a lot you don't know. You think I care if your nose isn't perfectly straight or you have some scarring. You must think me a pretty shallow person."

The movers came. "Ma'am, we're here to pick up your things."

"Yes. I've some boxes in the kitchen. You can start there."

The guy loaded up a stack of boxes on his dolly and walked out the door.

"Well, Rachel, I guess this is goodbye. I hope you let me know about my baby and where I can send money. I'm not Kenneth; I'm not forcing you to stay. I want an adult relationship with open communication. I thought we had that. I thought we had something special. But I can see I'm wrong. You can have this ring; I bought for you in Denver. You can hock it or give it away or whatever you choose. I never want to see it again, that's for sure. Oh, yes, and here are a couple of roses you can throw in the trash! Good luck with your life." He turns and walks out of the apartment.

She burst into tears. How could she have thrown away the best person in her life? Every part of her being screamed, go after him, stop him, but she froze, anchored to where she stood. In that moment she could've been turned into a pillar of salt, like Lot's wife in the Book of Genesis in the Bible.

He flew down the steps, two at a time. He wanted out of there, and he knew he'd never drive down Cherry Street again. He composed himself as best he could and called the office, telling Stacy he'd be unavailable for the rest of the day.

He drove through downtown Seattle, looking at all the Christmas decorations and the shoppers with packages walking down the street. It was hard to drive with the tears blurring his vision. He shouldn't be driving right now; it wasn't safe. He'd drive to the great wheel and watch the fishing boats and think of how he wanted to live the rest of his life without her. He should have seen the warning signs, but he had just chalked her behavior up to her being injured and the pregnancy. Bottom line, she didn't really love him. How could she have done this to him if she did? Running away. Maybe she'd been running for a long time.

The movers finished loading her things and she sat on the living room sofa, crying. Her tears soaked the little black velvet box. She flipped it open to see the most brilliant diamond ring, with a pearl on one side and an amethyst on the other. He didn't know about the pregnancy when he bought the ring! She cried harder. This was what her mother had been alluding to when she talked to her about leaving Seattle.

Wiping her eyes with some tissue she had in her jacket pocket and snapping the box closed, she placed it in her pocket. Her flight was leaving in a few hours and she needed to go.

She walked downstairs to the building manager's office and gave him the keys after the yellow cab loaded her luggage. Sitting in the back seat of the taxi, watching as it turned off Cherry Street, knowing she wouldn't be back to this apartment. This part of her life was over. The only piece of memorabilia was this angel growing inside of her. She thought she felt the first kick but wasn't sure. She'd read this is when the soul enters the womb. Some people believe we pick our parents and this thought comforted her.

Kenneth was summoned before the God Council and Rachel's grandmother, Emily Bender, was in attendance. They told him Rachel was going to the airport to leave and the two of them were being sent as a divine intervention to splice and mend these two souls. That being said, souls do have free will and their appearance may not make a difference. If the repair was successful Kenneth would have some of his negative karma expunged from the Akashic records. If not, the karma would be worked out in another lifetime.

They were on the freeway when she thought she smelled gram's perfume, Evening in Paris. Then she heard her voice quite clearly.

"Rachel Milicent Goodrich, whatever are you doing?"

Looking up, she sees her grandmother floating in the air in front of her, her hands on her hips. Standing beside her is Kenneth.

"Gram?"

"Did you say something, Miss?"

"No"

"Of course it's me. You're behaving just like your mother! Good Lord, I never thought you'd become so prim, proper, and stuffy like her! How could you throw away real love?"

"It's too late; I ruined it. He'd never want to see me again."

"Well, how do you know if you don't try? You know you were whisked out of heaven for a reason, not to just go off and be an unwed mother. A child without a father, what kind of life would that be? I never helped raise you to be so self-centered and selfish."

"Rachel, you're wrong" she heard Kenneth say. "Aaron really loves you. I want you to know how sorry I am for interfering in your life. I also want you to know how much I regret hurting you. Please, you belong with him; you are perfect for each other. He was the man I never was. Please forgive me and go to him. "

"Ma'am, which airline again?"

"American."

She heard the loudspeaker calling out, "for loading and unloading of passengers only."

"No, wait! I want you to take me to the Coffee Genie instead—the main office."

"Are you sure you're feeling okay, Miss?"

"Yes, I'm fine." She gave him the address

"Now that's more like the Rachel I know. Don't make us come down here again. You know the God Council is pretty stuffy about us meddling on the physical plane. They let us do it because they said divine intervention was needed. We don't want to watch you make such a ridiculous mistake. Now, get busy; go find your man. Geez, I can't get over how I spent my whole physical life trying to direct your mom and you're just like her."

"Goodbye Rachel," Kenneth said. "Go find him, trust him, and be happy. I love you, Rachel, and I always will."

She tried to call Aaron and there's no answer. She called the Coffee Genie and Stacy answered.

"Stacy, this is Rachel. Is Aaron there?"

"No. He called and said he wouldn't be in for the rest of the day."

"Do you know where he is?"

"No, Rachel. I'm sorry. I don't."

"Could you have a couple of guys come down and meet my taxi and put my luggage in my office?"

"Sure."

"I'll be there in about fifteen minutes."

Dropping off her luggage she had the driver go to Pike's Market, but she didn't see his car in the parking lot. Her only other idea was pier fifty-seven, near the Great Wheel. The driver drove the short distance and she saw his car in the lot directly across the street from the Ferris wheel on Alaskan Way.

She paid the driver and rushed down the sidewalk, looking for him. The wind was blowing her long hair and she had to stop to brush it out of her eyes. She's frantic to find him and every part of her being screamed, find him, you have to find him.

Like a crazed woman she looked at the people clustering in groups near the pier and brushed past them. She didn't see him at first, but there he is leaning on the railing looking off in the distance, a white paper cup in his left hand. Rushing to him, touching his arm with the side of her face and her hand, "Aaron!"

Jumping, he hadn't seen her; his mind was thinking of the day. He gazed down at her and she saw that his eyes and nose were red and swollen. "I thought you left."

"I'm such a stupid idiot." The wind tore at her hair and her eyes glistened with tears. "Can I have a sip of your coffee?"

"How do you know I'm drinking coffee? And no, you can't; you're pregnant and you shouldn't be drinking caffeine."

Handing her the cup, he said, "Just a small sip. It isn't as good as ours."

She took a sip. "I'm so sorry; I really love you. I was such a stupid fool. Could we start over? There's no one more important to me than you. I don't blame you if you don't want to."

305

Turning towards her, he extends his hand and says, "Hello. I'm Aaron Townsend, the owner of a little coffee shop called the Coffee Genie. Have you ever heard of it?"

"I'm Rachel Milicent Goodrich, and I believe I've sipped on some of your java." She places her hand into his and he pulled her tight against him. She could feel his heart beating and sobs rose from his belly button to the surface of his lips. They both stood there holding each other and crying, oblivious to the world around them.

"Rachel, I love you," he said, cupping her face in his hands. "I was so lonely before you. Please understand how much I love you and how much I want this baby. I can't help what happened to you just as you can't fix my broken heart over my wife and my son. We will have something special. Please, please trust me." He embraced her again, holding her tightly and stroking her hair. "Baby, I thought I had lost you forever!"

"I'm so sorry, Aaron, for what I almost did to us. I never trusted men before you. I feel safe with you. I know you and I can disagree and you aren't going to call me names or try to smack me around. I'm happy about our baby, too."

They pulled apart, each searching for a tissue.

"I was wondering, Ms. Goodrich, if you'd care to take a ride on the Great Wheel and see the bay?"

"Mr. Townsend, that's the best offer I've had all day. Love to."

They walked to the ticket booth and he purchased two VIP seats. They had their picture taken, were given two tickets for champagne toast at a fish place, and then they were escorted to their glass-enclosed gondola.

Although there were four seats in their gondola they were the only VIP passengers. They held hands while they looked at the city and then as they made the turn going forty feet out over the bay. When they were out over the bay, Aaron was the first to speak. "I'd ask you to marry me, Miss Goodrich, but I seem to have lost the ring."

Reaching into her coat pocket retrieving the black velvet box, she says, "Would this happen to be the ring you're talking about, Mr. Townsend?"

"Ah, the very one. I'd know that ring anywhere; it seems I've carried it from Denver to ICU. It's been practically everywhere." He lifts the ring from the box and it glitters in the sunlight. "Rachel, I'd like you to marry me. It'd make me very happy if you'd accept my proposal of marriage. Please marry me."

"Aaron, this is the happiest moment of my life, and yes! I'll marry you!"

He slipped the ring on her finger and kissed her. Rachel heard a soft bell ring and she arrived at that state of knowing that something wonderful had just happened in heaven. She had a fleeting thought that maybe Kenneth just received his angel wings.

"I can't think of a better place to propose to you than up here. It's so beautiful looking at the bay and the boats on the water. How did you know I'd be here?"

"I know you love this place, and I know you better than you think."

"When do you want to get married?"

"I think this has dragged on long enough. Besides I'm homeless. I see no need to wait. What about you?"

"I don't want to let you out of my sight, so right away is good for me. I wouldn't want to see a damsel homeless."

"Why don't we go to the justice of the peace in San Francisco; that way, my parents could come and be our witnesses?"

"Don't you want a wedding, Rachel? I thought most women wanted that?"

"I had that once, and no, to spend the rest of my life with you is all I want."

"Rachel, I love you. You are my finest treasure. Are you hungry? I'm hungry. Why don't we go collect these champagne tickets at that restaurant? Of course, you can't drink. I'll have to do it for both of us, and we can call your parents."

They placed their order and Rachel called her mother. "Mom, Aaron and I are going to get married!"

"I thought you were going to Denver, but I'm so relieved you came to your senses. When is the wedding?"

"We want to drive to San Francisco, and we want you and Daddy to be our witnesses at the justice of the peace."

"Your Aunt Amelia's here. Hold on." She heard her mother telling her aunt. She couldn't fully hear what was being said. Her mother came back on the line. "No. Let's do something nicer. How about we get Pastor Williams at the church to do the service in your aunt's living room?"

She tells Aaron what her mother said and they agree that would be great. "Sounds good, Mom!"

"Now you two get here, but drive safely. First, let me speak to Aaron."

Handing the phone to him. "Hello, Susan."

"Aaron, I want to congratulate you and tell you I can't think of a better son-in-law. In fact, just drop the in-law part. I was praying my daughter would come to her senses because I know how much you love her. Now drive safely; you've got my future grandbaby in that car. Amelia wants to say something to you."

"Hi, Amelia."

"Hi, Aaron. Congratulations! Don't worry about anything; we'll take care of everything."

"Thanks so much." He hands the phone to Rachel

"Hi, Aunt Amelia."

"Congratulations, dear! I'm so glad you accepted Aaron. You know a love like yours doesn't happen every day. You couldn't ask for a better man than him. I'm glad you stopped being so stuffy."

"I know I've been stuffy."

"Now drive safe and get here!"

Acknowledgements

*T*his is the area of a novel where authors express appreciation for all the help they received with their book. For me this novel could never have been written without all the love and support I have received throughout my life.

In 1950 when I was three, my mother refused to allow the Denver Children's hospital to do brain surgery. She took me home to die but really to live. At nineteen, the catalyst for change was my brother Bob, who told me in his military type way to stop feeling sorry for myself and go get a job. My younger brother, Dennis and sister, Cheryl, who have been very important people throughout my life.

My friend, Sandi, who I met when I was twenty-nine; she became the big sister I never had. She taught me to find humor in my experiences. She saw a potential for something greater in me that I couldn't see. The professors at UNC who encouraged me. Members of the National Federation of the Blind who taught and showed by example I could live the life I wanted.

Past employers who came to depend on my problem-solving skills and my ability to perform quality work. My coworker and best friend, Julieta, who went out of her way to give me rides to work when my journey to learn to drive with bioptics failed because I was too blind to drive.

I appreciate the opportunity I've had to work with abused women and their children. I was touched by their stories and proud to support them in their quest to regain control of their lives.

I would like to express my appreciation to Jean Boles for her great suggestions and editorial skills in improving this debut novel. In addition, she designed the book cover and formatted this book. She turned out to be the perfect person to take *Final Drive* the rest of the way to publication.

Lastly, but certainly not least, my husband, John, who has been my rock and the love of my life. He listened tirelessly to my screen reader reading this novel. He was always willing to listen and make suggestions on how to improve Final Drive. Spending my life with him has made my world a better place. I truly feel blessed to have someone as loving and giving as he is.

My life has been a fantastic journey, and when I think about the past, I can see my life is in perfect order. I know my life has always been guided by a higher source greater than me, even during those moments when it didn't feel like it. It seems to me that maybe we might not be able to fully appreciate the peaks in our lives unless we have walked in the valley of despair. Perhaps it was never really about arriving at destination /accomplishment, but rather the journey/process.

www.ingramcontent.com/pod-product-compliance
Lightning Source LLC
Chambersburg PA
CBHW031546240626
47153CB00002B/405